BORN ON THE BAYOU

An Eye on You Gabriel Ross detective novel

JOE HAMILTON

Eye on You – Born on the Bayou

A Gabriel Ross detective novel

by Joe Hamilton

978-0-9939999-5-6

Published 2019 by Joe Hamilton

DEDICATION

To my new Grandson, Thomas Fish

Thomas, I thought a great deal about you, your life and your wonderful parents, while writing this book. When you're older, maybe you will read it. I'm sorry about all the swear words, but it's the way some people like to talk. It made me think of the words of a great Bob Dylan song.

May God bless and keep you always
May your wishes all come true
May you always do for others
And let others do for you
May you build a ladder to the stars
And climb on every rung
May you stay
May you stay forever young

A PRIMER

This is the 6th book in the Eye on You mystery series. For you newbies, The Eye on You Detective Agency was formed in 1979 by Gabriel Ross and his silent partner Ben O'Shea, a Biloxi Police Detective. Jacqueline Cooper was the agency's first major client (Eye on You – Murder in Biloxi), and as luck would have it, she became Jacqueline Ross at the end of the first book.

Over the years, the agency has grown in business, reputation, and employees. The initial office was relocated to a bigger space in Gulfport, and Rachel Henderson was hired as a receptionist/associate. Arnie Sims joined as a part-time associate, mostly looking after his own clients. From the early days, the agency's mascot has been an orange tabby cat named Bourbon. A young protege named Travis Franklin has also been featured in most of the books.

This book details the opening of a second agency office in New Orleans. A veteran NOPD detective named Rutledge, who was featured in two previous books, was hired to run the office.

The characters in this story are fictional, and any resemblance to actual people is a pile of hooey.

I hope you enjoy the story. If you do, let me know. Some readers might think that the title of this book is based on the Creedence Clearwater Revival song by the same name. While I referred to the song in the novel, it has nothing to do with the title of the book. I can't tell you why I chose this title as it would spoil the surprise.

Books in the series:

1. *Eye on You – Murder in Biloxi*
2. *Eye on You – Rock you like a Hurricane*
3. *Eye on You – Mississippi Queen*
4. *Eye on You – Gimme 3 Steps*
5. *Eye on You – House of the Rising Son*
6. *Eye on You – Born on the Bayou*

PROLOGUE

Friday, February 11th, 1983
Somewhere in the Gulf of Mexico

Huge waves dwarfed the small cabin cruiser, causing it to ride up and down on the swelling Gulf like a child's toy. He hung on to whatever he could as a flash of lightning lit up the sky. There had been no warning of an impending storm. There was no mercy in that wind, no grace in the waves, only wrath. The untamed power of the storm roared and reverberated across the sea. Wind slammed the rain into his face, stinging like tiny stones.

He screamed to the person at the helm. They turned and looked at him, holding something in their hand. He struggled hand over hand to move forward along the bow so that he could be heard over the storm. A sudden flash of light lit up the boat, and he felt a searing pain in his chest. The shock caused him to lose his grip on the taffrail, and he felt his body slide backward just as the boat went upwards on a huge wave. He fell into the blackness of the Gulf.

The cold water shocked him. Waves washed over him as

he thrashed and flailed wildly. Each chance to breathe became further apart, each breath less than the last. He was a strong swimmer, but it didn't take long before he felt disoriented. Strong waves had him in their clutches, and he struggled to stay afloat. After only ten more seconds, he sank again. His legs were tired of fighting, and his lungs battled for air. With a superhuman effort, he broke the surface again. He gulped for air, but a huge wave pushed him under again.

With his last ounce of energy, he swam to the surface. "He...help..." he gasped, before realizing he was all alone. No lights from the boat. No lights anywhere. No stars, nothing but blackness. The rain continued to pelt down.

He started to shiver; the water temperature couldn't be more than fifty degrees. A wave crashed down on him, and once again he was under. He sank faster this time. His heart hammered against his ribs, muscles weakening. Every cell in his body screamed for oxygen. In full panic now, his movements were uncoordinated. He clawed furiously at the water; not even sure he was facing upwards. With his head about to explode, he gave up and opened his mouth, desperate for air.

Memories of the girl flashed through his mind.

CHAPTER ONE

Monday, July 9th, 1984
15 Months later
WGNO TV Studio,
New Orleans, Louisiana

Click, click...The flip clock on the make-up table was counting down. Lights glared in Gabriel's eyes. When Jacqueline had heard about the interview, she'd warned him that Suzanne Collings had a reputation for sandbagging her guests. He went over his planned responses and hoped things didn't get too tough. *Ben should be sitting here. Why did I let him talk me into this?*

A short, heavy-set make-up girl dabbed his face with powder and fussed with his hair. "If you don't stop sweating, you're going to end up looking like a Picasso painting." She stepped back with a look of concern.

"I'm sorry, the lights are hot. Any chance we can turn them off?"

"They don't like filming in the dark," she replied with a straight face, shaking her head at the suggestion.

"I'll turn off my sweat glands then."

She started to apply more powder, this time slapping his face a little too brusquely.

"Now I know how Tom Cruise feels. My wife tells me I look like him."

"Listen, the only way you'd look like Tom Cruise is to tape his picture to your forehead." A few more slaps with a makeup sponge. "Actually, Tom Cruise is 5 ft 8. He'd look like a giant compared to you."

"Hilarious." When the girl finished slapping him, he looked over at Suzanne. She was a slim, attractive brunette with a perpetual sly grin on her face like she knew your naughtiest secret.

"It'll be great publicity for your business," she'd said. "My program is very popular with the 'white women over fifty' segment. Just the kind of people who'd hire a private detective to check up on their cheating husband."

The news producer walked by as Gabriel took his seat beside Suzanne. Wishing him good luck, he flashed Gabriel a sympathetic look, then nodded at someone as he counted down from five.

The channel eight music started, and Suzanne, likely picking up on Gabriel's panic, leaned over and put her hand on his knee. "You'll do great, easy. I like soft balls," she whispered, making a cupping motion with her hand.

"Good morning New Orleans, and thank you for tuning into our program," Suzanne enthused while staring into the camera. "Today we have a special guest with us. You may have read about his exploits in the papers, or seen the billboards on the highway. I am pleased to have Mr. Gabriel Ross, owner and operator of the *Eye on You Detective Agency* with us today. Mr. Ross is here to promote his new location, opening up at 1300 Canal Street in our fair city. Welcome to the program, Mr. Ross."

"Uh, thanks. You can call me Gabriel."

"We have a shot of the billboard for your new office." Behind Suzanne, a screen displayed a cartoon image of an alligator wearing a golf shirt and a peaked hat, holding a magnifying glass. "Calling your New Orleans team 'Investi-Gators' is pretty cute."

"Thanks, it was a suggestion from the team." Gabriel shifted in his seat.

"Is that chair too big for you? Do you need a box for your feet?" Suzanne asked playfully.

"It's fine. I'm just a little nervous."

"Let's start with an easy one. Many of our viewers must be wondering, just how tall are you?"

"I'm over 5 feet," then because he couldn't think of anything else, "I'm not short, just concentrated."

Suzanne laughed at the attempted joke. "Seriously Gabriel, how much of a handicap has being short been for you?" She held up her thumb and index finger about an inch apart.

He shrugged, "I haven't thought of it as a handicap. People probably underestimate me because of it. I focus on rising to the occasion."

Suzanne smiled again and crossed her legs seductively. "Did you always plan to be a private "dick?" She used air quotes to ask.

"No, I went to school to be an accountant." He turned away from Suzanne to face the director, who was pointing at the camera. "That didn't work out, so I came down to Biloxi, where I met Ben O'Shea, my business partner. At the time, Ben was working as a Biloxi Police Detective, and he must have seen something in me. He taught me the business."

"You recently concluded a case where the Mayor of Biloxi was arrested on what he claims are trumped up charges. The case also involved a well-known businessman, can we discuss that?" Suzanne's mouth started seductively playing with the end of her pen.

"I can't say very much since it's still before the courts. The case started as routine and developed into something else."

"Weren't you also part of an FBI task force, a couple of years back, involving a man who became known as the Mardi Gras Killer?"

"Yes, Charles Bouvier, he grew up in New Orleans. He was working with an accomplice to abduct teenage girls. Sadly, Bouvier never faced justice or had to explain what happened to the girls. He fell overboard off his boat and drowned. Those families will likely never find out what happened to their daughters."

"That's a shame," Suzanne replied with a tone of concern. "When I was reading about your exploits, your job sounded very dangerous."

"I suppose it can be, but most of the cases we handle involve doing reference checks, looking for missing teenagers, doing surveillance on a cheating spouse...Pretty tame stuff."

"I read that you investigated a local sheriff. You stopped him from burying his wife alive. Is that what you mean by tame?" Without waiting for a reply, she continued, turning to face the camera, "So you killed him, and married his wife!"

So much for the soft balls. "Hearing it that way makes it sound like I made all that happen. No, I was hired by the Sheriff's wife to tail him. She suspected he was cheating on her. During the investigation, I learned that he was involved in many illegal activities with some very bad people. He got upset when his wife left him, so he kidnapped her. My partner and I were able to save her in time."

"And you killed him."

"No, well, yes. His wife and I developed a relationship after he was arrested. The FBI had cut a deal with him in return for testifying against others. He was put into the witness protection program. It was quite a bit later when he came back to Biloxi and tried to kill us. I had to, you know, put him down, kill him, you know, with a gun." Gabriel took a long drink of water from the glass they'd put on the table beside him.

"I sense some nerves over the whole killing thing, Gabriel, which might surprise some of our viewers. They've probably read in the papers that you've been compared to a miniature Charles Bronson or an itsy-bitsy Clint Eastwood. Just how many people have you 'put down'?"

"I'm not keeping track. I've never killed anyone who wasn't threatening to harm someone else. Anyway, all of that is in the past. As I said, most of our cases are pretty routine."

Suzanne gave him a disbelieving look and smiled before turning towards the camera. "There you have it, folks, Investi-Gators coming to a location near you. And of course, our very own, not dangerous, crime fighter-avenging angel. Thank you, Gabriel."

CHAPTER TWO

Monday, July 16th, 1984
Slidell, Louisiana

My name is Gabriel Ross, private detective, or as Suzanne Collings called me, a private dick. A few months ago when Mayor Baxter was arrested, I was feeling good. The business was expanding, and we were bringing on experienced staff. We'd hired a black detective named Rutledge, who had 40 years of experience in policing. But after that interview, I began to question myself. My self-image bore no resemblance to Dirty Harry or that guy in the Death Wish movies. Ben - my mentor, my partner, my best friend - in his no-nonsense manner, told me to quit acting like a girl. Later, when I brought it up again, he quoted Satchel Paige, the famous ballplayer, and said, "Don't look back, something might be gaining on you." So here I am, sitting in a bar staring into my beer, wondering what any of this means.

Jacqueline thought the WGNO interview was hilarious, and that I needed to steer the Agency towards attracting more mainstream clients. Ever since that business with her ex-

husband, she had been very clear that she didn't want to live a life worrying whether something terrible was about to happen. Now her best friend Chevon, who feels the same way, was about to marry Ben..

On last night's news, Gabriel and Jacqueline had watched former Biloxi Mayor Baxter being interviewed at the courthouse. Because the trial judge had denied his bail request, he was surrounded not only by his attorney, but also a posse of Harrison County Deputy Sheriffs. Baxter had stopped midway in the hallway to answer a reporter's question. "There has been a lot of bad reporting in the papers," Baxter said pompously. "Fake news, I call it. Fake, fake, fake. I expect that when the public hears the truth, I'll be completely vindicated. Biggly. I'm the true victim here. Ben O'Shea, a corrupt former city detective, and his friend Gabriel Ross conspired to frame me. They're evil."

LIKE A HUNDRED OTHER bars down south, the Hideout Bar and Tavern's décor was chosen by someone who thought the South should have won the war. Confederate Flags, old muskets, bugles and dozens of paintings showing battle scenes decorated the cheap imitation paneling. The décor went with the band; a rock group called Southern Cross, which was butchering their way through a rendition of Lynyrd Skynyrd's *Gimme Three Steps*. There had to be sixty, maybe more, base-ball-cap wearing rednecks squished into the place. Gabriel did a quick count and discovered that the John Deer tribe outnumbered both the U.S. Marine Corps and the New Orleans Saints.

The bar was located in a town called Slidell just east of New Orleans. The town where Tommy Huffman lay almost comatose in a psychiatric hospital, likely to never leave. He was under constant care, suffering from what has been diagnosed as mutism — an inability to communicate. He had been perfectly normal until he'd seen what the thugs named the Nantois brothers did to his parents. They say his mind was stuck like a broken record, playing the same horrible track over and over again.

The bartender, a squat man with his long, blonde hair tied in a ponytail, lifted Gabriel's half-empty beer bottle and gave him a sad look. *You're not going to get rich on me buddy.* Gabriel spied a man at the end of the bar who kept looking in his direction. *Slim with long stringy, oily, dirty blonde hair – check; mid-thirties with a bleached, pasty white complexion - check; alligator tattoo on his arm – check; overgrown chin strip – check; scumbag – check. The man was peeling the label off his beer bottle as if he was waiting for someone or something to happen. I' d seen a picture of him earlier that day. Petr Tadic. His wife Lana suspected his late-night rendez-vous for bowling lessons was bullshit.*

I kept my eye on him through the cloud of smoke that hung over the bar. The city was in the midst of a hot spell to end all hot spells and the cigarette smoke wasn't helping. The kind where you woke up sweaty, went to bed sweaty, even got out of the shower sweaty. A breath of fresh air interrupted his thoughts in the form of an attractive blonde who sat down on the stool next to him.

"Can you make me a High Tide?" the blond asked the ponytail behind the bar. When the bartender gave her a blank look, she explained that it was a concoction of rum, curacao and pineapple juice. She turned to Gabriel, "Believe it or not, I learned of it on a cruise. I had enough of my little brats, so I dumped them on hubby, and spent some quality time dancing."

Gabriel laughed and said he'd have to give it a try. He made eye contact with Petr Tadic. He was checking out the woman. Gabriel turned slightly towards her and gave her a quick once-over. *Likely thirties, wearing jeans and a gingham shirt tied in a knot above her waist. The kind of outfit you'd wear if you wanted to be noticed.*

She returned the look and noticed that Gabriel's feet didn't reach the ground. A confused look came over her. "Smoke too much?"

"Excuse me?"

"I'm sorry. I was wondering if you'd smoked too much when you were younger."

"No, never smoked, but there's so much smoke in here, I was 6 feet tall when I came in."

She laughed. "Funny."

They watched as the bartender mixed her drink. When he put the drink in front of her, Gabriel held up his beer, "Enjoy your High Tide."

She clinked her glass with his Budweiser. "To cruises."

"My name's Gabriel." He added, "The non-midget."

She laughed and said her name was "Brenda, the no-longer-married."

They chatted for a few more minutes about music and movies. It was typical bar chatter. The band started to play a fast, out-of-tune rendition of *House of the Rising Sun.*

"Oh! I love this song," said Brenda.

Clearly, an "I want you to ask me to dance prompt." I'm not comfortable dancing. Jacqueline says I'm painfully awkward. But compared to Ben O'Shea, I think I'm Fred Astaire. Chevon once compared his dance moves to a rooster having a seizure.

Likely sensing his reluctance, Brenda took pity on him and changed the subject. "I just attended a Star Wars revival.

All three episodes." She stirred her drink, using one of those plastic swords. She deepened her voice, "Come here often, you do?"

"No, but thinking about it, am I," Gabriel Yoda'd. *Tadic is getting up . He's likely heading to the washroom.* "Excuse me for a second. Nature calls."

Gabriel bumped and jostled his way through the crowd. When he turned the corner to go towards the men's room, he saw Tadic about twenty feet away with his back to him. He was cradling a pay phone between his shoulder and his ear. Gabriel edged his way down the hallway trying to look nonchalant, checking out the band posters pinned to the wall. With the music blaring, he was having a tough time doing any quality eavesdropping. He thought he heard the name of the bar, followed by what sounded like "I'm here, where are you?" *Maybe his bowling coach stood him up?*

The consolation was that Tadic was also having trouble being heard over the band. The man raised his voice. "A pretty small package, but don't worry; it'll be smooth as silk." A few moments later, he laughed and said, "Yeah, I can't wait, the bigger, the better."

Was Tadic speaking to his bowling coach about meeting later? The conversation sounds sexual.

Gabriel watched as Tadic hung up. When he started to turn around, Gabriel pulled a flyer off the wall and acted like he was checking it out. He looked up just in time to see Tadic go into the men's room.

He made like he was using the payphone while he waited for Tadic to finish his business. After a couple of minutes, Gabriel followed him back to the bar and found that Brenda had bought him a High Tide.

"Thought you'd like it."

"Thanks." They clinked glasses again.

Brenda was fun and attractive. *She seemed unfazed by my wedding band.* Brenda lit a cigarette and passed him the matches. *She's written her number on the inside cover.* One High Tide led to another, and Gabriel started to feel woozy. *Could I be drunk after just a few drinks?* The feeling intensified; like a kid on a tilt-a-whirl, the room seemed to be spinning out of control. Gabriel looked up, and Tadic had disappeared.

"Where'd that guy go?" Gabriel called out to the bartender. When the bartender shrugged, Gabriel stood up and almost fell over before yelling, "The one who was sitting right there." He pointed to the end of the bar.

The bartender poured him a coffee. "I think that's enough for tonight, champ,"

"Man? What man?" Brenda asked. Her face seemed to be zooming in and out like someone adjusting the lens on a camera.

"He's gggg...one," Gabriel slurred.

"Gabriel, I think I better take you home." Her voice showed concern as she held his arm.

He was suddenly consumed with an overwhelming need for fresh air. He reached into his wallet and threw cash at the bartender.

"Hey champ, you want me to call a cab?"

In response, Gabriel said, "Got to call Jacqueline," except it came out Wackoline. He couldn't get his mouth to work properly. "Need some air."

"What's wrong, Gabriel...are you sick?" Brenda called after him as he staggered out the door.

Gabriel tried to press the little button on his Casio that

illuminated the screen. It took an eternity before he could focus his eyes to see that it was a few minutes before 11 PM. There were people on the sidewalk, seemingly trying to get in his way. He bumper car'd in the direction of where he thought he had parked his car. Looking up at the crescent moon, he pointed it out to some people passing by. "Look the moon...it's half awake." It struck him as funny as he staggered along the sidewalk, carefully holding on to the side of a building.

"My poor little Bug...they painted it pink. Thought it would make me get a new car. Well, hell no. I'm a loyal man," he said to an older woman, who quickened her pace to get away from him. "They think they're so cute, leaving little messages under my windshield about feminine products. You know ... pads and stuff. I'm not going to do it. No, not going to," he yelled after the woman. Gabriel slid down the side of the building and sat on the sidewalk. "Not going to do it. Oh, Wackolin how could you do that? No, it wasn't her, it was Wachel. That Wachel, she's trouble. Lovely, sexy Wachel." He started to chuckle at the sound of his voice. He thought he sounded like Elmer Fudd.

He must have dozed for a few minutes before looking at his watch and seeing that twenty minutes had passed. He pulled himself up and stumbled down the sidewalk. "I can drive. It'll sober me up." He found his VW and wrestled with the keys, trying clumsily to stab them into the door lock. Finally successful, Gabriel opened the door and collapsed onto the driver's seat. He sat up and let his head fall back against the seat and closed his eyes. *So tired, just for a moment.*

Gabriel woke with a start and grabbed the steering wheel,

swinging wildly to the left to avoid what he thought was a tree. When the fog cleared, he realized that it was the pine-scented air freshener hanging from his rearview mirror.

He laughed to himself as people walked by, giving him funny looks. *Got to find some coffee. That'll do it.* He got out of the car and zigzagged past a poorly lit alley, pausing for a moment. *A sound. "Ow," or was it "Meow?"* He heard it again. It might have been a call for help, or maybe it was just a cat, or maybe a cat meowing for help. His ears strained to hear. There it was again, this time clearer, more desperate. *I should have brought a flashlight. But that's stupid. Who goes to a bar carrying a flashlight?*

"Hello, is someone there?" He didn't like the sound of his voice, so he regrouped and dropped down a couple of octaves and belted out more confidently. "Need help? I mean, do you need help?"

Gabriel tentatively inched his way into the dark alley waiting for his eyes to adjust. *This alley smells bad.* He could make out a huge garbage bins. Once again, he heard a noise, just one word, "Meeeowelp."

What if it's Bourbon? Bourbon is such a great cat. I miss Bourbon. But why would Bourbon be here? There's a shape lying in front of the bin. He inched close. *A six-foot-tall kitty wearing black cowboy boots?* Gabriel knelt before the cat and touched its leg, "Hey, wake up little kitty." He was trying to come to grips with how big a cat's paws had to be in order to wear cowboy boots when he sensed a quick movement from behind him. Next came a gush of wind followed by a siren and a searing pain in his neck. Doubling over, he would have face-planted into the gravel if the cowboy-boot-wearing cat hadn't caught him. Holding him up, the cat let loose with a vicious slap causing Gabriel to fall back and into a puddle of something disgusting.

CHAPTER THREE

DAY 2

Tuesday, July 17th, 1984
Slidell, Louisiana

Darkness. *My eyes are open, but everything's black. I feel like I have a toothache in my brain.* Gabriel struggled to sit upright but immediately felt woozy. He tried to stand but the gravel beneath him started to shift. *What the hell? Okay, okay, calm down, think, think, pink, blink, bada-badabink...* Incoherent thoughts were popping in and out, like ping pong balls in a bingo machine.

Noises, people, I hear noises, street noises...people. He tried to yell for help, but couldn't get his mouth to work. He sat back down and tried to organize his thoughts. A flash of a cat wearing cowboy boots came into his mind. He shook his head, causing more pain. *I remember yelling at a woman on the sidewalk about my car being painted pink and Rachel leaving little notes under the windshield. Why does my head hurt so much? Wait, I fell asleep in my car and almost hit a tree.* He lay back down on the gravel for what he thought would be just a minute.

GABRIEL WOKE ONCE AGAIN. *Someone's there.* His body was being tussled from side to side. His eyes tried to adjust to what little moonlight there was. The shape was rooting in Gabriel's pant pockets. He tried to sit up but couldn't. His muscles seemed to have taken the night off. The aching in his skull continued to ebb and flow like the Biloxi tide.

He could make out a man wearing a trench coat. *Maybe it's going to rain. That would be nice, cool things off. He's looking at my wallet.* He watched as the man turned the wallet sideways. He was mumbling something interspersed with faint guttural sounds. *He's looking at the picture of my wife.* Gabriel wanted to tell him that it was from their wedding, but again, he couldn't form the words.

The man is looking at me now. He's got rotten teeth. I should give him the name of my dentist. The man bent over Gabriel and moved closer until he was lying on top of him like he was a blanket. *He must think I'm cold. That's nice.*

He's sniffing me. Trench coat moved within inches of Gabriel's face. *His hair is hanging down. He needs a haircut. Wait, this guy is doing something with his mouth, maybe he wants to tell me a secret. Ugh! I think he just licked me.*

"Whar's yer money?"

Gabriel couldn't make out what the man was saying.

"Whar is th' cash?"

Gabriel shook his head and stretched his neck away from the man.

"Come on, yo' got rich fella clo'ese, rich fella shoes, yo' smell like a richie rich. Whar's yer money?"

Gabriel closed his eyes. *I don't understand this guy. He must be a tourist.*

"Don't yo' back t'sleep on me. Yo' drunk? Whar's it at? Yo' doesn't git t'have thet kind of pussy wifout money."

I think he said pussy. Maybe he knows the cat with the cowboy boots. After a couple of moments, Gabriel felt the man lift himself off of him. He opened his eyes in time to watch him slip into the shadows.

He had no idea how long he'd been asleep. It was still dark. He tried to sit up, but once again found he had no hand-eye coordination, Noises were coming from the street. His stomach turned, and he swallowed down what had come up. *I remember going into this alley. I remember someone hit me. But what am I doing here?* Gabriel tried to stand again only to find that the earthquake had returned.

He lay down and tried to remember. *I thought Bourbon needed help. Wait, that's stupid. Bourbon doesn't wear boots. What's more, Bourbon's in Biloxi. It couldn't have been Bourbon. I'm in New Orleans. I'm here to help, Ruthe....Rutherford? Rutledge? The guy doesn't have a first name. How silly is that? Everyone has a first name. Did his mother call out, Rutledge, it's time to come home now?*

He knew he needed help. Gabriel crawled over to the garbage bin and used it to pull himself up. The exertion made his heart race. Sweat dripped down his face as he inched along the side of the bin. He used the side of a building to make his way to the mouth of the alley. Once there he heard the sounds of car horns and tires screeching.

CHAPTER FOUR

Tuesday, July 17th, 1984
Ocean Springs, Mississippi

"This is by a famous painter called Lorin Thompson. He's respected for his painting of Native American tribes," explained Jacqueline as she approached the well-dressed couple looking at a painting on the gallery's wall. The couple gave her a blank look. From behind her, Jacqueline was momentarily distracted by the chime signaling the opening of the gallery's front door. A person wearing a brown monk's tunic walked in, the hood hiding their face.

Jacqueline turned back to the couple. "Have you heard of the legend of the singing river?"

The attractive, well-dressed blonde shook her head. The man, who had to be twice her age, smiled at Jacqueline, giving her a creepy once-over before winking. She ignored him and focused her attention on the blonde. "This depicts the Pascagoula tribe and the river that bears their name. The legend suggests that if you listen closely at night, you'll hear the sound of singing coming from the river. Some say it's mermaids."

"Wow." The blonde was chomping on gum. Her eyes went wide. "I think I heard them last night. Our Best Western's balcony faces the river." She turned to look at her companion, who was still ogling Jacqueline.

"That was the television," replied the man, without taking his gaze from Jacqueline. "We were watching Hill Street Blues."

"No, I think it was Love Boat. I remember, Pookie, because we had just finished, you know, and well I thought, how cool is that?" Turning to Jacqueline, "We're on our honeymoon."

"Congratulations."

"Larry Oglethorpe," said the man, his tone a verbal hitching up of his pants. He extended his hand and flashed a lustful smile.

"Jacqueline Ross." She shook his hand. "Welcome to the Moran Gallery."

"Awesome," said the blonde, looking around the small shop, "This is such a quaint town. My name's Pebbles. Pebbles Oglethorpe," she repeated, chuckling at the sound of her new married name.

"What do you think of the painting?" Jacqueline asked, wanting to refocus their attention on the art.

"I like the colors. I can see this hanging in our foyer, don't you think, Larry? You know, instead of that moose head thing."

Once again, he ignored her. "Say, isn't this the shop with the skeletons under the glass floor?"

"Yes. That's a real tourist draw. Not nearly as beautiful as the Thompson though." Jacqueline led the couple to the back of the gallery near a plexiglass area in the floor. She flipped a switch on the wall and spotlights illuminated some skeletons as well as Indian artifacts.

"Oh," cooed Pebbles. "Kind of creepy. Isn't it, Larry?"

Once again, Larry ignored her.

"There was a big hurricane that hit here in 1969 called Camille. It pretty much destroyed everything. The owner of the gallery, Mr. Moran, had to do a lot of reconstruction. During the rebuilding, they unearthed this find. Mr. Moran says it's a sacred Indian burial ground. Likely for the local Biloxi tribe. Other experts disagree though, claiming the find might date back to 2200 BC."

Larry nodded as if he agreed. "Interesting. I'm in the funeral home business myself. I own a slew of them from Philadelphia to Pittsburgh. I'm pretty much the big wheel up there."

"That's interesting," repeated Jacqueline, distracted by the monk who was now handling some Indian artifacts. She was used to the gallery's upscale clientele. Seeing a monk enter the store was unusual.

"So, how much?"

"Sorry?" she said, returning her attention to the man.

"For the painting she likes. It is for sale, isn't it?"

"Oh, yes, I'm sorry." Jacqueline reached under the counter for a brochure that gave more information on the painter and his works. "This brochure has it listed at $2000. But I suspect it's worth a great deal more."

"Yeah right," sarcasm dripped from Larry's voice. "I wouldn't pay more than $500."

"If you want to make an offer, I can present it to the owner. But I should tell you that he recently turned down three times that amount."

"Larry, I like it," pleaded Pebbles. "Could we get it?

Pleeeease?" She rubbed up against him. "It could be a wedding present for ...the house."

After fifteen minutes of back and forth, Pebbles got what she wanted. Jacqueline agreed to ship the painting to their Philadelphia home.

Once the couple left the store, Jacqueline noticed the monk was up front looking out the shop's window, "Welcome to the Moran Gallery," she said, approaching from behind.

The monk turned to face her and removed the hood revealing a young, attractive face. Her head was shaved, her face devoid of makeup. She smiled. "Are you Mrs. Ross?"

"Yes, my name's Jacqueline. Do I know you?"

"We met a few years ago. I'm not surprised you don't remember."

"What's your name?"

"Star." Jacqueline waited for the girl to clarify, but she occupied herself, looking at some of the paintings on the wall. "Did you know the Pascagoula were murdered by the Biloxi tribe?"

"I didn't know that." Jacqueline was tempted to ask the girl if she was a real monk but didn't want to offend her.

"It was a romance thing. Despite being promised to a dude in her tribe, the local Biloxi princess fell for the Chief of the Pascagoula. He must have been a hunk. There was a big battle..." she shrugged her shoulders, "and it didn't go well for the Pascagoula."

"You appear to know quite a bit about this. Is that from studying at the monastery?"

The girl gave Jacqueline a smile, "I'm not a real monk. We wear this because we've taken a vow or something." She moved on to another painting. "We've also taken vows against a whole bunch of other fun stuff." Jacqueline hadn't been sure of the girl's age but based on her choice of words, figured her to be in her late teens.

"Was there something you wanted to see me about?"

"You really don't remember me? I bet Gabriel would."

"You know my husband?"

"I was looking for him, but the receptionist, a girl named Rachel, told me he was out of town. I let her believe we were family. She told me you worked here."

That morning Jacqueline had dropped off their son at her parents, surprised that Gabriel hadn't yet called from New Orleans. "But what is it you wanted to see me about?"

The girl stared at Jacqueline with eyes showing emotion for the first time. "Do you remember the Mardi Gras Killer?"

"Of course, he terrorized the Gulf Coast a couple of years back. He died in a boating accident before my husband had a chance to catch him."

"I wish." She rolled her eyes, "Yeah, well." She paused and bit her lip before continuing. "That's not totally correct. My name used to be Jessica Grant."

CHAPTER FIVE

Tuesday, July 17th, 1984
Ocean Springs, Mississippi

"You don't seem like the Jessica Grant I remember." They sat in a booth of a diner kitty-corner to the gallery. Jacqueline had agreed to meet the girl for lunch once the owner came in to cover her break.

"That's because I'm not," Jessica said as she read the diner's menu. "I'm famished! Are you buying? Like, I'm busted."

"Sure, but I'm confused. Who are you?"

Jessica put down the menu, having made her selection. "The Jessica you met had big Farrah Fawcett hair and spoke and acted like a hosebag. I'm not that Jessica anymore. I'm Star now."

"Oh, I get it." A waitress approached the table to take their order.

"I'll have a stack of blueberry pancakes, a side order of bacon, toast, and two fried eggs. Oh, and coffee...lots of coffee."

Jacqueline ordered a small salad. When the waitress left, she said, "You didn't take a vow against eating."

"Don't tell anyone. What happens outside the camp isn't anyone's business."

"You live in a commune? When did that happen?"

"Well, when fucktard, I mean Bouvier went overboard, I was rescued by the Coasties. After that, I had a big row with my parents. My dad had a shit fit. He thought I was leading an 'immoral' life and that everything that had happened was my fault. Yeah, like I kidnapped myself and those other girls. So, I told him to fuck off and bunked with girlfriends. That's when I met Stevie. They call him the Governor because he runs the camp and makes the rules."

The waitress brought coffee. "Keep' em coming. I haven't had coffee in, fuck...I mean years." The waitress was momentarily taken aback by a monk's profanity and left to get their food.

"Sorry, I don't talk like that at the camp."

"Tell me about it. Where is it?"

"It's north of Mobile. That's in 'Bama. I had to thumb a lift down here. Amazing how easy it is for a monk to get a ride." The waitress brought a tray of food to the table, and as soon as she was gone, Jessica/Star started in like a hungry alligator.

"Are you in touch with your parents?" Jacqueline watched Jessica gobble down her meal.

"No. At least not until recently. That's why I wanted to talk to Gabriel." Star's mouth was full of pancakes.

"Your parents must have been very worried about you."

"At first, my Dad just thought I was pissed. But when I didn't come up for air, he went to the cops and filed a missing person report. For a while, I was in the news again. Stevie told me to keep a low profile. He said it was important to cleanse the impurities out of my system."

"You said you thought the Mardi Gras Killer was still alive..."

"I know he is," Star said matter-of-factly as she chewed a piece of toast.

"How?"

She reached into a small cloth handbag and pulled out a folded-up postcard showing a street scene with eight children dressed up in costumes wearing different Mardi Gras masks. The picture had a creepy feel to it. Jacqueline turned the card over. It was postmarked from Mobile. The one-line message on the back was written in neat script using a blue felt pen. *Looking forward to you joining the group.*

Jacqueline looked up into Jessica's eyes. "How do you know it's from him. This might just be someone playing a joke. As you said, you saw him fall overboard in the storm, right?"

"He did fall over. I shot him with a flare gun." She downed the last of her coffee and held her cup up, signaling to the waitress. "Hey, babe!" Star turned back to Jacqueline, "The cops never found the body."

The waitress came over and filled her cup. "As for this being a friend playing a joke, I don't think so. A friend might do it once. This fuck...I mean guy, has been sending these to my parents for months."

"Charles Bouvier," Jacqueline was so shocked at what she was hearing, she had barely touched her salad.

"I used to call him fucktard. Another reason these cards are legit is that he referred to something personal."

"What's that?"

"On one postcard, he asked if I still wore yellow panties."

"You and your parents need to go to the police. Right,

now!" Jacqueline said in alarm. "This guy is a monster. He could be abducting girls, killing people. Oh my God, Jessica!"

"We tried. The Harrison County Sheriff said they'd look into it; they said that everyone at the post office would have handled the postcards so dusting for prints was a waste of time. They thought it was a prank, or I was sending them to myself to get attention. And get this, the cards all come from different places, and they all have to do with a Mardi Gras parade. The first card my parents got was mailed from New Orleans. The next one came from Gulfport, The last from Mobile. It's like he's getting closer. Like he's figuring it out."

"What does he mean, join the group?"

"I don't know unless the eight people on the postcard represent the other girls."

"I think Gabriel told me there were six girls."

Star just shrugged and took a last bite of pancakes.

"You must be scared out of your wits, Jessica. How did you even know about the cards?"

"I stay in contact with a friend near where my parents live in Gulfport. The card about the yellow panties must have creeped Mom out, and she talked to my friend's mother. My friend came to the camp and told me. I've been staying at my parents place the past couple of days while we tried to get the cops to do their job." After a moment, Star added, "There's one other thing. My parents have been getting calls."

"What kind of calls."

"At first, it was just hang-ups, then it was heavy breathing. Lately, the creep just says, Jessica."

Jacqueline felt a wave of panic wash over her. "Gabriel will be beside himself. As I said, he's in New Orleans. Let's go back to the shop, and I'll call him. He'll know what to do."

CHAPTER SIX

Tuesday, July 17th, 1984
New Orleans, Louisiana

"Afternoon, er... *Eye on You Detective Agency*, Rutledge."

"Hello, Mr. Rutledge, it's Jacqueline Ross. Put me through to my husband, please."

"Uh, I can't...he's not in the office yet this morning."

"It's not morning. It's almost 1 PM. Do you know where my husband is?" For good measure she added, "It's important."

"Not really, likely at the hotel. He's staying at the *Hotel Provincial*, I think. I have the number somewhere..."

"I called there, and they said he wasn't answering." Jacqueline was conscious her excitement over the Mardi Gras Killer was making her impatient and tried to calm herself. "Where else might he be?" she asked slowly, gritting her teeth.

"I don't know. I was expecting him this morning."

Jacqueline was about to hang up when she thought of something else. "Is Ben O'Shea in the office?"

"He just walked in a few minutes ago." There was a clunk as Rutledge put the phone down heavily on his desk. Jacqueline could hear a whispered, "Gabriel's wife?"

"Jackie, is that you? Is everything okay?" Ben asked as he picked up the receiver.

"Yes, and no. I need to find Gabriel. He didn't call me this morning, which is very unusual."

"I'm sure it's nothing Jackie, he might have just gone out for lunch, or maybe he's working on something. Did you call Rachel? He's not likely there, but she usually knows what he's up to."

For some reason, Rachel knowing more about Gabriel's whereabouts annoyed Jacqueline. "No, I haven't. That's a good idea. I'll hang up and call."

"Call me back, meanwhile I'll make some calls from this end."

Fifteen minutes later, Jacqueline called back, "Ben, we have a problem."

"What did Rachel say?"

"She hasn't heard from him, she also checked with Arnie Sims, and he hasn't either."

"That doesn't necessarily mean ..."

Jacqueline interrupted, her voice rising, "I then called the hotel back and spoke to the manager. He checked with the cleaning staff, and they said Gabriel's bed hadn't been slept in."

"It's almost 1:30."

Jacqueline heard Ben yell at Rutledge. "Start calling your buddies at the police station. See if there were any reports last night." Then she heard a whispered, "Accidents, assaults, you know the drill."

Ben then came back on the line, his tone reassuring. "Jackie, try not to worry. I'm going to get right on it. Maybe that car of his finally bit the dust."

"Check the hospitals, please, Ben. I'm on my way."

CHAPTER SEVEN

Tuesday, July 17th, 1984
Gulfport, Mississippi

Rachel called Arnie again. He'd barely said hello when she cried out, "It's Rachel. All hell is breaking loose. Ben's in New Orleans; the phone is ringing off the hook; Jacqueline's going crazy."

To his credit, Arnie didn't waste time with questions. "Bourbon and I are on the way."

WHEN HE ARRIVED at the agency, Rachel hugged the older black man. Arnie had joined the agency part-time after developing a friendship with Gabriel. "Something big is happening, Arnie. I just got off the phone with Jacqueline again. She wants you to head out to an address in Gulfport, and to introduce yourself and make sure nothing bad happens."

"Anything bad," repeated Arnie, handing the cat to her. "Can you be a little more specific about 'bad?'"

"I don't know. First, Jacqueline called and asked if I knew where she could reach Gabriel. When I said he was in New Orleans, she almost bit my head off. She hung up on me and then called back and apologized, saying Gabriel hadn't slept in the hotel last night. No one at the agency knows where he is. She has Ben and the new guy, Rutledge, calling the hospitals."

"There might be a straightforward explanation."

"Maybe, but in all my days of knowing her, she's never barked at me like that. There must be something else. Rachel said she was going to drive to New Orleans. Something's very wrong, Arnie."

"And this address in Gulfport?"

"The name is Grant; all she said was to ask for the monk."

"The monk?"

"Yeah, the monk. That's all I know."

"I'm going to go to this address, and ask for the monk? Oh, and then, I'll make sure nothing "bad" happens." Arnie rolled his eyes. "I'd better get going then. Speaking of mysteries, maybe you should ask that Don guy to help. That is, if that's his real name." Arnie was referring to Rachel's latest romantic interest, whom she'd met while investigating a stolen car ring. At one point Don had gone by the name Drake, then Dan, and finally Don. Don worked undercover for the Mississippi Bureau of Investigation, the state's version of the FBI, and was evasive about his true identity.

"The last lie he told me was that his name was Don Purplinski. He blurted that out, but if you remember, I had a black eye at the time."

"Sounds like what my Grandma used to call horse pucky."

"Yep. It's too bad; we were pretty good together. I told

him I wouldn't see him anymore if he was going to lie to me. It's been three weeks since we last spoke, so I guess Don loves his bullshit more than me."

Arnie gave her a sympathetic look. "All right, I'm off to see the monk."

CHAPTER EIGHT

Tuesday, July 17th, 1984
New Orleans, Louisiana

Ben called hospital after hospital, drawing a blank on white John Does brought in the previous evening. Similarly, Rutledge called his pals at the NOPD and was told there was nothing reported on a man meeting Gabriel's description. Rutledge had been Ben's former partner back when they had both worked for the Biloxi PD. Now he was 'the Invest-Gator' at their New Orleans office.

"Hold on, Ben, is this like Gabriel, to go off the reservation?"

"Not at all. The guy's a straight arrow. Besides, Jackie would kick his ass."

"Who would have a grudge against Gabriel and want to hurt him?"

"Lots of people. That's one of the hazards of the profession. You saw that interview on WGNO yesterday, Gabriel has made more than a few enemies. We both have."

"Speaking of interviews, I heard that Baxter guy in front of the cameras saying the charges were all trumped up."

"Baxter's in jail but between him and that Frank Reznikov I wouldn't put it past them to do something. What happened on Monday, when I was taking marriage classes?"

"Not much, we picked up a case, a walk-in. Pretty straightforward, but now that I think about it, Gabriel didn't like the lady."

"Why?"

"He didn't believe her story. Her name was Lana, Lana Tadic. She came in with one of Gabriel's business cards. She thought her husband was fooling around. She's been getting hang-ups, and her husband Petr was cooking up some excuse to go out every night. Said he was taking bowling lessons."

"It could just be a misunderstanding."

"Maybe so, but when she took the checkbook out, I thought it was worth a look-see. She said she'd overheard her husband on the phone say he would be at the Hideout at 10 PM on Monday night. That's a country and western bar east of here in a town called Slidell. It was pretty straightforward. Take a drive out to the place and see what the bowling teacher looks like."

"How would Gabriel be able to recognize this guy?"

"She gave us a picture of the two of them on some beach getting married. Here, I took a copy for the file."

"Tadic, what kind of name is that?"

"I assumed it was her married name. It might be Croatian; there's a large community here."

Ben looked at the photo. "Not a bad looking dame, if you like tough broads with big tits. So maybe Gabriel goes out there, sees a little hanky-panky, tries for a Polaroid, and this Tadic nabs him. That what you're thinking?"

Rutledge shrugged his shoulders. “I don’t know what to think. There is one other thing,” he paused and looked up at the ceiling. “It should have been me. I’m the manager. But I had tickets to a Saints game.”

“Better get me everything on these people.”

CHAPTER NINE

Tuesday, July 17th, 1984
Gulfport, *Mississippi*

The sky was darkening. Arnie rolled up the van's windows as he heard the rumble of thunder. Maybe it was the confederate battle flag hanging from a flag pole in the side yard, but the thunder sounded like cannon. The battle between the States carrying on in the heavens. The weatherman had forecasted a round of thunderstorms because of all the humidity.

It took Arnie twenty minutes to arrive at the small bungalow on 60th Avenue. The house looked in good shape and had an empty one-car driveway leading to a garage that had been converted to living space. *Not exactly a monastery. Why would a monk be living in a plain residential area?* He pulled his van into the driveway and sat, staring at the house. *Why would a monk be in danger living here? And what does this have to do with Jacqueline?*

Arnie looked up at the house and saw curtains in the front window move. Getting out, he made his way to the front door and knocked. After a second knock, he was startled by an older white man who had come up behind him.

"Ain't buying anything, so best be getting on, boy," The man appeared to be in his fifties, wearing a John Deer cap and dirty overalls.

Arnie ignored the slight. "My name's Arnie Sims. Would you be Mr. Grant?"

"That's right, and this here's my property. So state your business."

"I'm a private investigator, and I was told to ask for the monk."

"You're a private investigator?" Mr. Grant asked in a tone of disbelief. After a moment of staring followed by snorting and spitting something disgusting on the ground, he added, "Ain't no monk here. My daughter Jessica is around back, but believe me, she ain't no monk."

Arnie figured Grant wasn't about to invite him to walk through his home, so he stepped off the porch. As he approached the man, he smiled and extended his hand.

Grant ignored him and turned around, walking to the side of the house. Arnie followed him and saw he was working on a rusty old car. "Wow, I haven't seen a Belvedere in years. Is it yours?" The sedan was mustard yellow with a white roof and white sidewall tires.

The man looked at Arnie with surprise. "Yep, she's a '54, built up in St. Louis. Just changing up her plugs. I figure I'm gonna restore her and enter her in some shows."

"She's a beaut. This was their first full-size model, right?"

The man nodded, "Don't make 'em like this anymore. All you find now are those little Jap cars. We beat the crap out of them in WW Two, and we end up driving their little shit-boxes." Grant accentuated his disgust by spitting on the grass again.

"I hear you, man." Arnie was thankful he was driving a North American van. "Needs a little body work; can you do that?"

"'Spect, so," came the reply as the man bent over the engine. "Say, you aren't in with that outfit that was chasing this Mardi Gras Killer, are you?"

"Yes, I am. Gabriel Ross is my boss. I came on board after, but I followed the case. That was one sick guy. I wonder what gets into people."

"If you're asking me, boy, I would say it's all on account of the lefty pinkos — this whole hippy culture with their drugs. The country's going to hell. Just look at all of this free love crap. Women are walking around just putting it all out there."

"That so?" Arnie's internal voice was cautioning him not to antagonize the man.

"What'ya'll want with Jessica?" Arnie noted a hardening tone.

"I was sent here to make sure the monk was alright. I don't even know her."

"You carry a gun, Mr. Private Detective?" Grant asked from under the hood, pronouncing private detective as if it had a dozen syllables.

"I have a gun, but I don't have it with me."

"Well, how the fuck you going to protect her?" Grant straightened up and glared at Arnie, "You can't protect shit without a gun. If something happens, cops won't come until it's too late. I keep my 12 gauge right handy."

Arnie thought he was losing any goodwill he'd built up. "Where did you say Jessica was?"

"Hey, Jessica!" Grant yelled towards a raised deck on the other side of the yard. "Y'all got a caller. He come here to protect ya."

A young woman dressed in a brown tunic came out of a

screen door, stood on the patio, and waived. She was bald but appeared to be young. She flashed a smile. "You the guy Jacqueline was going to send over?"

"Yes, name's Arnie Sims." He walked over and extended his hand.

"Would you like some lemonade?" Jessica shook his hand and gestured inside. "I was sitting outside watching Pops work on that car, but it's way too muggy with this on."

"I think it's supposed to storm. Are you a real monk?"

"No, Jacqueline asked me that too. We wear this on account of the vow. I'm so hot, I feel like taking it off."

"If you want to take it off..."

"I think Daddy might mind. I have nothing on underneath."

"Whoa," Arnie said a little embarrassed. "You'd better not. He told me about his 12 gauge." Arnie smiled at Jessica, who poured two large glasses of lemonade. "Thanks."

"The name's Star actually, but my parents keep calling me Jessica. I guess they're not copacetic." She invited him to take a seat at the kitchen table.

"Star? How did you get a name like that?"

"When I first arrived at the camp, Stevie, he runs things; we were talking, and he told me that I had to shed my skin and part of that was picking a new name. We were looking up at the stars, so that's what he suggested."

"So, if you're Star, who is Jessica Grant?"

"You don't remember her?" She seemed a little disappointed. "Jessica was this blonde teenager who got abducted by some asshole, I mean man, who sold her to another sicko on a boat. That guy was not cool."

"You're that Jessica? I read about this in the papers. And the company I work for helped uncover the guy."

"Gabriel, yeah, that's right. I met him and his wife a couple of times. She has beautiful hair."

Arnie pointed at her bald head. "Having second thoughts?"

"Yeah, sometimes, but I'm glad I look like this now. That sicko had a thing for blonde teenage girls who looked like Farrah Fawcett. I'm hoping he hasn't developed a fetish for baldies," she giggled.

"Well, he's dead, anyway."

A look of surprise came over her face. "Jacqueline didn't tell you?"

"Tell me what?" Arnie took a sip of his lemonade.

"He's not dead. We all thought he was, but he's been sending these Mardi Gras postcards to my parents, saying he'll see me soon."

Arnie stared at Star for a moment trying to determine if she was kidding. "Do the police know about this?"

"The cops around here are pretty useless. There was so much publicity. They said it was just someone playing a sick joke. A copycat. So I pointed out that on one of the cards, he asked if I still wear yellow panties."

"And that's right? You wear yellow panties?"

"When I wear panties...yes."

"Okay, are the cops still looking into this? This was a pretty big case."

"The Harrison County Sheriff said there's nothing they can do." Jessica lowered her voice as if someone might be listening, "My parents have been getting phone calls from some man looking for me."

Arnie picked up the panic in the young girl's voice. "Oh Jesus, maybe I should have brought my gun. What does your Dad say?"

"Pops? Well, Pop kind of feels I brought this on myself.

Let's say he's not the most enlightened creature on the planet. He just told the creep he had the wrong number."

"And your mom?"

"She's scared. She doesn't go near the phone; she can't sleep. Just the opposite of Dad."

"Is she upstairs?"

"No, my Gramma up in Jackson isn't well. So Mom is there helping." A flash of lightning was followed quickly by a crack of thunder, and the lights went out.

CHAPTER TEN

Tuesday, July 17th, 1984
New Orleans, Louisiana

"Ben, I just got off the phone with the NOPD. I have some bad news." Rutledge had a panicky expression on his face.

"Please, please don't say something bad happened to Gabriel."

"The good news is there are still no reports of accidents involving anyone matching Gabriel's description. A lot of the guys remember him from that business with the Nantois boys last spring. They're going to get right on it as if he was one of their own."

"Get to the not so good news."

Rutledge took a deep breath, "There is no record of Lana Tadic."

"The client? What? Like they don't have a police record? That doesn't..."

"No, I mean, she doesn't exist anywhere. No police

record, no driver's license, the address she gave us is a vacant lot north of town. The check she gave us is on a bogus account."

"So ...you're saying this was a setup?"

"Kind of looks that way."

"That's a little out there. Let's go over this again, tell me again everything you remember about this Tadic lady." Ben took a chair and sat down in front of Rutledge's desk and listened as Rutledge went over everything again.

"So, she gave you a check?"

"She said, how much do you need to take care of this? Gabriel asked her what she meant by taken care of because some customers might want pictures, timelines, and stuff. She said all she wanted was confirmation and where she could find the little slut, so she could beat the crap out of her."

"Then she wrote out the check?"

"$1000, even recorded it in her little bogus check register." Rutledge shook his head.

"Anything else you can remember about her?" Did she have an accent?"

"No, no accent. Oh, wait a minute, she smoked Lucky Strike cigarettes, the menthol kind because they stunk up the place."

"Did you say this Hideout bar is in Slidell?"

"Yeah, do you know it?"

"I know Slidell." The agency's front door opened and Jacqueline walked in, looking frantic. Ben stood up and hugged her. "Don't worry Jackie, we'll find him."

Jacqueline wiped away a tear. "Have you learned anything?"

"Come sit down with us, and we'll bring you up to date. By the way, I don't think you know Rutledge."

The large black man stood and extended his hand. "Why don't I go next door and get you a cup of tea?" he asked.

"Yes, please, that would be nice," Jacqueline shook his hand.

Rutledge left to go to the diner and Ben brought Jacqueline up to date about the calls to the hospitals and what they'd learned from the NOPD about the client.

"Ben, it sounds like someone went to a lot of trouble to do this. I'm scared, and I know why."

"What does that mean Jackie? I don't follow."

Jacqueline explained about Jessica Grant, the postcards, and how she had asked Arnie to watch the family.

"You're saying the Mardi Gras Killer is...alive? That's hard to believe. I haven't read about any girls disappearing. But Jackie, that happened over a year and a half ago. If he did survive why abduct Gabriel now?"

"I don't know Ben, but one thing Gabriel always says, there is no such thing as a coincidence."

Ben was still shaking his head in disbelief when Rutledge came back carrying a tray of coffee and tea. He took a look at Ben's face. "Okay, what'd I miss?"

Jacqueline filled him in on the Mardi Gras Killer and the theory that he might be responsible for what had happened to Gabriel.

Rutledge shook his head in disbelief. "I can't believe that psycho is alive. Well, you're right; this does feel personal. People don't go so far to cook up a story unless they have a serious ax to grind. Jesus, I'm sorry, Mrs. Ross. I was telling Ben, I feel bad because it should have been me."

"Why is that?" Jacqueline drank her tea.

"I'm the manager; it would have been natural for me to have gone. But I had tickets to see the Saints play on Monday night."

"When did you buy the tickets?" asked Ben.

"They showed up in my mailbox one day. There was a retirement card. It said something like, 'thanks for all the great years'. I took my ex-partner, and the funny thing is he said he didn't know anything about it."

"Maybe that's how they knew it would be Gabriel," said Ben

Jacqueline listened impassively, trying to read Ben's expression, looking for signs of hope. "So we have no idea where my husband is, who might have done what to him, or why."

"You're right Jackie," said Ben. "Right now, there's much that we don't know. But have faith in Gabriel. He's been in tough spots before. We'll find him."

Jacqueline cradled her head in her hands. "I know something bad has happened. I can feel it."

Rutledge shook his head as if he was trying to dispel a bad thought. Before he could say anything, the phone on his desk rang.

While Rutledge answered the call, Ben shifted the topic. "Is Benjamin with your parents?"

"Yes, thank God. I sent Arnie to babysit Jessica. With the postcards and phone calls, Bouvier knows where they live."

"We should assume he knows where everyone lives," Ben responded as Rutledge hung up the call.

"That was my old partner. They put out an APB on Gabriel's car. A patrol found it in Slidell, about two blocks from the Hideout. The driver's door was unlocked, and the keys were in the ignition."

"Gabriel would never have left the keys in the ignition." Jacqueline's voice was tinged with panic.

"I'm heading to Slidell to talk to the people at this bar." Ben stood up.

"And I'm coming with you," Jacqueline's tone dared someone to argue.

"Call me if you get anything," Rutledge requested as they left the building.

CHAPTER ELEVEN

Tuesday, July 17th, 1984
Gulfport, Mississippi

The back door to the house opened suddenly, and a wild-eyed Grant ran in, yelling at Arnie and Jessica to keep their heads down. He opened a closet door and pulled out a Remington, then reached into a box on a shelf to grab a handful of shells. "What'd I tell you, boy? A real man's gonna have to take care of business. You best hide under a bed with Jessica."

The darkening sky had bathed the kitchen in shadows. Outside, the clouds opened, and rain started coming down in a torrential downpour.

"Did you see someone out there?" Arnie stood up to look out the kitchen window.

"Get down, you fool." Grant moved from window to window, brandishing his shotgun.

Arnie and Jessica shared a look. She shook her head and nodded towards the staircase leading upstairs. "I think it's just the storm." Arnie watched Jessica leave the kitchen.

"Someone's out there. On the other side of your van."

A sound of breaking glass came from the front of the house, followed by Jessica's scream.

Arnie flashed a look at Grant and ran to the living room, carrying a spatula that had been on the stove. He found Jessica on the ground hiding under the broken window. "Are you alright, Jessica?" She was lying in the fetal position, muttering to herself. "Jessica, are you alright?" Arnie repeated.

"There was someone out there. He broke the window."

The words had no sooner left her lips when her father came running in, shotgun at the ready. He went to the window, broken glass crunching under his boots. After a moment he said, "Can't see shit with all this rain." He noticed Arnie holding the spatula above his head. "We can all feel safer, knowing you can make him breakfast."

Arnie ignored the comment and went to the phone. "No dial tone." He looked out the window anxiously before bending down and helping the girl up and away from the window. "You're safe, Jessica. Did you recognize the person?"

"No, they were wearing something over their head."

"Like a hoody?"

She nodded. "He threw that," she pointed to a rock the size of a baseball. It had landed under the coffee table and had a piece of cardboard attached to it with an elastic band. Grant put his shotgun down on the table and reached to pick it up.

"Stop! There might be fingerprints," yelled Arnie. Grant looked over at Arnie and backed away as if the rock was about to explode.

"We better find a place to hide, maybe the cellar," suggested Arnie.

"I ain't fuckin hiding. You go on, and take Jessica with you."

"What are you going to do?"

"Meet the enemy head-on," A look of defiance was written on his face.

Arnie reached for the man's arm."That might not be wise. You don't know who's out there." Before Grant could say something sarcastic, Arnie asked, "Do you have a pair of scissors and some tweezers?"

Grant looked at Arnie as if he had two heads. "First the spatula, now tweezers? What-cha- gonna do? Offer to mend his clothes?"

Jessica stood up. '"Mom has a sewing basket in the kitchen. I'll get it."

Grant went back to the window, searching for something to shoot. "Rains coming in. I got some old wood in the crawlspace," he said, moving to the stairs.

Jessica returned from the kitchen and gave the kit to Arnie.

He moved the coffee table, then got down on his hands and knees. Using the scissors from the basket, he snipped off the elastic band from the rock. The front of the card had a picture of eight traditional Mardi Gras masks, and the words, *Greetings from Gulfport, Mississippi*. Arnie looked over at Jessica, now slumped on the floor and holding her knees, a look of sheer terror on her face. Grant had interrupted his move to the crawlspace to look over Arnie's shoulder. Using a pair of tweezers, Arnie flipped the card over. It had been mailed locally and was written in a blue marker. "*Sorry, we missed Mardi Gras. But we have the World's Fair.*"

CHAPTER TWELVE

Tuesday, July 17th, 1984
Slidell, Louisiana

Ben drove his truck at full speed, weaving in and out of traffic. To settle him down, Jacqueline asked Ben what he knew about Charles Bouvier.

"Gabriel was the one that found the connection between the girls; he found Boone Cooper, then traced everything back to New Orleans. From what I know, Charles was a spoiled little rich kid with some serious Mommy issues. His mother died when their mansion burned down, with Charles conveniently out on his boat at the time. Charles' father had previously disappeared suspiciously during a hurricane."

"All the girls had that Farrah Fawcett hairstyle, right? Why the fixation?"

"I don't know. When Bouvier went overboard, and they couldn't find the body, they had an inquest. They needed it to close the case. I remember hearing that when they recovered his boat, they found all kinds of Betamax tapes of Charlie's Angels and all kinds of posters of Farrah on the walls. Kind of like a shrine. Why the fixation? Your guess is as good as mine. If he's alive, maybe we can ask him. Maybe find out what happened to all of those girls."

"Oh, he's alive. Jessica is convinced."

"Tell me about Jessica." Ben turned onto the highway leading to Slidell.

"She's gone spiritual. Says she's been living in a camp north of Mobile. Her hair is all shaved off, and she wears this brown monk outfit. She says she's taken a vow of poverty, but from talking to her, I'm not sure she's fully drinking the kool-aid."

They drove past an area known as the Irish Bayou, a small village surrounded by wetlands. Jacqueline pointed out a structure off to the right, "What's that?"

"A castle. A developer had it built as an attraction for the World's Fair. Rutledge told me he thought it was a bust."

They crossed Lake Pontchartrain on the Highway 10 bridge and arrived at the outskirts of Slidell, a small town experiencing rapid growth. "Isn't this where Tommy ..."

"Yes, he's at the Northshore Psychiatric Hospital. His aunt lives here too."

"Terrible thing, it makes me so sad when I think of what happened to him and his family."

"Rachel still goes to visit. She hasn't lost hope. She thinks he understands more than the doctors claim and that they have a bond."

BEN AND JACQUELINE had no problem finding the Hideout which was on the western edge of town. Ben pulled up to the curb in front of an older building. "Let me do the talking."

"Whatever you say, Ben."

"Do you have a picture of Gabriel?"

Jacqueline took out a wallet from her purse and pulled out a picture of her husband. He was looking sheepishly back at the camera in front of the Biloxi lighthouse. "Gabriel always hated this picture. Because of the angle, the lighthouse makes him look like he's two feet tall."

The bar was dimly lit, and the Scorpions big hit *Rock You Like a Hurricane* was playing on the jukebox. A heavy-set bartender, his blonde hair in a ponytail, was wiping the counter. Ben noticed he had a swastika tattoo on his neck.

They sat at the bar and took the place in. A dozen or so rough-looking men were sitting at tables and another couple perched at the far end of the bar. Ben made eye contact with the bartender and asked for a couple of Buds. When the bartender put the beer and glasses in front of them, Ben asked him if he had been working the previous night.

"Yeah, it's my place so, I pretty much work all the time," he replied, pouring the beers.

Ben put a twenty dollar bill and the lighthouse picture of Gabriel in front of him.

'You a cop?"

"No, just a guy looking for a guy. My name's Ben, and this lady is Jacqueline. It's her husband in the picture."

The bartender picked up the twenty. "You still owe me for the beer."

Ben smiled and nodded, pulling another twenty from his wallet. "Do you remember seeing this man?"

"He looks like the guy that was here last night, except smaller. He was with some blonde." He shot Jacqueline an uncertain glance. "She was all over him. You know, constantly touching him, caressing his arm, rubbing her you know whats, into his side. They were drinking fancy drinks. Like they were on some romantic vacation. But your buddy couldn't hold his liquor. He was slurring his words pretty good. I cut him off and offered to call him a cab, but he said no. He threw some cash at me and stumbled out the door."

"What about the woman?" Jacqueline jumped into the conversation.

"She was concerned. She offered to take him home. Left shortly after him." The bartender winked at Ben, "If you know what I mean, but frankly if you saw how blitzed this guy was, I'd be pretty impressed if he could perform."

"Have you seen this woman before?" Jacqueline leaned forward.

"We get lots of her type. But nah, I don't think so."

"And what type is that?" Jacqueline asked. Ben detected her growing hostility.

The bartender flashed a look at Ben. "Blonde, nice enough looking, phony tits, pushed up, she was wearing a checked shirt tied in a knot below her hooters. She might have had a bit of an accent. Just the way she said stuff."

"Like, Croatian?" asked Jacqueline.

"I don't know, maybe."

"Did you catch anything else that was said?" Ben took a big sip of his beer.

The bartender paused for a moment, trying to remember. "It was a busy night."

"Was there another man at the bar, kind of skinny, straggly hair, had one of those chin strips?"

"That describes most of my regulars."

"His name is Tadic. Do you know him?"

The bartender shook his head again. "Look around, of the dozen guys in here at least half of them look like that."

CHAPTER THIRTEEN

Tuesday, July 17th, 1984
Gulfport, Mississippi

It took an hour before anyone from the Harrison County Sheriff's office arrived. The barrel-chested deputy in his twenties had a boxy head topped by a brush cut. He was struggling to piece together what had happened, with Jessica, Arnie, and Mr. Grant talking excitedly over each other.

"Okay, slow down. I'm Deputy Sheriff Weber. I'm a professional peace officer." He pointed to his name tag, "It says Deputy Sheriff, not speedwriter. Why don't we have the monk do the talking for everyone?"

Jessica explained what had happened while the deputy scribbled notes on a pad. "Just so I'm sure I have this right, you're saying that a man, this Charles Bouvier, aka, that means also known as, the "Mardi Gras Killer," he used air quotes, "Who died in some boating accident a couple of years back, has come back to life and is stalking you. You say this dead man threw a rock through your window." He pointed to the rock on the floor. "That rock. You're saying it had this postcard attached to it. That about it?"

"He's not dead; his body was never found. He's now calling and hanging up, and sending these postcards. You need to arrest him before he hurts people. The guy's insane," said Star.

"Could you tell it was him that threw the rock? Can you give me his description?"

"No, he was wearing a hoody, but I know it was him."

The deputy nodded his head knowingly. Turning to Mr. Grant, "Can you describe the individual who threw the rock?"

"It was raining like a pissant out there. I couldn't see past two feet. But if my daughter said she saw someone, then she saw someone. The rock didn't throw itself."

"I know that," the deputy smiled. "Doesn't mean that some dead man threw it though." He used a golf pencil to flip the postcard over. "Doesn't sound threatening to me. Not against the law to send postcards."

Arnie looked up at the ceiling in frustration. "Listen, Deputy, is it against the law to throw a rock through someone's window?"

"Of course, it is. I know that. Before I came here, I did a full sweep of the area and found no one lurking. I checked with both your neighbors, and neither of them said anything about a stranger, except, well, for Mr. Sims here."

Arnie ignored the comment. "This is related to a very big case. You need to notify your sheriff."

"We've been having a lot of vandalism lately, at bus shelters, people spraying graffiti. Sadly, there isn't much I can do here."

"Jessica, didn't you say that your mom had already spoken to someone in the Sheriff's office?" asked Arnie in frustration.

"Yes, a few days ago. We brought all the postcards, there was at least a half-dozen, and they agreed to look into it."

"Alright, Deputy," said Arnie. "You have an open case; someone in your office is looking into this."

"Listen, folks, if this here dead man is alive, why aren't there any missing girls? All we have are a bunch of postcards which could have just as easily been sent by anyone, including yourself." The deputy looked at Jessica.

"Why would I do that, fuckhead?"

"Young lady, do you think that kind of language is appropriate for a...woman of the cloth? But to answer your question, maybe you were missing the publicity."

CHAPTER FOURTEEN

Tuesday, July 17th, 1984
Slidell, Louisiana

"That was all bullshit. Gabriel wouldn't be interested in some cheap slut. There is no way Gabriel would fall for a tramp with big pushed up tits. I know him; he wouldn't." Jacqueline said, mainly to herself as her anger bubbled over.

"I know, Jackie. Gabriel is the least likely guy to cheat. He worships you. It sounds like the blonde slipped something into his drink."

"Why would she do that?"

"I don't know, but the woman who set this up is a foreigner, and apparently, the blonde had an accent."

As they drove down the main drag, they noticed Gabriel's car parked along the curb. A couple of uniform cops were dusting the car for prints. Ben pulled the truck in behind the VW Bug.

"Hey guys, I'm Ben O'Shea, and this is Jacqueline Ross, the missing man's wife."

"Officer Don McRae. I remember you from that shootout in the spring. You helped save my partner's life."

"I remember. How's your partner?"

"Getting better, but likely done on the force."

The police officer's partner had taken a bullet to the leg, and Ben had tied a hasty tourniquet. "Shit, I know what that's like. Did you find anything in the car?"

"Keys are in it. Other than that, no sign of foul play. We've dusted for prints; we're checking them now. Lots of fresh scratch marks around the driver side door lock might mean he was under the influence. We have a team out talking to merchants, asking if they saw anything."

"Any luck?"

"One possible hit so far. A gal who works at the chicken restaurant across the street said a short man, clearly hammered, was walking westbound yelling about someone painting his car pink and a bunch of other stuff that she didn't understand. We showed her Mr. Ross' drivers license picture, and she said it was him. We narrowed the time to around 11 PM, give or take a few minutes."

"That helps." Ben looked around the area and tried to put himself in Gabriel's shoes. *If he were too drunk to drive, he wouldn't. He'd call a cab or someone for a lift.* "How about that coffee shop down the street. Would it have been open last night?"

"Absolutely, but we canvassed, and they didn't recognize the photo."

Ben told them what he'd learned from the bartender at the Hideout. The officers said they'd check out the bar a little bit later. There might be more people who might recognize Gabriel's picture.

As Ben and Jacqueline were about to leave, the police received a call on their car radio. The officer went to his cruiser, only to return a few minutes later. "Your lucky day, folks. That was the St. Tammany Parish Sheriff Department. They're holding a street person who tried to use a credit card belonging to Gabriel Ross."

IT TOOK Ben and Jacqueline less than five minutes to get to the sheriff's office, which was located on Brownswitch Street at the center of town. They were greeted by a uniform officer sitting at the reception desk.

"Afternoon officer, my name is Ben O'Shea. I was told by the NOPD to speak to Sheriff Hardie."

They were directed to sit in the waiting area while Hardie finished a meeting. The wait was only a few minutes, and a thin, older man came down the hallway and introduced himself as Sheriff Hardie. Ben smiled and introduced Jacqueline while explaining he was ex-Biloxi PD.

"I heard about Mr. Ross. It's very concerning. We picked up a male suspect trying to buy bourbon using Mr. Ross' Visa. The clerk called us because when he asked for identification, he produced a Mississippi Driver's License that clearly didn't belong to him. "

"That was pretty smart of the clerk," commented Jacqueline.

"Not only did the photo not look like the guy, but the clerk got suspicious when he saw that Mr. Ross was only five feet tall. The guy we arrested is over six feet."

"Do you mind if we speak to the man you arrested?" asked Jacqueline.

"I'm sorry, Mrs. Ross, I know you must be going through a tough time right now, but our procedures don't allow the public into our interview rooms. We can set you up to watch the interview through one-way glass. If you'll follow me, he's this way."

Ben turned to Jacqueline, "Jackie, keep your fingers crossed, this our best lead yet."

THEY WERE STANDING outside the interview room watching a man through one-way glass. Sitting in the room was a skinny, fiftyish man with long straggly hair, wearing a dirty beige trench coat. He was sitting quietly with his hands folded in his lap, gently rocking on his chair.

"You know this guy?" asked Ben. "He looks harmless."

"He's a regular. When we booked him, he asked straight up if the kitchen was still open for dinner like we were some fancy restaurant. His name is Jerome Pichette. His family are longtime residents of Slidell, but they don't want anything to do with him. We pick him up a couple of times a month. He's not technically homeless. He lives in the shelter down the street. This is a first for him. Public drunkenness, disturbing the peace are his thing. Tell you the truth, most times, we feed him, clean him up, and let him go. This is the first time we arrested him for anything serious."

"It's your shop. How did you want to handle this?"

"You go ahead and take the lead. I'll sit in just in case I can add something." The sheriff opened the interrogation room door.

Jerome immediately looked up when they walked in, his eyes as expressionless as ice cubes.

"Jerome, my name is Ben O'Shea. I'm a detective looking into the disappearance of the man whose identification you stole."

Jerome mumbled something to himself, continuing to rock back and forth on his chair.

"What was that?" Ben's voice grew louder.

"I say, I didn't steal nuthin." Jerome avoided eye contact with Ben by looking at Sheriff Hardie.

"That's just fine. What time do you have?" Ben pulled out a chair across from him.

The man looked at the clock on the wall instead of the watch on his wrist. "Dunno."

"How did you come to have Gabriel Ross' wallet?"

Jerome looked up at the ceiling and took a deep breath. "He give it to me. Told me he wanted some sippin' likker, so ah went t'git fo him."

"He gave you his wallet?" Ben's skepticism rode on his voice.

"Yup. Said he was partial to Wild Turkey. I'm a Jim Beam man mahse'f. Ah like my drink t'have a rich, full-bodied taste."

"What time was all of this?" Ben tried to catch the man's eye.

"When's dinner time?" Jerome changed the subject and looked over at the sheriff. "Ah kind of haf a hankerin fo' some gravy and biscuits."

Sheriff Hardie replied, "Y'all doing real fine Mr. Pickett. When we're done, we'll get you something."

"My name is Pichette; it's French. How menny times does ah have t'explain thet t'yo'?"

"Mr. Pichette," said Ben. "What time did all this take place?

"Mebbe midnight. Time ain't important to me."

Ben looked at Sheriff Hardie. "The convenience store is open all night."

"Tell me, Jerome, where were you going to give Mr. Ross his whiskey?"

The question seemed to stump Jerome for a moment. "Ah c'd pow'ful use sumpin' t'eat." The sheriff reached into his pocket and tossed him a Marathon bar.

Jerome snatched up the bar "Mareethon, they're crap. Yo' got a Milky Way, o' an Oh Henry o' sumpin'?"

"No. Answer Detective O'Shea's question. How were you planning on giving Mr. Ross his bottle?"

"Wal, th' next time ah sar him, of course," he said indignantly, ripping the cover off the *Marathon* bar.

"Jerome, why would Mr. Ross need you to get his whiskey for him?" asked Ben.

Jerome took a bite of the candy bar and took his time chewing before responding. "Ah don't rightly knows fo' a fack. Most likely, on account o' he was in no shape t'ax fo' it hisse'f."

"And what kind of shape was that?"

"Drunk. Ah watch mah cornsumpshun of likker, but sometimes it kin kind of creep up on yo'. This hyar guy was drunker than I've evah been. Drunk as Cooter Brown, they say."

"You're a liar. You stole his wallet then you took his watch."

"Thet ain't so, he gave me th' watch as payment fo' gittin' him his likker." Jerome looked down at the floor. He resumed his rocking back and forth on his chair.

"Hey Jerome," Ben demanded. "Where was this?"

Jerome went back to chewing his candy bar. Finally, he turned to the Sheriff. "Thar's an alley off th' main drag jest a ha'f-block fum thet bar. Ah reckon th' bar is called th' Hideout o' sumpin. Ah wouldn't know, they don't let me in there."

Ben stood up and brought his chair over so that he was sitting inches away from the man. "I think you're lying, Mr.

Pichette. I think you came across the rightful owner of the wallet and stole it." Ben let his voice go loud. Pichette recoiled, moving his chair back, trying to put distance between Ben and himself. "You tried to buy some whiskey for yourself by impersonating this man. You're in a lot of trouble here. This is not some petty crime. If anything bad happens to him, I'll make sure you go to Angola State Pen for the rest of your useless life. Now 'fess up. What happened to Mr. Ross?"

"As ah said, he was drunk. Ah gather eff'n he ain't still in th' alley, then he took off. '

Ben slammed his fist on the table, "You're lying, and when we find out what happened to him, you'll be held responsible. His wallet and his credit cards were your motives."

Jerome made eye contact with Ben for the first time. "Ah don't know nuthin about thet."

Ben looked over at the sheriff and shook his head, "Show us exactly where Mr. Ross gave you his wallet, and the sheriff will get you some real food."

CHAPTER FIFTEEN

Tuesday, July 17th, 1984
Slidell, Louisiana

Ben and Jacqueline followed Sheriff Hardie's cruiser to the alley. They all got out and followed Jerome, who stopped and pointed to a spot by a dumpster. "He was right hyar. Drunk like ah said. But he told me t'take his wallet an' git him some likker. Thet's all ah know."

"My husband rarely drinks. You're a liar!" yelled Jacqueline.

Hardie wisely moved in between Jerome and Jacqueline.

She walked away to join Ben, who was searching the area.

Near the dumpster, Ben found a matchbook from the Hideout. The matchbook felt damp but otherwise was unused. Inside the cover was a phone number and the words, *for good time, me you call, Yesssss.* Ben showed it to Jacqueline. "What do you make of this?"

Jacqueline read the inside a few times before saying, "Sounds weird. Who talks like that?"

"It might be a coincidence, but I'd wager that blonde from the bar."

Ben waived the deputy over and showed the matchbook to him. "I think this is a clue; he might have got this from a woman in the bar. I want to follow up on it."

"Alright, but let me know what comes from it, this is a crime scene. What do you think about Jerome's story?"

"Bullshit. But it's pretty clever. I think he either found the wallet and the watch, or worse, stole them, but I can't see this guy hurting anyone."

"Without Gabriel to contradict him, not sure many judges around here would find him guilty of much."

"How long can you hold him?"

"Knowing Jerome, he'd be happy to stay as long as he can," replied Hardie.

Ben and Jacqueline thanked the sheriff and got back in the truck. They pulled out, heading west to New Orleans. It was a good five minutes before Jacqueline spoke. "What's going on, Ben?"

"I don't know."

"What else can we do? The clock's ticking on this. We're running out of time."

"We need to call the FBI and get someone who can help us."

They drove in silence until they got to the outskirts of the city. Jacqueline spoke up, "I have two questions. First, why Slidell? There are a ton of bars in New Orleans; they could have picked any of them."

"I don't know. Maybe they wanted an out of the way place," Ben drove onto the highway that crossed the bridge.

"Or maybe there's some significance to it. Maybe the Tadics live near there?"

"Maybe that's where they're holding Gabriel. Somewhere local."

"Could be. We can call the Slidell Sheriff and see if there are any abandoned warehouses or buildings." For the first time, doubt started creeping into Ben's mind. *Was Slidell chosen because of some connection to what happened with Tommy in the spring? If Reznikov is involved, it would likely be to silence Gabriel from testifying at the upcoming trial. Has Gabriel been abducted or is it more likely he was murdered, and the body dumped somewhere?* He tried to shake the thoughts from his mind. "You said two questions."

"Why Croatian? Even if they're Croatian, Tadic is not their real name. Rutledge said she didn't have an accent, so why pick that name, why not Smith or Jones?"

"Another good question." After driving in silence for ten minutes, Ben pulled into the agency parking lot. He turned to Jacqueline. "One thing that Gabriel liked to say is that the best lies are usually 80% true. So maybe they are Croatian."

CHAPTER SIXTEEN

Tuesday, July 17th, 1984
Gulfport, Mississippi

On the drive to the Agency with Arnie, Star expressed her concern about leaving her father behind.

"I understand, but you heard what your dad said. He wanted to stay and guard the homestead and wait for your mom to show up. Besides, this maniac isn't interested in him. He wants you. We need you to keep moving. We'll spend the rest of the day at the agency."

"And then what? Maybe I should go back to the camp."

"I can't protect you there. You'll be fine if you stick with me." Arnie hoped he was right. He kept an eye on the rearview mirror, watching for a tail.

JESSICA AND ARNIE walked into the agency and saw Rachel busy at work. Bourbon was sleeping, all scrunched up in a much too small shoebox on Rachel's desk.

"You're back!" Rachel exclaimed enthusiastically.

"Any word on Gabriel?" Arnie pet the cat.

"Not a thing. How did you make out?" Rachel gave Jessica a broad smile.

"I don't know if you know Jessica Grant. Jessica, this is Rachel Henderson."

"I remember you from a party we had at the end of the case. But you look different."

"It's all part of my new persona. My name is Star."

"Okay, I'll call you Star from now on." Rachel turned to Arnie and asked if anything transpired. Arnie quickly brought her up to date on the rock throwing.

"You must be frightened out of your wits." Rachel gave Star a hug. "I remember that case; that man was crazy."

"I thought, since the killer knows where Star lives, she could hang out here for a while," Arnie suggested.

"Of course, and you're welcome to spend the night with me at my apartment. I live alone and have plenty of room."

"Thanks, Rachel," said Arnie. "Is there a file on the Mardi Gras guy? I need to get caught up."

The phone rang before Rachel could respond. She answered and a few moments later said, "Yes, Ben, he's right here with Jessica Grant, who now goes by the name Star. Why don't we huddle in Gabriel's office, and I'll put you on the speakerphone."

Once they were seated around Gabriel's desk, Ben kicked things off. "Jacqueline and I are back from checking out this bar that Gabriel went to last night, and we've learned a fair bit, so I wanted to give you a quick update. Rutledge, our new associate here in New Orleans, is with us." Ben went through what they had discovered at the bar and from Jerome, and then about the matchbook they'd found at the scene.

"I'm scared, Ben," said Rachel once he had finished.

"Gabriel always says he doesn't believe in coincidences. With this Mardi Gras thing resurfacing, do you think there's a connection?"

"Jacqueline wondered the same thing. It's possible, but let's not forget about other possibilities. Both Gabriel and I are scheduled to testify against ex-Mayor Baxter and Reznikov. Even though they're locked up, they could have hired people to ...." Ben stopped mid-sentence, his voice cracking with emotion.

Jacqueline jumped in. "Arnie, how did you make out in Gulfport?"

Arnie filled them in on the rock and postcard thrown through the window at the Grant's, and about convincing the reluctant deputy to have a patrol check the house. "In the meantime, I brought Star with me, and I believe she is going to stay with Rachel tonight."

"That's great, thanks, Rachel," replied Jacqueline. "You know this is crazy. Yesterday we weren't even thinking about Charles Bouvier. The dead are supposed to stay dead."

"Listen, everyone," Ben had recovered his composure. "Thank you for helping to find our friend. We need to turn the tables on whoever is responsible. If they're holding Gabriel, we need to find out where. Rachel, maybe you and Star can canvas the homeless shelters in Slidell, and then in New Orleans. It sounds like Gabriel has no identification and no money. He's likely disoriented and confused. Arnie, use your contacts with the sheriff's office, and find out if there are any missing teenage girls."

"I'm on it, Ben."

"Jackie suggested there might be a Croatian gang, so Rutledge is going to talk to his former NOPD partner about people who might be connected to either Frank Reznikov or a Croatian gang. I think that might be our best lead. I'm going to call the FBI and see if I can get some help, and then I'm going to check out the number in the matchbook."

"Ben, I'd like to go back out to Slidell. Maybe the sheriff would be willing to have a deputy take me around to check out some vacant warehouses," said Jacqueline.

"Good thought, Jackie. Thank you, everyone, for scrambling. It's important that we find the trail before it goes cold. Anyone finds a lead, call it in and share it."

CHAPTER SEVENTEEN

Tuesday, July 17th, 1984
New Orleans, Louisiana

Ben dialed the number for the FBI in Jackson, expecting to have to settle for a callback the next morning. When the receptionist answered, he asked to be put through to Dr. Bayliss, the FBI profiler. He'd met Bayliss on the original Mardi Gras case. This past fall, he and Gabriel had met again with the older gentleman to develop a profile on a case involving a white supremacist responsible for a series of random killings.

"Dr. Bayliss." Ben recognized the no-nonsense voice immediately. Bayliss had a unique personality and approach to his role.

"It's Ben O'Shea. We met when I was working for the Biloxi PD."

"Very good, yes, I remember you, and your sidekick, Gabriel Ross. I heard something about you being on disability. You took a bullet in the shoulder."

"I'm still on disability, but I'm keeping sharp by helping Gabriel at the agency."

"That's the ticket. We can't lose your experience," Bayliss enthused. "How is Gabriel?"

"I'm glad you asked." For the next ten minutes, Ben brought Dr. Bayliss up to date on Gabriel's disappearance and the resurfacing of the Mardi Gras Killer. Bayliss listened actively and held his questions until Ben was done.

"My, my Ben. I'm glad you called me. I remember doing a profile on ...Charles Bouvier. You both did some fine work on that case. You would have arrested him had he not disappeared."

"Wil Graham ran the taskforce on that case. I understand he retired."

"Wil Graham, yes, one of the smart ones, retiring when he's still young enough to do things."

"Do you stay in touch with him?"

"Not in the past couple of months. I understand that he and his wife are traveling. She was diagnosed with something, and Wil wanted to accomplish some things on her to-do list while they could."

"That's too bad," said Ben. "Dr. Bayliss, I need some help. We need to reverse the tables on this guy. If he abducted Gabriel, we need to find him before its too late. Is there someone taking over for Wil?"

"Of course, but are you jumping to conclusions? What do you have that leads you to believe that Bouvier is responsible?"

"Just the coincidence of him resurfacing now."

"Resurfacing now? You are just learning about him now. He disappeared fifteen months ago. One of the first things I teach new agents is not to go down the rabbit hole until they've considered all of the potential suspects."

"The guy has a history of abductions."

"There you go down the hole again. How do you know Gabriel's been abducted? Has there been a ransom demand?"

"No, and you're right, of course. It's just easier for me to believe he's alive being held somewhere."

"I understand, and don't get me wrong - if Bouvier is alive then this is very alarming, but he might have nothing to do with Gabriel's disappearance."

Ben thought of a different approach. "You know the case as much as anyone. I suppose I understand why a maniac might keep a girl tied up on his boat, but why Gabriel?"

Bayliss took a moment to answer. "I can think of any number of reasons, and I'm not bat-shit crazy like he is. My original theory was that he had developed an obsession with the actress Farrah Fawcett. When he realized he couldn't get the original, he went looking for a surrogate. Ultimately these young girls were bound to disappoint him. So he would move on to the next girl. As for why he would take Gabriel, the abductions were about power, a need to possess. I guess it could be that Bouvier needs to control someone who was pursuing him."

"We need help, Dr. Bayliss. Any chance we can get the task force together again?"

"Things have changed around here Ben..." Bayliss lowered his. "More red tape. But I can make a few calls, call in some favors. I'll call you back as soon as possible. In the meantime, I'll pull the file."

"Thank you, Dr. Bayliss. I'll be at this number waiting for your call."

Ben hung up from Bayliss and walked over to Rutledge. "Anything?"

"My old partner put me in touch with someone from the gang task force. He looked into known associates of Frankie

Reznikov. He said there are a couple of Croatian guys that ride with the Sons." Ben had survived a run in with the Sons of Silence a couple of years back. The *Herald* nicknamed them the "Lugnut Killers" because their MO was to loosen the lugnuts on the target's car and sit back and watch the action. Ben had lost a rookie partner when his cruiser went out of control. "They're pulling likely candidates for us. If you want, I can head over and look at some mugshots. I know I would recognize Lana."

Ben thanked Rutledge. He had the matchbook in his hands and began to pick up the phone before changing his mind. "I was going to call the number, but now I'm wondering if we had an address, it might be more effective to do a house call."

"You're right. Let me make a call. I'll get the address, and we can go knock on the door."

While Rutledge called the NOPD, Ben answered the other phone when it rang.

"Ben, it's Dr. Bayliss again, I spoke to the Director, who was at a dinner party up here in Jackson. He was quite skeptical that Bouvier could have survived. He peppered me with questions to ask you. Did you get the handwriting on the postcard analyzed?"

"I hadn't thought of that. I guess I was going with how certain Jessica Grant seemed. But it's not a bad idea."

"How many teenage girls are missing?"

"I have an associate running that down. I should get an answer soon."

"Bouvier's psychosis runs pretty deep. It would be rare for a sociopath to change, but not unheard of. Lastly, and you'll likely find this frustrating, are the local authorities officially asking for the FBI's help? You're no longer on active duty, Ben. The director wants to know what the locals think."

"Dr. Bayliss, Charles Bouvier was responsible for multiple abductions and disappearances. In answer to your question, the local sheriff is aware of the situation, but I understand they are not convinced. So I guess the answer is no."

"Get back to me with the name of who to call in the sheriff's office, and I'll contact him myself."

"Thank you for that."

"One other thing that I found in the file. We know that people who own boats tend to be social, always waving to passing boats. This doesn't fit with Bouvier. For that reason, Gabriel stopped canvassing the marinas and started looking at boats moored offshore."

"The timing of all this seems pretty tight. We believe the killer was in Gulfport this afternoon. If Gabriel was snatched last night, he would need to be transferred to the boat quickly so the killer can make it to Gulfport from New Orleans."

"I'm going to have to start calling you Bugs. You're getting ahead of yourself. Gabriel could be stashed away somewhere until the transfer to Bouvier can be made."

Ben thanked Bayliss for the help and promised to call back the following day. He sat heavily in his chair and closed his eyes. "Here goes the runaround."

Rutledge got up and slapped Ben on the back. "Hey, buddy, don't lose hope. I got that address."

CHAPTER EIGHTEEN

Tuesday, July 17th, 1984
New Orleans, Louisiana

As they got in Ben's truck, Rutledge quipped. "Yellow and red stripes. Can't be too many of these on the road. You know it just struck me. Your truck matches your clothes." Ben was wearing a yellow golf shirt and red polyester slacks.

"Funny guy." Ben had a reputation for throwing on whatever was in his pile of laundry without much thought as to how it went together.

"Gabriel told me the reason he had to do the TV interview was that you didn't want to get all fancied up."

Ben ignored the comment and deflected. "How are you enjoying day two of your career as a private detective?"

"I don't know if this is what it's going to be like, I'll have to get new batteries for my pacemaker."

"You're getting a baptism under fire. Gabriel always says his job's pretty routine. When I was with the Biloxi PD, I used to refer the odd open case to him. You know, those cases where police red tape has your hands tied?"

"Yeah, I'm not going to miss those. How about that Huffman case in Slidell a couple of months back?" asked Rutledge.

"That was unique. Because I was on leave, I didn't want to mess up my disability, so I agreed with the Picayune Sheriff to take another look at it. As it turns out, there was a sizable reward which I turned over to the Agency. That's part of the Reznokov case where Gabriel and I are scheduled to testify."

AFTER ABOUT TWENTY MINUTES, they came to a farmhouse just off Highway 11, east of Slidell. "I think this is the house coming up on the left." Rutledge pointed to the long laneway. "The phone company said the number belonged to a B. LeBeau. That matches the name on the mailbox at the end of the lane." Looking up at the house, he added, "If I were going to snatch someone, this place would be perfect, totally isolated, away from the road. I'm getting a feeling about it." Rutledge pulled a Smith and Wesson from his shoulder holster and checked the ammo. "How did you want to play this?"

"Let's leave the truck on the shoulder and hike up to the house. Maybe look in the windows see if we see Gabriel bound and gagged. If we do, then we go in, guns blazing before they can do anything." Ben checked his own .38.

"Should we call the sheriff?"

"Yep, just as soon as we empty our guns into these bastards. You ready?"

"We need to talk about danger pay, boss," Rutledge muttered as he got out of the truck.

When they got to the front of the house, Ben gestured for Rutledge to go around to the back while he tried the windows facing the front. The owner of the house had put thick curtains up, so there was no way to see inside. He tried to slide one of the windows open but found that they were nailed shut. *Who nails their windows shut?* He rapped on the window, "Gabriel, are you in there?"

Rutledge came around from the back of the house."Windows are all locked with the curtains drawn; the back door is locked."

"Let's go knock on the door." There was no doorbell, so Ben knocked loudly, holding his revolver out of view. They waited a few minutes before concluding that no one was home.

"I don't hear a dog," said Rutledge.

Ben took a quick look around and saw no cars on the road. He turned and gave the door a hellish kick, splintering the wood and popping the door open.

"I could have picked the lock."

Ben rolled his eyes. "Now, you tell me." They walked into the hallway, letting their eyes adjust to the shadows. Ben could see that the place was sparsely furnished as if someone was in the process of moving in or out. He nodded to the staircase leading to the second floor and Rutledge started up the steps, his gun at the ready.

Ben cleared the main floor, which had a combined living-dining room, as well as a spacious kitchen in the rear. *Whoever lives here doesn't eat here very often,* he thought once he looked in the icebox. There was a carton of milk, some juice, and half a dozen eggs.

Rutledge returned to the kitchen. "Upstairs is clear. Just one bedroom being used. The other two are empty. Feminine products in the bathroom. Condoms by the bed. Ladies clothes in the closet."

"Check for a basement or a hidden room."

Both men fanned out and found a locked door leading to a shed. This time Rutledge used his lock picks. Other than the sound of scurrying rodents, there was nothing but abandoned furniture and junk. When they returned to the foyer, Ben pointed to an answering machine sitting by a black rotary dial phone in the hall. Rutledge pressed the message button and heard a cheerful woman's voice.

"Hello, this is Brenda from the Northlands Psychiatric Hospital. Press #1 if you are an egomaniac; Press #2 repeatedly if you are obsessive-compulsive; Press #3, #4, and #5 if you have split personality disorder; Press #6 if you're depressed, but it doesn't matter because no one will call you back. If you have paranoid delusions don't press anything, we know who you are, and we know where you're calling from. Hang up, and we'll call you back. Everyone else, leave contact info."

Rutledge chuckled and looked at Ben, who was intent on something out the front window. Rutledge followed his gaze. A pickup truck had just turned into the laneway.

"I'M CALLING THE POLICE!" Brenda brandished a can of mace in her hand. "You creeps broke my front door. What the hell are you doing in here?"

Ben and Rutledge were sitting on the couch, still chuckling at the voicemail greeting. "Do you really work at the psychiatric hospital?" Ben picked up a ceramic Yoda ashtray off the coffee table and examined it.

"Yes, and this is my house, well, at least I'm renting it. What the hell do you want? And put my ashtray down before you break it."

Ben and Rutledge pointed to the wallets they'd placed on

the table showing their police identification. They were gambling that Brenda wouldn't call their respective departments.

"Cops? I've seen enough TV shows to know you can't just break into someone's house."

Ben pulled the matchbook out of his pant pocket and tossed it to her. She caught it and looked at the message inside, a puzzled look on her face. "So what?"

"Are you Croatian, Brenda?" asked Rutledge

"Croatian? You have me mixed up with someone else. The name on the mailbox is LeBeau. That's French, you dumbasses. Now, are you going to explain yourself, or do I need to call the sheriff, who's a personal friend of mine?"

Ben sat back and smiled at Brenda. "You're free to call Sheriff Hardie if you want. We're looking into a possible abduction. That matchbook was found in an alley where the gentleman was last seen."

"I gave this to a man I met last night at a bar. He seemed nice, so I asked him to call me."

"Was that before or after you roofied his drink?" asked Rutledge.

"What? Do I look like I need to drug people to get a date?" After a moment, she added, "Don't answer that!"

"So you're saying you didn't spike his drink?" Ben carefully watched her expression.

"No, I didn't. I met this man. He was cute, funny, and easy to talk to. All of a sudden, he started slurring his words. And what's weird is, he might have had a couple of drinks. Maybe short people have a lower tolerance."

Ben shared a look with Rutledge. "Tell us everything you can remember Gabriel saying or doing."

"I already have. We were at the bar together. I asked the bartender to make me a High Tide." When she saw their confused looks, she added, "It's a cocktail. Hardly has any booze in it. Gabriel and I struck up a conversation. After a bit, he got up and went to the bathroom. So he probably took something in the can. When he came back I bought him a drink; then he bought me one. Then all hell broke loose. He starts yelling and talking gibberish. I offered to drive him home. The bartender offered to call him a cab, but he just waved us off and stumbled out the door."

"What was he yelling?"

"Gibberish like I said. I work at the Psychiatric Hospital. My bet is he had a psychotic episode."

"Okay Brenda, if you think of anything else I can be reached at this number." Ben picked up his wallet and handed her a card.

"Hey, it says private detective. Thought you were a cop?"

"I was, still am. It's complicated. The guy who was abducted owns the detective agency, and he's my best friend. Any help you can give us would be appreciated."

"So this Gabriel's missing? Have you checked the hospitals?"

"Yes, and the shelters, and the police stations, and the parks. He was last seen in an alley, near that bar." Ben stood up.

For a moment Brenda looked like she was debating saying anything else. "There was one thing he said. It was, 'he's gone.' He said it a couple of times. It just came from nowhere. He hadn't mentioned anyone before. But he seemed pretty upset about it. That was just before he left. Now, who's going to pay for my door?"

CHAPTER NINETEEN

Tuesday, July 17th, 1984
New Orleans, Louisiana

It was several minutes before Ben or Rutledge spoke on the drive back to the police station. Finally, Rutledge asked what Ben had thought of Brenda.

"Pretty genuine. I had no problem believing she was pissed when she saw us, and no problem believing her story. I'm not sure where that leaves us. I sure hope you can identify one of these mug shots."

"My contact from the gang unit said he'd have a binder ready for us."

"Let's think this through," said Ben. "Gabriel was at the bar around ten last night. He meets Brenda, and they have a drink. Presumably, he's watching Tadic. He probably followed Tadic into the washroom. He comes back and shortly after, Brenda said he goes berserk. Now, I know Gabriel pretty well, he would not be drunk after a couple of cocktails. When he comes back from the washroom, Brenda buys him a drink; then he starts going crazy when he notices that Tadic has skipped. Maybe Tadic left early to set up a trap for him. Then sometime between eleven and twelve, something happens in the alley, and Jerome Pichette ends up with Gabriel's wallet."

"Something happened in the washroom, but what?" asked Rutledge.

"I don't know. He wouldn't knowingly take anything."

"I saw a movie once where they smeared something on a toilet seat. It was a powerful drug. The guy sits on it, and when he stands up, he stumbles out of the cubicle and falls flat on his face."

"Pretty far-fetched. Let's back up. Let's assume someone snatched him. Why? If this is about revenge, why didn't they kill him? It would be simpler, neater."

"They might have, and maybe they took the body with them."

For some reason, Rutledge's last comment hit a nerve. "I'm clinging to the belief that since we haven't found a body, Gabriel is still alive." Ben turned into the NOPD parking lot.

Ben and Rutledge went straight to the gang task force on the 3rd floor. Rutledge said hello to a couple of his old colleagues before they were given a binder of mug shots that had been put together for them. The binder had about two dozen photos of people who had connections to the Croatian community. Rutledge took his time looking for the man he knew as Petr Tadic. As far as he could tell, none of the photographs matched the picture of the man on the beach. He was about to give the binder back when he took a second look, this time looking for the woman who called herself Lana. He found a possible match about half way. "This might be a match, but the hair is a different color, and the face is thinner. The woman who came in yesterday was blonde and full-figured. There's something about the face."

"She was likely wearing a wig, maybe some padding." Ben looked over Rutledge's shoulder. "Plus, this picture was dated a few years ago when she was booked for extortion. Her name is Gadzinga. Lana Gadzinga."

"The name cinches it. It's the eyes, that impudent look."

"Look through the rest of the book. I'll see if someone has anything recent on her." Ben got up from the table.

A few minutes later, the desk sergeant printed off Gadzinga's rap sheet. Ben took it over to the table and went over it with Rutledge. "Hmm, in addition to the 1981 extortion rap, where she got a suspended sentence, there's a drug offense. That case was dropped because the evidence mysteriously disappeared."

"It lists her as being single and living in an apartment on McCowan Road," said Rutledge. "That 'just married' picture looked legit, not something they just cooked up."

"She might be married. That part of the sheet is based on booking data. Maybe she didn't feel like disclosing her husband's name."

"Why isn't Petr's mug shot in this binder?"

"Let's go ask her."

CHAPTER TWENTY

Tuesday, July 17th, 1984
Gulfport, Mississippi

Rachel and Star had been working phones non-stop, with no luck. While Star made more coffee, Rachel picked up the phone and dialed a familiar number.

"Hello, it's Don!"

"It's me, stranger," Rachel said, only to realize that she was talking to a voicemail greeting.

"... I'm currently out having fun and unavailable to rescue you but leave me a message, and I'll see what I can do."

Rachel's lips tightened as she felt a tinge of humiliation, followed by anger that he was out enjoying himself. She blurted, "I wonder how many people you catch with that voicemail. I bet you listen to them and yuck it up. It's Rachel if you haven't figured that out. I know I said I didn't want to see you again, no, strike that. I know I said that you should go live with the animals seeing how much you like bullshit. But Don, things have changed. I need your help; we really need your help. Some crazy we thought was dead is really alive, and

Gabriel's missing. Call me, please." As soon as she hung up, she regretted making the call and everything she'd said.

Arnie had heard the call. He came out of his office and said there were no reports of teenage girls being abducted in any county near Biloxi. "Any luck on your end?"

Rachel shook her head, stifling a sob.

"Don't worry, Rachel. We'll find him. Maybe Jacqueline found something while looking for warehouses."

"No," said Star, exiting the kitchen carrying a tray of full coffee mugs. "She called a few minutes ago to say it was a massive waste of time. In between visits to Dunkin' Donuts, a deputy drove her around to a half-dozen empty warehouses, a boarded-up school, the house he grew up in, and where he made out with his last girlfriend."

"Maybe Ben and Rutledge are getting somewhere," said Arnie hopefully.

CHAPTER TWENTY-ONE

Tuesday, July 17th, 1984
Gulfport, Mississippi

Star and Rachel sat on the floor around the coffee table in Rachel's living room. "I haven't had Mac & Cheese in ages, this is fantastic," said Star. Rachel had changed into pajamas and found a pair of with a picture of Winnie-the-Pooh on the front, equipped with a trap door and little footsies, for Star.

"What does it mean when Mac & Cheese is the best part of your day?"

"I'm not kidding. You'll have to share your recipe." Star started to laugh. "Dad would never let Mom buy it for us. He called it wop food."

"I can give you the box; the directions are on the side. Tell me about what it's like to live in a commune."

"No one calls it that. Everyone calls it the camp. It's nice. No one bothers you."

"Come on, girl. Tents? How many people? Hippies, Drugs? Do you all wear tunics? Spill it, girl."

Star took a forkful of her meal before answering. "It's kind of hush-hush, but I guess I can blab a little since you made me this lovely meal and lent me these sexy PJ's. There are cabins, nine, no ten," she paused, counting to herself in the air. "Yeah, ten. They're all arranged in a circle with a firepit in the middle. There's the learning cabin. The Governor, Stevie, calls it that because he wants the focus to be on learning and not on teaching. There's an eating cabin where everyone has their meals. We're all vegans. We grow most of our food, and everyone shares. There's the quiet cabin, that's for prayer if you're into that, or just silent meditation. There's no organized religion, no ministers, everyone is encouraged to share their insights about life. Everyone is respectful, and yes, we all wear the tunics."

"Sounds very peaceful. Is it?"

"Stevie has a rule. If you disagree with someone, just shut up, nod your head and say 'peace be with you.' People, for the most part, mind their business. There's a woodworking cabin, where some build furniture. Some of it is nice, so they sell it at craft fairs. There's a storage and supply cabin. That's where they keep the supplies; we need to work the gardens. The rest of the cabins are for sleeping."

"Sounds cool, how many people live there?" Rachel said, finishing her dinner.

Star started counting in the air again. "Including the kids, I would say around 40. There are some couples, and then some singles like me."

"Do you practice free love?" Rachel asked, then laughed at the awkwardness of the question.

"That's just in the movies. No more so than anywhere else."

"What's an average day like?"

"We work most of the day. There's no TV — no electricity. If you get cold, grab a blanket. Stevie has a transistor radio in his cabin. That's pretty much the only contact we have with the outside. At night we usually have a bonfire. There are a couple who like to dance, some who like to play the guitar, others sing. Whatever floats your boat."

"It sounds like a pretty big place, who owns it?"

"That's a mystery. I overheard Stevie one day talking about the Guardians. They're people who live outside the camp who give us money and stuff. I think one of them might own the camp. Another Guardian owns a store nearby and keeps us supplied with stuff we can't grow."

"Are you happy there, Star?"

Star took a few moments before answering, clearly wrestling with her feelings. "I feel safe, because of what happened on the boat; that was what I needed. At first, I was living on adrenaline. I had no idea just how pumped I was. When the crash came, I went into a huge depression. Pops wasn't helping. He was having a cow about how I'd brought everything on myself. I met Stevie at a party, and he convinced me to check out the camp. It's been over a year, so I guess I must be happy."

"You didn't mention drugs. Is that part of the lifestyle?"

"It's not any different than it is on the outside. I smoked more pot in high school than I did this past year. We grow our own, and anyone who feels the need can help themselves." Star looked around and added, "Say you wouldn't have anything, would you? After today, I think we deserve it."

"No, I'm sorry I don't do that. I have a bottle of Cold Duck in the icebox. I was saving it for...."

"I love cheap wine," Star said, her eyes going wide.

Rachel went to the kitchen and came back with the bottle and a couple of glasses. She sat back down on the carpet and poured the wine.

"You were saying you were saving it for..."

Rachel let out a deep sigh and sipped her wine. "I was going with this guy, Don. Except it might be Dan, it might be Drake. He told me his last name was Mangina, which is bullshit, and it tells you what he was thinking about." She shook her head and downed her glass. Star quickly picked up the bottle and poured her another glass.

"He's in law enforcement, and we got along pretty well." Rachel lay back again and started to giggle. "I honestly thought, felt in my heart, that he might be the one. But like, he has this one big flaw." She sat up quickly and pointed at Star. "He lies like a rug. I don't even know his real name."

"Well, Star's not my real name. Maybe there's a reason..."

Rachel made a motion to cut her off. "So, one night after hot sex, we had it out, and I told him that I couldn't be with a man I didn't trust. If he loved me, he had to tell me the truth."

"Wow. What did he do?"

"He lied to me about his name again. Said his name was Don Purplinsky. When he realized I was serious, he nodded that he understood. Like it had all happened before. It was no biggie. He put his clothes on, and adios. I haven't seen him in three weeks."

"How was the sex?"

"Incroyable, as the French say."

"Well, fuck him. He's not the one. What about others?" Star refilled their glasses.

"There's no one else."

"Bull. Rachel, have you looked in the mirror? You're beautiful. You've got a great figure, nice rack. I love your hair."

Rachel laughed, "Of course you'd love my hair. There's been others, one in particular. We went out a few times when he was separated from his wife. But she came back, and that didn't work so well for me. Before Don Purplinsky, I went out with a university professor who was twice my age, and according to Gabriel, talked like Kermit the frog."

"You mean like this." Star deepened her voice, "You have nice boobs, Rachel."

This led to some hysterical laughter. "That was a pretty good impression. You even did the bulgy eye thing."

"I can do a lot of voices, plus read lips."

"That must be fun at parties."

After a few minutes, Star yawned, and Rachel said, "You can sleep in my bed, and I'll take the couch."

"I don't want to put you out, but I'm too tired to argue. What's on tap for tomorrow?"

"I think we head into the office early and pray that Ben or Rutledge found Gabriel."

As Star got up and went towards the bedroom, she turned around. "Thanks for everything, Rachel. It's cool how you guys rallied like the cavalry for Gabriel. That was special. It made me feel like I was part of something good."

"Thank you for your help, Star. Have a good night."

Rachel got a blanket and pillow down from the hall closet and put them on the couch. She was emotionally drained and physically tired. Despite this, she tossed and turned on the couch, trying to find sleep. She finally gave up and turned on the local news. She went to the kitchen and poured herself another glass of wine, bringing it back into the living room just as the news anchor was talking about an apparent suicide that had happened earlier in the day.

"The victim, well known in the business community, was recently in the news as a key witness in the case against former Mayor Baxter." Rachel's heart missed a beat as she turned up the volume. The camera was focusing on a body on the sidewalk covered by a sheet. "Oh, ...oh,....oh, please no, don't let it be."

The coverage went to a hectic scene in front of an eight-story heritage building. The news reporter was speaking to an English couple who was vacationing on the Gulf coast.

"We were walkin', mindin' our own, comin' back from 'avin' a drink at a local establishment when out of nowhere, this body landed in front of us. It made kind of a splat noise. Weren't more than six feet oray...It was all pretty orful," said the middle-aged man.

"It was more of a splat-glump noise, I'd say," added his wife from behind him.

The man rolled his eyes, "Back home ah wawk in th' slaughterhouses, I'd say it was jest a splatt."

The coverage changed to an interview with a deputy sheriff. "I'm here with Deputy Sheriff Weber of the Harrison County Sheriff's Department. Can you tell our viewers about what's happened?"

"At approximately sixteen hundred today, that's 4 PM, this man," the deputy gestured to the body under the sheet, "did a swan dive off this building. He was pronounced dead at the scene."

"There seems to be some conjecture about this being a suicide?" asked the reporter.

"The name tag says Deputy Sheriff, not psychic. We'll have to wait for the coroner's report, but we found some poker chips on him from a local bar called Lucky's. A man matching the deceased's description was seen at the bar losing heavily." The deputy hitched up his pants and added, "Wouldn't have been the first man to jump from a tall building after losing heavily at a casino."

"Yeah, but what's the victim's name, fuckwad?" yelled Star from the bedroom. "That's the same jerk that came to the house today. Totally useless."

Rachel hadn't been aware that Star was listening and

called to her. "Sometimes they don't release the name until they notify the next of kin."

"You don't think it could be Gabriel, do you?" Star came into the living room and sat down cross-legged on the floor.

Rachel's voice quivered, "I don't know, but he was supposed to testify."

As if on cue, the coverage shifted back to the television studio where the anchor was speaking. "We've received the go-ahead to release the name of the deceased. He has been identified as Hollis Huntley of Gulfport. Until recently, Mr. Huntley was employed by The Heritage Savings and Loan Company. That firm was recently forced to close its' doors after being audited by financial regulators. A court case is pending, where Mr. Huntley was scheduled to give testimony against former Biloxi Mayor Baxter and New Orleans businessman Frank Reznikov. Reasons behind Huntley's fall are still being investigated."

Rachel breathed a sigh of relief and hugged Star. As Star went back to bed, Rachel thought about Gabriel and Ben scheduled to testify at the upcoming trial.

Rachel debated the merits of it before picking up the phone and dialing the number she had for Chevon. Ben's fiancée answered on the second ring. "Chevon, it's Rachel Henderson."

"Oh, hi, Rachel. I made Ben take a sleeping pill, and he just crashed. I can already hear the snoring through the bedroom door. He filled me in on what's been going on, and I just got off the phone with Jacqueline. You must be going crazy. I'm almost too scared to ask if anything else has happened?"

'There is something. A man who was working at the bank in Biloxi, the bank involved in the fraud that Ben and Gabriel were investigating, just fell off the tallest building in Gulfport."

"Oh, no. Are they saying it was more than an accident?"

"The initial guess from the deputy was suicide over gambling losses, but that might be wrong." After a moment, Rachel added, "I thought Ben would want to know."

"Do you think this has anything to do with Gabriel's disappearance?" Chevon's voice showed her concern.

"I'm worried. There's too much happening. First, this killer resurfaces, then Gabriel disappears, and now this."

"I'm worried too. Jacqueline is beside herself. Ben said I could go to work with him tomorrow and answer phones, make calls, that sort of thing. That will leave Rutledge and Ben free to keep looking. I wish there were something else I could do."

"Did Ben happen to say how the leads panned out?"

"He said that they don't have much. They found the real name of the woman who hired the agency yesterday. So at least they have that. But when they went out to her last known address, they found she hasn't lived there in ages."

Rachel's attention was drawn to the window where a flash of lightning illuminated the room. "I think we're about to get a storm," said Rachel. As she spoke, a crack of thunder ripped through the silence. "I bet everyone is going to need a sleeping pill tonight. Tell Ben to read the paper tomorrow morning."

CHAPTER TWENTY-TWO

Friday, February 11th, 1983
Ship Island

He was awakened by a sudden flash of lightning followed by a loud crack of thunder. He'd expected to be dead. His teeth were chattering as the rain continued to pelt down. He looked up at the sky; storm clouds had blotted out all the stars. *I'm on a boat. Jesus, someone rescued me.* He sat up and retched over the side onto a sandbar. He felt the skiff being pulled forward. He lay back down, wiping the rain from his face. He was about to attempt to sit up when a large face entered his view.

An older, bald man with a big round bowling ball-like head was looking down at him. His expression was kind and reassuring. "I've got a tent set up on shore with a Coleman heater. We better get you out of this rain and under some dry blankets." The man extended a meaty hand, which hung awkwardly for a few moments. Finally, the man said, "What's your name, young fella?"

It took another moment, but finally, he reached for the man's hand and lied, "Gabriel Ross."

It was still dark when he re-awakened. He was in a large tent covered in warm, dry blankets. The man with the big head was sitting in a beach chair looking over at him with concern. A light came from a lantern casting shadows in the tent. Now that he could see him, he could see that the man was barrel-chested, with muscles that rippled like the waves in the Gulf.

"Welcome to the land of the living, buddy. That was one close call. I think you were going down for the last time when I grabbed ya." The man chuckled. "The name's Nelson Gallant. Not that it should matter to you, but you should know who saved your life. Got some coffee here, Folgers, just instant though." Gallant started to sing and do a jig while standing to make the coffee, "*The best part of waking up is Folgers in your cup.*"

My chest is sore; something struck me. He lifted the blankets and saw that he had a nasty burn. He moved the blankets again and discovered he was sharing the blankets with a full-size dog.

"Now where are our manners? This here is Molly, the only other inhabitant on this island." At the mention of her name, Molly looked up and turned to face her master. Nelson threw her a treat. "Molly tells me she's purebred Golden, but I don't know. She might have a little hound in her. She's getting a little long in the tooth just like me. Her hind legs give her some problems 'specially on nights like this. I think she knew you were in bad shape and she crawled right in there to keep you warm. About that coffee, I imagine after what you've been through, even instant will taste pretty good. Got no fancies like lemon or sugar on account it's just Molly and me, and I like the taste of coffee just as it is."

This guy talks like a runaway train — each sentence running into another.

Nelson held the cup of black coffee out to him. "Yessiree boy, you were just about a goner. Or as they say in these parts, going up that golden staircase." He chuckled again.

When the man called Gabriel Ross made no attempt to take the coffee and rolled over on his side, Nelson shrugged his shoulders. "So, buddy, what in God's name were you doing out in the middle of the Gulf?"

Silence filled the tent for five seconds before Nelson drank the coffee, "You must be just about as confused as a fart in a fan factory. Well, as I said buddy, my name is Nelson Gallant. Most folks call me Nellie. You're on the one and only Ship Island. Hold the presses. I shouldn't say that. No, that's not correct. You see Gabriel, there used to be only one Ship Island, but this big hurricane, called Camille, came right through here and made two Ship Islands. This here, is what we call West Ship Island. Not much here. No one lives here, that's why I like it. I like the solitude. Just me and Molly." Once again, the dog lifted her head and looked at Nelson expectantly. Once the dog had been rewarded again, Nelson spoke to her, "Now ole girl. We were brought up Christian like. When we saw you going down for the third time, we knew we had to do something. Didn't we, girl? It was Molly who saw you first and started barking. Were you out fishing and then got caught in the storm? That's what happened to my dad back in '78."

The man rolled over and covered his head with the blankets.

"Still feeling poorly, are you? I guess almost drowning can

do that to ya. Ya'll look plum tired. I remember almost drowning in Miller's crick when I was just a youngin'. Not as bad by a mile as what happened to you." Nelson had finished the coffee and got up and opened the tent zipper and started urinating on the beach. Looking back at the man, "It's always better to do your business outside the tent. That rain is coming down like a cow pissing on a flat rock." After a couple of minutes, Nelson came back and sat in his chair. "So yeah, this here is West Ship Island. East Ship's a lot smaller but has some trees and birds. Give you a little history on your new home, Gabe. This here used to be owned by Injuns, then the Frenchies, then Spaniards, then of course by the good ole U.S. of A. There's a fort down the beach, Fort Massachusetts. You can check it out once daylight hits. It's a pretty popular spot for tourists during the season. I stay away from them. We like our privacy, don't we Molly? Did I already say that? Anyhoo, the fishing out here is pretty good, and if it ain't raining, you can see right to the bottom."

The man curled into a fetal position. Nelson was undeterred and continued, "As I said, we were out in the boat coming back from a spot. I guess our secret spot. Can't tell you where, else I'd have to kill ya, you know?" he said chuckling. "When this big wind came up and all of a sudden it started pissin'. I was maybe a couple of miles offshore when Molly saw your head bobbing in the water. At first, I took you for a dolphin on account of them being all over the place. Say, maybe it was a dolphin leading me to save ya. Do ya figure?"

The man fell back to sleep. When he woke, Nelson was still talking.

"...Anyhoo, tourist season starts in late March. That's when old Nellie stays away. Say, you feel up to having some of that coffee?"

He desperately needed Gallant to shut up. Not wanting

to see him dance and sing again, he nodded that he would like a cup. Nelson repeated the line about not having any of the fancies, like lemon or sugar. After taking a sip of the coffee, he started feeling a bit better.

"Searched your pocket thinking I might need to call your next of kin. No wallet, did it go into the brink?"

He instinctively reached for his wallet, only to find he had no pants.

"I couldn't let you lie in those wet clothes. Don't worry; I'm no homo. I like pussy as much as any man. Yep, quite the ladies' man, aren't I, Molly? While you were sleeping, I slipped your wet clothes off and found some keys, but nothing else. No watch, no rings, I started thinking maybe someone took a dislike to you, stole your shit and threw you in the Gulf. That what happened to you?"

The man took a deep breath before answering. *Maybe if I satisfy his curiosity, he'll shut up.* "I fell off the boat. It was an accident."

"My, my, an accident." A tone of skepticism crept into Nelson's voice. "Why didn't the boat turn around and fish you out?"

"I don't know; it was dark. They probably couldn't hear me over the storm."

Nelson nodded his big head, seeming to weigh the answer. "I suppose you got people, Gabriel. Someone who might have been on that boat?"

"No. And how would you have called people? Do you have a radio?"

"As a matter of fact, I do. I can radio the Coast Guard, or as I call them the Donald Duck Navy, and tell them I fished you out. Maybe they can tell your family. Betcha they're worried sick. I know if my boy fell into the Gulf and almost drowned, I'd be beside myself. Of course,

I don't have a boy," he started to laugh. Finally, he stopped laughing. "What line of work are you in, Gabriel?"

Fuck this guy. "I work for...a private detective firm."

"Private De-Tect-tive. Well, my, my. Now I'm gonna think someone threw you off the boat. You know, to throw you off the case. My favorite detective flick is the *Maltese Falcon.* Ever see that one?"

"No, never have. Like I said, an accident."

"Are you on a big case, Gabriel?" Nelson dropped his voice to a whisper as if someone outside the tent might be listening.

"Yeah, you could say that."

"Well, don't keep us in suspense. We did save your life."

"Have you heard about this serial killer in New Orleans responsible for all the missing teenage girls?"

"Can't say that I have. Don't get the paper delivered out here," Nelson belly-laughed.

"There's this man, who's responsible. I was on his trail."

"That so?" Nelson's voice grew serious. "What would make someone take them girls?"

"The doctors say he's a nutcase. They say he killed his father the night of that hurricane. Then, his mother burned up suspiciously in a house fire."

"Oh, my Lordie, that sounds like one sick puppy," Nelson laughed a little less heartily.

"That's why it's important I get back to the office, so I can keep tracking him."

"With that storm, no one's going anywhere. Once it stops raining, I'll run ya back. My skiff's got a 250 horsepower Johnson engine. She'll do us fine. Maybe I should call the Coast Guard now. Say, what was the name of the boat?" Nelson asked, turning away from the man and pulling a generator-powered radio from a leather bag. “Maybe they found it. I remember one time...”

“I don’t know; it wasn’t mine,” the man said quickly, not wanting to hear another story.

“Okay, what was the guy’s name? The fellow that owned the boat.”

“Ben O’Shea.” *I can’t risk the Coast Guard.*

“Alright, what about your home address so that the locals can send someone over?” Nelson asked over his shoulder as he turned on the radio.

“You know Nelson, let’s leave it until the morning. My wife said something about staying with friends. I’m exhausted. I’d like to lie here quietly and go to sleep.”

Nelson turned back to face the man, giving him a confused look. After a moment, he broke into a grin and said, “Good idea, Gabriel. Things always look better in the morning.”

CHAPTER TWENTY-THREE

Saturday, February 12th, 1983
Ship Island

The man woke to the sound and smelled the cooking outside the tent. He got up and retrieved his dry clothes. He could see through the mesh of the tent that it was light outside. Nelson was hunched over his Coleman, cooking something in a cast-iron skillet. The dog Molly was nearby, chewing on something sh'de likely dragged up from the beach.

"Good morning, buddy," Nelson said, sensing the man behind him. "The rain finally stopped and left us with a beautiful day. How're you feeling this morning? Care for a couple of eggs and maybe a little Folgers?" he turned around and smiled, "You know what they say, *'The best part of waking up is Folgers in your cup.'*"

"Sure, thanks Nelson," he said, climbing out of the tent. "I feel much better. I don't think I properly thanked you for saving my life."

"It's Nellie, and not to worry my friend. You were busy just making sense of what happened to you. I am curious though, you never really explained what you were doing on the boat."

"You're right; I didn't."

"Well, no time like the present." Nelson poured him a cup of coffee.

"A client. We were meeting to discuss a business matter when the storm hit." He took the coffee. "Looks like it's going to be a nice day for a boat ride," he tried to change the subject. He watched as Nelson fussed over the eggs.

"You know buddy; I've been thinking about what you said about this maniac. The one who took those girls."

"Yeah?"

"He'd be smart to have a boat. Something big enough to allow him to stash the girls below deck. He goes out in the Gulf and does what he wants to them, you know, without anyone to stop him." Nelson turned and stared at the man. "Then, when he's tired of them, he guts them and tosses them into the Gulf. The Gulf is over 5000 feet deep in places, and no one would ever know. That is if you weighed them down proper-like."

The man flinched a moment and then looked out onto the Gulf to watch a couple of seagulls dive for fish. "You should be the detective, Nelson."

"Maybe I should. How do you go about finding a killer like that? I mean, you said he had killed his family. I bet he's a loner. Like he wouldn't want people to find out about his dirty little secrets." Nelson lifted the eggs onto a paper plate. "Ain't got but one chair, but the sand's already dry."

"Thanks." The man sat down on the beach holding his plate, looking up at Nelson.

"Like I was asking," repeated Nelson taking his plate and sitting in the beach chair. "Just how would a private detective go about finding a man like that?"

He took his time answering. "Think about what's known about him. Where did he grow up? Who were his friends? What can you find out about his interests? For example, all the girls are teenagers with blonde hair. Why is that? Was there something special about the first girl that triggered something? Go to the last known place the girl was seen. Did the neighbors see anyone suspicious? You get the idea. Then work things from there." He took a bite of his eggs.

"You have this pretty down pat, don't you? I bet you're pretty close to catching the guy. You probably know him better than he knows himself."

"I don't know about that." He leaned back on his haunches with his face turned towards the sun. He grabbed fistfuls of white sand and let it slip through his fingers.

"You know you can tell a lot about a man by the way he sits? Like crossed legged injun style, upright with their back straight, or like you, lounging back."

"Yeah? What does that tell you about me?"

"I'd say you're confident; you know what you like. But in contrast, the way you are grabbing at that sand might suggest you have something eating at you. Releasing slowly through your fingers would tell me you like to be in control." When the man ignored the comment, Nelson added, "After what you went through last night I'd be surprised if you weren't a little jittery. Say, wouldn't this be something for the police to investigate? Why are you on the case?"

"I'm working as a consultant for the FBI."

"My, my, the FBI, that's impressive. You're like a G-Man."

"There's no one else on this island?"

"Not a soul. It's not that big. There used to be a wooden lighthouse, but back in '72 a bunch of hippy campers burned it down. Come the end of March, a ferry runs from the mainland and takes people out here to lounge on the beach for the day. The place gets crowded."

"How do you and your dog survive out here?"

"I only come out to camp and fish a week or so at a time. That's about the limit of my generator. Kind of need it to run my stuff."

"Do you live in Biloxi?"

"I have a place in D'Iberville. Pretty modest. I live on a pension from my days at the cannery. My ex moved out a while back. She left Molly and the bills."

"What would happen if you got hurt out here? How long before someone might come looking?"

"Why? You thinking of killing me?" Nelson chuckled nervously.

"No, just concerned. They say that when someone saves your life, you have to look out for them."

"All I need is Molly. The Coast Guard swings by every once in a while to chat. I guess they might check the tent if they suspected something. But more likely, I'd lie here until the damn tourists arrive."

The man nodded, his mind wandering. *God that sun is warm. I could sit here for days and still not be rid of the chill from last night. I remember Ship Island. This was party central when I was growing up. Not that I've ever been in the in-crowd. I took particular delight in torching their lighthouse. Watching the flames from my boat, I knew the hippies would be blamed. So, what about you, Nelson? Do you suspect something? As much as I'd like to continue playing Twenty Questions with you, I need to get out of here. There's a chance that Jessica got my boat docked somewhere and the Coast Guard is looking for me.*

"Enjoying the sun, buddy? Say, would you like to check out the fort while you're here?"

"No, I'm kind of anxious to get back and see my wife. How long will it take to get to Biloxi?"

"The ferry makes the trip in a couple of hours, but I've been thinking. If I radio the Coast Guard, they might even agree to stop by with one of their patrols."

"Good idea," said the man getting to his feet, wiping the sand from his khakis. He grabbed a piece of driftwood and showed it to the dog; then he tossed it into the surf. The dog limped down the beach after it. Nelson had taken his chair into the tent and was getting the radio set up. Following closely behind, the man spied a hook-like tool among some fishing equipment. He thought it was called an angler, used to haul big fish into a boat. While Nelson still had his back to him, he grabbed the angler. *I might only get one chance at this.*

"Coast Guard. Calling the Coast Guard, come in, this is Nelson Gallant out on Ship...."

Taking a deep breath, Bouvier swung the angler, impaling Gallant in the neck. He then pulled upward as if he was hoisting a barracuda. Nelson's eyes bulged in shock as he tried to form words. He started making gurgling noises. The dog started to bark outside the tent as the man wrestled the angler from Nelson's throat, only to swing it again, this time ripping Nelson's Adam's apple. Blood was spurting everywhere as he heard a voice coming through the radio.

"This is the Coast Guard, go ahead, Nelson."

The man continued to wrench the angler back and forth until he heard a death rattle. The older man slumped to the ground. "You disappoint me, Nelson," he gasped, trying to catch his breath, tired from the exertion.

He was thinking about what to do when he was propelled suddenly forward on top of Gallant. Molly was growling and snarling like Cujo in the Stephen King movie. He felt a sharp pain in his lower leg as the dog clamped onto him with her fangs. He dropped the radio handset and used his fists to punch the dog repeatedly. The pain was shooting up his leg, blood spurting from where she had broken the skin.

"Ship Island, come in. What's happening there?"

Molly continued to dig her teeth into his calf. He reached down and picked up the angler. He screamed as he swung the angler, striking the dog in her side. The blow momentarily stunned her, but not enough to loosen the grip. "Fuck, fuck, fuck," Bouvier screamed again, striking the dog over and over again. Finally, he felt her grip loosen, and Molly slunk back to the front of the tent.

"Ship Island, come in. This is the Coast Guard. Come in, Ship Island."

If I don't answer, they'll get suspicious. After a moment to compose himself, he picked up the handset and pressed the talk button. "This is Ship Island again, disregard my last communication. Everything is fine. Going to be a great day." After a moment he added, '*The best part of the morning is waking up to Folgers in your cup.*" Bouvier then used the angler to destroy the radio.

CHAPTER TWENTY-FOUR

Saturday, February 12th, 1983
Ship Island

I *need to find a first aid kit. Old farts like him always carry one.* The dog was lying at the front of the tent licking her wounds. Molly let out a growl as he limped to the front of the tent, blocking the entrance. He made a threatening gesture with the angler, which only brought on more snarling. "Yeah? You want some more? You bitch!" He looked down at the broken radio. *Now I'm fucked if I can't get out of here. The Coast Guard will come and find me here with a dead body.* He noticed a container of dog treats on the small table that Nelson had been using for the radio. He reached in, took one of the treats and slowly approached, holding it out to the dog. Molly looked at the treat, but when Charles got to within a few feet of her, she bared her teeth and tried to snap at him. "Okay, we'll do it your way. You're going to bleed out, you old fuck."

He resumed his search for a first aid kit and found it in a cooler in the back corner of the tent. He sat in the beach chair, keeping one eye on Molly as he tore off his blood-soak pant leg. He was repulsed by the huge rip in his thigh. "You bitch, look what you did to me." He used a wet cloth to staunch the blood and clean the wound. Inside the kit, there was a bunch of condoms. *What are these for? There's no one else on the fucking island.* There was a bottle of something called chlorhexidine. He knew it was to ward off infection. He screwed off the cap and poured it on his wound. The pain seemed to run up his leg and up into his brain like a scorching fire. "OH, FUCK! JESUS ON A STICK, YOU FUCKIN DOG! He tried to stand, only to find that it made the pain worse. After a few moments of cursing, he looked over at the dog. Molly appeared to be smiling. He sat back down and wrapped his calf with gauze as tightly as he could.

Once done, he thought about his predicament. *The Coast Guard has surely headed out, which doesn't leave much time to clean up the place up and get out of here.* He looked at the dog again, and as if on cue, Molly bared her teeth. He still had the angler close at hand, but he didn't want to risk another fight. He picked up the remnants of the radio and threw it at the dog. The dog struggled to get up and hobbled pitifully out of the tent.

Bouvier limped after the dog, picking up the skillet Nelson had been using, and holding it over his head as a weapon; he started yelling at the dog. "GET THE FUCK AWAY, GO ON BITCH."

The dog moved fifty yards down the beach and lay down, continuing to lick her wounds while keeping an eye on him.

Charles had a lot of work to do and precious little time. He went back into the tent and dug Gallant's wallet out of his jeans. Other than a picture of the dog, Nelson had a couple of credit cards, a driver's license, and about $50 in small bills. He also had a set of keys. There was a fob that said, "*Taking the backroads in my Jeep.*"

It took almost twenty minutes and most of his strength to drag Nelson's body to the boat. He remembered that one of the reasons big ships came to the island was that the water's depth dropped off quickly. He assembled a makeshift anchor using rope and part of the tent, along with some rocks he found along the beach. Next, he checked the gas levels and found a reserve can. Using the skillet, he dug a hole big enough to bury the rest of the tent. He debated about burying the angler, but at the last minute, decided to take it with him.

It was exhausting work. The gash in his leg had started to bleed again and the pain seemed to have gotten worse. He carried the supplies that were in the tent to the middle of the island so that they wouldn't be seen from the beach. Molly was still lying in the same spot; her eyes closed.

The position of the sun suggested it was almost noon. He kept looking out toe sea expecting to see the Coast Guard. He started to panic and worked as quickly as he could. He struggled to drag Gallant's body into the boat. He started up the Johnson and was about half a mile offshore when he pushed, heaved and rolled Nelson's body overboard. Watching it sink, he decided it marked the end of a chapter in his life. It was time for a new beginning, a new direction.

Biloxi was over a dozen miles away. The swells of the waves were tame compared to what he'd endured the previous evening. With a little luck, he'd make the trip to Biloxi in good time and without seeing the Coast Guard. He looked back one last time. He was struck by the beauty of the beach, "I should send someone a postcard."

The sun hung high in the cloudless blue sky, entirely impervious to the carnage that had just happened. Charles kept the little boat on a due north heading. He planned to veer east at first sight of land and put in at the Port Cadet Marina in Biloxi. It was the largest marina on the coast, and the one closest to nearby D'Iberville. With any luck, there would be a Jeep in the parking lot just waiting for him.

He had cut his pants into shorts, mainly because of all of the blood. With temperatures in the mid-sixties, he was thankful that he had brought one of Nelson's blankets. He passed some pleasure crafts, mostly heading west to New Orleans. His mind flashed back to what had happened on the boat. Jessica had surprised him by fighting back and trying to kill him. Her actions had shown courage and determination. All the others had wilted in fear and begged for their miserable lives. Every strong man needed a strong woman. *Yes, Jessica, you are a painting for my eyes alone. One day we will be reunited. I will be your lover, and you will be mine. I will be the one who will marry you, make love to you, and you will bear my children. You will be mine to love forever. How sweet that will be.*

He was about halfway through his journey when he saw a Coast Guard cutter heading towards him at full speed. His heart started to race. *Could they already know what happened? Have I forgotten something? Will they recognize Nelson's boat?* He decided to change course and veer east. The cutter was still far enough away. If he was seen, they'd likely interpret his maneuver as a small boat getting out of the way.

When the cutter was a hundred yards away, Charles was already well to the east. He could see sailors on the bridge looking at him through binoculars. He waived, but they ignored him and continued heading south. *At their top speed, they'll get to the island in thirty minutes.* At his rate of speed, he figured he was still ninety minutes from the marina, plenty of time for them to get to the island and radio an alarm back to Biloxi.

He pushed the Johnson motor as much as he could.

IT WAS mid-afternoon by the time Charles docked the little boat at the Port Cadet Marina. Thankfully, there were plenty of fishermen and boaters out on the dock, so he was able to slip anonymously among the people. He passed a newspaper box on his walk to the parking lot and was startled to see his picture on the front page. The headline was about the manhunt being led by Gabriel Ross and his FBI task force.

He ran to the parking lot, looking for a jeep. He was frustrated when he saw that just about every fisherman drove a Jeep. It took the better part of twenty minutes to find the right one – a bright green Laredo.

CHAPTER TWENTY-FIVE

Saturday, February 12th, 1983
D'Iberville, Mississippi

The sign outside the Glenmark Apartments indicated there were vacancies for one and two-bedroom units. Gallant's driver's license showed him living in apartment four. After parking the Jeep in the visitor's lot, he made his way to the front of the building.

When he opened the door to Nelson's apartment, he found a tidy one-bedroom apartment. A picture of Nelson stood on an end table by the couch. He was holding up a large bluefish for the camera. Molly was sitting at his feet looking up wistfully at the catch.

Charles kicked off his shoes and looked in the bedroom for clothes. Nelson's jeans were about 6 inches too short and that much again too wide. They'd have to do. The shirts were also ridiculously large on him, but they'd have to work until he could get to a store and buy his own stuff. He found another picture on the night table by the bed. It showed a middle-aged woman with a deadpan expression, standing with Nelson in front of his jeep.

He made himself at home on the couch with his feet resting on the coffee table, then got up and turned on an ancient black and white Electrohome, selecting the local news channel. President Ronald Regan was meeting with Reverend Jesse Jackson at the White House. The reception on the television was crap. Nelson had used aluminum foil on the rabbit ears to try to improve the picture. Charles played with it, but no matter what he did, ole Ronnie had three eyes. After a few minutes, the newscaster reported a late-breaking story.

"This just in, a reminder to everyone, please pay close attention to weather forecasts before setting sail out onto the Gulf. Even if the weather looks clear, things can change quickly. This was the case last night when a flash storm hit the Gulf. Luckily for a Gulfport woman, the local Coast Guard was in the vicinity and rescued her. She had lost control of her cabin cruiser and had become disoriented."

Well, Jessica. They don't know everything yet. Glad you survived. I bet at this point, you're telling them quite a story. Once the news ended, he got up and changed to a channel airing The Hawaiian Open Golf Championship, and went hunting for beer in the icebox. He found a couple of pieces of fish hastily covered with Saran Wrap. Upon closer inspection, they smelled horrible and had started to spoil. There was no beer, no juice, no cokes. *Jesus Nelson, what do you drink?* The answer lay on the shelf over the sink. There were a half-dozen jars of Folger's coffee. On a whim, he checked them all and found one empty containing a bundle of cash. *Good man, Nelson, I'll need this.* He counted slightly over $400 in small bills.

Charles opened the cupboard above the stove looking for food. The only thing he found was a half dozen boxes of

Lucky Charms cereal. He opened a box and sat down on the couch, trying his best to get interested in a three-eyed Tom Watson putting a ball. He picked up the phone directory sitting under a black rotary dial telephone on the end table and looked up the name Grant. He found almost two dozen.

His thoughts were interrupted by a banging on the apartment door. He immediately assumed they'd found the dog, guessed what had happened to Nelson, and followed the trail to the apartment. He got up and turned down the television. Looking out the living room window, he didn't see anyone checking out Nelson's Jeep. If worst came to worst, he could go out the window. He sat down on the couch and prepared to wait them out.

A few moments later, there was another round of banging, this time louder, followed by a woman's voice. "I know you're in there. Open this fucking door."

A cop? A neighbor who'd heard the television? She might have seen me and wants to know what I'm doing in Nelson's apartment.

"Come on, come on. It's Freda. You remember, baby? Are we going to have this conversation out in the hallway?"

He decided to go to the door and check the spyhole. What he saw frightened him. A woman with a cigarette in one of those plastic holders, looking back at him. She must have been in her fifties and had red hair in pink curlers. She was wearing a ratty old dressing gown.

He recoiled from the door when he heard her voice. "I see you in there, Nelson. Now give it up. I rendered the services. Just because my name's Freda, doesn't mean it was free." Her laughed was more of a cackle. "I didn't hear any complaints.

Now open the door unless you want me to tell our neighbors about all the little games you like to play."

Charles opened the door; the woman was even more frightening in person. "Listen, I don't know who you are, but Dad isn't here. I can leave him a message."

"Your dad? What's his Jeep doing in the parking lot?"

"He lent it to me."

"What's your name?" She pushed Charles aside and entered the apartment.

"Gabriel."

"Good Jewish name. Gabriel what?"

Charles took a little too long to answer, "Gallant, like Dad. Of course."

"Of course. I don't believe you; Nelson never said he had a son." She marched into the living room. She spied the box of cereal on the coffee table. "Have you been eating me Lucky Charms?" she asked, combining a Jewish inflection with an Irish accent.

"It's the only thing edible in the place."

"Did he also give you permission to wear his jeans? You look like a schmiel; where's the flood?" she asked sarcastically.

"I spilled something on my clothes and needed to borrow his."

The woman seemed to consider this for a moment before speaking again. "Something seems hinky here. I don't know what. You don't look like Nelson at all." She blew smoke out of the side of her mouth.

"I look like my mother."

"Is that right?" She noticed the angler that Charles had left on the bureau. "What's this for?"

"It belongs to Nelson; it's a fishing thing."

"Yeah? But what's it doing here? If he's out fishing, why did he leave it here?"

Charles shrugged.

"Nelson owes me $50. Since you're so buddy-buddy, you might want to pay his bill for him."

He pulled out Nelson's wallet. "You have to leave; I'm expecting company."

"Entertaining, dressed like that?" she cackled.

Charles took fifty dollars from the wallet and handed it to the woman. As he handed over the cash, he noticed that a twenty had a bloody thumbprint on Jackson's face.

She took the cash, but instead of pocketing it, as he had hoped, she held the bills up to the light, snapping them to ensure they weren't counterfeit. He thought she was satisfied and had turned to lead her out of the apartment when she said, "Hey, wait up sonny boy. There's something on these bills." She gave him a puzzled look. Let me see that wallet."

He knew he couldn't let her leave the apartment. She was suspicious and would rat him out first chance she got. Charles picked up the angler and swung it while she was still holding up the twenty. She had the same look on her face as Nelson had when the angler went into her neck. It wasn't just the surprise; it was disbelief. Like this wasn't supposed to happen. There was blood everywhere as he hit her over and over again. She was a fighter and continued to thrash around even though her neck was ripped open. He had to hit her a dozen times before he was sure she was gone. Even then, her legs continued to twitch. Charles grabbed a handful of Lucky Charms and watched until it stopped.

In the middle of the night, he rolled her body up in the rug she was lying on and lugged it out to the Jeep. He drove the backstreets until he spotted a dumpster behind a fast food restaurant. Charles dragged the body from the Jeep and after a couple of attempts, hoisted it into the bin. If the stench got to be too much, people would assume it was coming from Burger King.

He kept thinking back to the look on Freda's face when she'd realized she was going to die. It gave him a rush. He'd read somewhere that police in England had been able to capture the image of the killer in a victim's eyes. It had sounded like bullshit when he first read it, but now he wondered if it could be true?

He'd now killed two people using the angler. He liked swinging the tool. It had a good weight to it. He relived the sensation of killing Freda over and over again. He felt a new passion grow.

CHAPTER TWENTY-SIX

Sunday, February 13th, 1983
D'Iberville, Mississippi

Charles figured he was safe to stay in Nelson's apartment for a few days, but he'd soon need to find somewhere else. Over a breakfast of Lucky Charms and Folgers, he made a list of some of the things he would need. After a long, hot shower, he changed the dressing on his leg and drove the Jeep a few miles to where he'd noticed a K-Mart. He bought clothes, shoes, a gym bag, and some essential toiletries before heading to the grocery section and buying some decent food. He would soon need to find a source of cash, as he was down to his last $200 and still needed to put gas in the Jeep.

He thought back to the cover of yesterday's *Herald*. They were using an old high school yearbook picture taken when he wore his dark hair longer. Outside the K-Mart, he bought the early edition of the paper.

SUSPECTED SERIAL KILLER THOUGHT TO HAVE DROWNED

A freak storm on the Gulf may have put an end to the search for a man thought to be connected to the disappearance of at least six teenage girls. A representative of the Harrison County Sheriff's Department confirmed that Charles Bouvier of New Orleans is believed to have fallen into the Gulf during a violent storm. Gabriel Ross of the Eye on You Detective Agency and part of the FBI's Mardi Gras Task Force, said that they had been closing in on Bouvier and an arrest had been imminent. Jessica Grant, a resident of Gulfport who had been abducted by Bouvier, was found frightened but unharmed on Bouvier's boat. The bodies of the other missing girls have not been found, and some people have suggested that Bouvier sold them into white slavery. Others wondered if he disposed of their bodies in the Gulf.

The story continued on page three, where it showed file pictures of each of the girls taken, including Jessica Grant. Looking at each of the photographs, he remembered each one, how they had excited him and ultimately disappointed him. There was a write-up on each, as well as a story about Boone Cooper, his dim-witted partner that had brought him the girls. A separate article on Gabriel Ross explained how he had used an FBI profiler to understand the killer's mind. Now when Charles looked at Jessica's picture, he felt a longing, an emptiness inside. When he looked at the pictures of the other girls, he felt nothing. It was like looking through a window at someone else's life.

Charles drove back to Gallant's apartment and changed into his new clothes. He put Nelson's stuff in a garbage bag. As he was putting away the grocery items, he turned on the local news. The lead story was all about Jessica Grant, who had finally been released from the hospital and was being interviewed by a reporter from the Herald. Judging by the uniforms worn by the police, he figured she was being interviewed at the Harrison County Sheriff's Office. If he went there now, he could watch her leave and follow her to her parent's house. There was just one thing he had to do first.

THE SHERIFF's office was located on Larkin Smith Drive in Gulfport. Parking across the street gave him a perfect view of the front doors. Hopefully, she was still in there. While he waited, he admired his new look in the rearview mirror. Now, with bleached blonde hair and dark sunglasses, even Jessica wouldn't recognize him.

He wasted over an hour parked outside the sheriff's department, thinking about the cops interviewing Jessica. Jessica, poor Jessica. The survivor. Brave little Jessica. Oh, how horrible it must be for you. How clever of you to think of the flare gun. He debated walking into the building and asking whether she was still being interviewed, but he didn't want to press his luck.

He turned his attention to a pressing problem. He needed money. More than just walking around money. He had plenty of money in the bank but going there was out of the question. Or was it? With everything that had been happening, they may not have flagged his accounts yet. Without identification, he would need to go to his home branch in New Orleans. He finally discounted the idea. Right now, the cops probably think I drowned. If I go into the bank, they'd have proof I survived.

* * *

On his way back from the sheriff's department, Charles

stopped at a Texaco station. The colored attendant bounded out of the building as soon as he drove up to the pumps.

"Sure be a fine day for February," said the attendant cheerfully as he approached the driver side window. "Want me to fill her up with supreme? It's better for a vehicle like this. Say, how long have you had the Laredo?"

Charles ignored the man's questions. "Just fill it up and get me a map of Gulfport."

"Ain't got a map just of Gulfport. They all come with Biloxi," replied the man, starting to pump the gas. "Kind of like you buy Gulfport, and you get everything else for free."

Charles rolled the window up and closed his eyes. After a couple of minutes, the sound of a squeegee broke his daydreams. The man was cleaning his window. Once the attendant saw that Charles had his eyes open, he rapped on the window and gestured for him to roll it down. He made the man wait before he lowered it.

"If y'all pop the hood, I'll check the oil. You don't want to take a chance of running low and your engine seizing up."

"Fuck off," he said, rolling the window back up.

The attendant stared at him for a moment before shrugging his shoulders and going back into the building. While Charles was waiting, three motorcycles rode up to the pumps. He noticed Sons of Silence stitched on their jackets. The attendant came back moments later carrying a map. Once again, he gestured for the window to be lowered. "That'll be $19 for the gas and another dollar for the map."

Charles took a twenty from Nelson's wallet, the same twenty that had gotten Freda killed, and held it out to the man. As the attendant reached for the money, Charles dropped it to the ground. He started up the Jeep and put it in gear. The motorcycles had given him an idea.

CHAPTER TWENTY-SEVEN

Sunday, February 13th, 1983
D'Iberville, Mississippi

When he got back to the apartment, he was about to shower when the phone rang. Initially, Charles planned to ignore it, but at the last minute curiosity got the better of him, and he picked up the receiver.

"Hello, I'm looking for Mr. Nelson Gallant; this is Captain Rosman of the United States Coast Guard Service." The man's voice was pleasant and confident.

It took a moment for Charles to register. "I'm Nelson," Charles replied, hoping Rosman wasn't already acquainted with Gallant.

"Oh, I'm glad I caught you. We're doing a routine check. If you've been watching the news, you might have heard that the Coast Guard is undertaking a search for a man who was last seen falling overboard during Monday night's storm. I know you like to camp out on Ship Island and we were wondering if you might have seen anything."

"Seen anything? No, there's nothing on the island. I didn't see anyone."

"We checked the fort and didn't find anything. We think the man drowned, but since we haven't recovered his body, we thought we should check that he isn't hiding out somewhere."

"I didn't see anyone. Maybe the sharks got him."

"Thanks for that." Before hanging up, Captain Rosman said, "Listen, I'm sorry to hear about your dog."

"My dog?"

"Yes, one of our patrols went to the island the day after the storm. You had already cleared out, but we found your dog."

There was another pause on the line before Charles responded. "My dog? Yes, pretty sad. I'm still shaken up."

"The patrol said it looked like your dog had been in a fight and was gored to death. What happened?"

"I don't know. I was upset. That's why I left, to get help."

There was a long pause before the captain asked again, "Sure you didn't see anyone? Maybe the night of the storm."

"No. Nothing. I was hunkered down in my tent."

"But...then, how did your dog get hurt?" The Captain's tone was shifting from friendly to suspicious.

"I don't know, Captain. She ran off in the morning and came limping back to the tent. She was hurt pretty bad and needed a vet. I'm getting old; otherwise, I would have lifted her into the boat, but she was too heavy."

"Did you find a vet willing to go back out there?"

"No, of course, I tried, but they all wanted me to bring the dog in. I figured there likely wouldn't be any point. The dog was getting pretty old anyway."

There was another pause on the line before the Captain spoke up, "Mr. Gallant, sorry to have interrupted your day, if you happen to remember anything else, my name is Captain

Rosman." His tone had grown icy. "Oh, by the way, what was your dog's name?"

It took a few seconds for Charles to respond. He resisted the urge to hang up and make a run for it. "Molly," Charles said, finally remembering. After hanging up, it took almost five minutes before he stopped shaking. *There was something off about the call. The last question was a test.*

Charles drove down to the waterfront, parking again across the Coast Guard office. The rain was coming down pretty hard as he watched the umbrellas come and go. *It was a mistake to leave the dog. I should have killed it and buried it with everything else. That Captain suspects something.*

He sat there watching for a half an hour before the rain let up. He got out of the Jeep and walked down to the pier. The Coast Guard kept all of the impounded boats in a locked fenced-off area. It took a few minutes to find the *Jill*. Charles was sure that by now the Coast Guard had thoroughly searched the boat, but was also sure they wouldn't have found his hiding place. In the forward berth, there was a framed poster of Farrah Fawcett wearing an orange bathing suit. Behind the poster was a secret compartment almost invisible in the paneling. If you pushed on the wall in just the right spot, it would pop open revealing a compartment. Inside was a metal box with a thumbwheel combination lock containing $80,000 in cash, a set of new identification papers, and a Colt .45.

CHAPTER TWENTY-EIGHT

Wednesday, February 16th, 1983
Gulfport, Mississippi

Later that week Charles parked in front of a seedy bar called Boogie's along the beach strip. Most of the joints here doubled as illegal gambling houses. He saw a bunch of Harleys parked in front as he settled in to wait. Shortly past midnight, a tall skinny man wearing a sleeveless leather vest came out and urinated against the building. Sons of Silence was embroidered on the back of his vest.

Charles approached the man as he was getting on his bike. "Nice bike."

"Yeah? Who the fuck are you?" The biker had an accent, maybe Polish or Russian.

"Why don't we call me Smith. I'm looking to hire someone to perform a service."

The man hawked up a phlegmy loogie, hitting Charles' new shoes. "Fuck off, homo."

"I'm not a homo. The money I'll pay will probably cover your gambling loss tonight." In response, the man kick-started his Harley. Charles yelled over the noise, "Fifteen minutes and you earn $500. That's $2,000 an hour."

This got the man's attention. "You a cop?"

"Nope, just an average guy willing to pay to retrieve his property."

"$500 for fifteen minutes? It's either illegal or dangerous." The man turned off his bike and eyed Charles suspiciously.

"It's nothing you can't handle. The cops impounded my cabin cruiser, and I need to retrieve something. You get it for me, and I'll give you the cash."

"Yeah, what is it?"

"Just a locked case containing some important papers. Nothing of value to you." Charles noticed the man had tattoos up and down his arms. His dirty blond hair was straggly as was his chin strip.

"I get the money up front."

"No, only when you give me the case."

"Listen, fuckwad. That's not the way it works. But for a grand, I might consider it."

Charles looked at the man. *I don't like being called that.* He considered going to the Jeep to get his angler. "$500 tops. If you don't want it, I'll offer it someone else."

"Give me your address; I'll think about it."

"No, if you want to think about it, I'll be back on Friday night."

The man nodded and started the Harley and then backed out of the parking space.

Charles shouted over the roar of the motorcycle. "What's your name?"

"Petr."

Charles watched as Petr turned east on Beach Boulevard, before following in the Jeep. He wondered about using Petr. He could go get it himself. The problem was that he didn't know what to expect. There might be a night watchman, a guard, a dog, or some kind of alarm. Not that using Petr wasn't risky. He could easily figure out that whatever was in the box was worth more than $500. Charles had an idea on how to stack the deck.

CHAPTER TWENTY-NINE

Thursday, February 17th, 1983
Gulfport, Mississippi

The next day it was raining when Charles woke up. The weatherman on WLOX was forecasting a low-pressure system coming in from the north, bringing cooler temperatures and a chance of thunderstorms. In the weatherman's sign-off he once again warned people to be careful if their plans involved boating on the Gulf. Charles waited to hear an update on the Mardi Gras case and was almost disappointed when the story was no longer news.

After breakfast, he drove back to the Hidden Acres trailer park where he'd followed Petr the night before. There was a thicket of pine trees beside Petr's trailer, which was perfect for surveillance. There was no sign of the Harley. He was surprised to see a tough-looking woman come out drinking a beer. *A little early, wouldn't you say?* He watched as she sat on the steps and lit up a cigarette. She had blond hair piled up on her head and looked in her mid-thirties.

After a few minutes of watching the woman, he drove the

Jeep up to the trailer and got out. The woman flicked her cigarette butt at him as he approached. "We don't want anything, so fuck off."

"I'm looking for Petr." She took a long swig from her Bud. "My name's Smith. Is he around?"

"Do you see his bike, numbnuts?"

Charles wished that he had brought the angler. "Too bad, I need to talk to him about business."

"What business?" She spat a stream of something at his shoes.

What the fuck is wrong with people. "Are you his girl?"

She laughed and repeated, "What-cha want, numbnuts?" Charles approached closer. "He went to meet some of his ... associates."

"I have some money for him. Hey, do you have another Bud? I'm thirsty."

The woman seemed to weigh his request before replying, "Wait here." She got up and went into the trailer. Charles followed right behind her. Before she realized what was happening, he pushed her into the trailer and slapped her hard across the face. Stumbling, she landed on the dirty floor of the trailer, her beer spilling. He looked around. "What a fucking dump!"

"You're going to be sorry. Petr's gonna make you pay, shithead."

Charles let out a laugh. "I'm quite willing to pay. What's your name?"

"Fuck off." She started to get up.

"That's quite the name." He let her get almost fully up before kneeing her viciously in the gut. She let out a gasp and then fell to the floor again, lying in the fetal position and sobbing.

"Now, your name is not fuck off; what is it?"

"Lana."

"That's good. I wouldn't get up, Lana." He went over the small fridge and opened the door. Other than beer, there wasn't much that was edible. He opened the freezer section, and beside a bunch of Swanson Hungry Man dinners, he found some baggies of marijuana. "Well, look at this. How much is all this worth, Lana?"

"Fuck off! Asshole. I think you broke a rib."

Charlie took all of the baggies out of the freezer and put them on the counter. He noticed an envelope on the counter addressed to Petr and Lana Gadzinga off the counter. "You have a lot of unopened bills." He looked at the dirty dishes in the sink. "You need to clean up around here, Lana. You never know when people might drop in."

She was still lying on the ground, holding her side.

"Ah, here let me help you." Charles grasped her arm and pulled her up. He led her to a chair. "Now I'm sorry, Lana, but you called me a bad name. I don't like being called bad names." He picked up a dirty, serrated knife from the sink. "Now, Lana, did you want to call me another name?"

She watched him, fear in her eyes for the first time.

He was holding the knife menacingly. "I should confess, the last person who wasn't very nice to me, got her throat ripped open. She's now in a garbage bin in an alley being eaten by rats. Now let me give you another chance, Lana. Did you want to call me another name?"

She shook her head, this time with tears welling up in her eyes.

He pulled over another chair and sat down across from her. "Lana, I'm a reasonable person. I don't want to hurt you, or Petr. I want to be your friend. Do you want to be my friend?" She didn't immediately reply, so he pointed the knife at her with a questioning look.

"Yeah, let's be friends," she said sarcastically.

"Good," he said, smiling. He ran his hand down the side of her face, then down to her breast. He squeezed her breast, watching for a reaction. "I met Petr last night and offered to give him $500 for fifteen minutes of work. Did he tell you about it?"

She shook her head.

"I hope I didn't ruin a surprise. Well anyway, Lana here's the deal. On one side of the scale, if Petr does this little job, then I'll give him $500. I'll also return all this pot plus another $500 just for you. Our little secret." He winked. "Now on the other side of the scale; if he screws me, then I'll keep the cash, I'll smoke his pot, and then I'm going to come back and fuck you. That is before I rip out your throat. While you're twitching away on the floor, with blood spurting everywhere, I might eat your TV dinners. Do you still want to be my friend?"

She nodded frantically.

"When Petr comes back, I want you to treat him special, tell him how much you love him and that you met a friend of his. Then make sure he doesn't fuck this up."

CHAPTER THIRTY

Friday, February 18th, 1983
Gulfport, Mississippi

Charles was in his Jeep, looking at the front door of Boogie's again. He worked through how he expected the conversation to go. *What if he comes out with his biker friends? Well then, I'll play bumper cars with their Harleys and run over a few of them before leaving.*

He was still watching the door when the passenger door of the Jeep opened, and Petr got in. It took a moment for Charles to regain his composure.

"Mr. Smith, I'm in. What's the plan?"

"We have a deal, $500 for the return of my property?"

"You told Lana you'd return my weed."

"Good enough, I enjoyed meeting Lana; is she your wife?"

"Yeah, she said you were a major league psycho, and I'd be best not to fuck with you."

"Delightful girl and smart. You might want to keep her, Petr. Are you familiar with the Coast Guard impound lot... ?"

Charles followed the Harley down to the waterfront. He had given Petr instructions about the boat as well as a flashlight and a prybar to take care of the lock on the fence of the impound lot. Once again, he parked across from the Coast Guard station, approximately a hundred yards before a short hill led down to where the boats were moored. To watch Petr in the impound lot, Charles would have to get out and walk to the hill.

Petr got off his bike and nodded to Charles, then started walking towards the impound. Charles could see the light from the flashlight as he made it to the hill. *Five minutes to break the lock and get to the boat, five more to retrieve the box and another five to come back.*

After about three minutes, the Jeep was illuminated by a car's headlights coming down 23rd Avenue in his direction. Charles slumped down in his seat, watching the car from the side mirror. The vehicle passed the Jeep slowly and turned into the Coast Guard parking lot. He watched as a deputy sheriff got out of a cruiser, climbed the steps, and tried the front door of the building. Finding it locked, he shone his flashlight through the door and then slowly walked back to his car. *By now Petr must have made it to the Jill.* The cop backed his cruiser out of the lot and waited a minute before pulling out onto 23rd, heading towards the impound lot. *Did Petr leave the gate open? Will he see Petr's flashlight on the boat?* As he watched, he saw the cruiser's brake lights come on. A minute later, Charles heard a car door slam. Under the streetlight, he saw the deputy. He was pointing his flashlight at the impound yard.

Deputy Nolan had just turned 22 years old. To celebrate the occasion, his buddies had taken him to a Creedence Clearwater Revival concert the night before. The previous late night explained why he was dragging his ass on patrol tonight. A recent graduate of the academy, some of the deputies had said Nolan was too young to be on patrol alone. The Harrison County Sheriff's Office, however, was undergoing staffing issues, and Nolan had volunteered, hoping to build up his reserve of brownie points. He was familiar with the routine, having done the patrol with a partner over a dozen times before.

Nolan checked the Coast Guard building and then used the police radio to give Dispatch the all-clear. He sat in his cruiser for a couple of moments humming *Born on the Bayou.* He debated taking a quick nap before checking the impound lot, but decided against it and turned the car onto 23rd heading towards the waterfront.

He parked his cruiser on the side of the road and kept it running with the headlights illuminating the road ahead. He noticed a Jeep and a Harley parked at the curb and wondered why anyone would park so far from the residential houses. He took his flashlight with him and got out of the car. There were maybe a dozen boats in the impound, most of which had been confiscated from drug dealers. While he had yet to find anyone breaking into the yard, the sheriff had told him that he'd rousted a bunch of neighborhood punks trying to steal booze or drugs.

He was halfway to the fence when he thought he saw a flicker of light coming from the big Chris Craft moored at the dock. *I should go back to the car and call for back-up. That's what I'm supposed to do. But the guys will never let me forget it if I call in the cavalry to handle some punk-ass kids.* Nolan turned off his flashlight and pulled out his service revolver and waited. A couple of moments later, he saw a flashlight appear on the deck of the boat. He watched as the light bobbed up and down, heading his way. He heard the screech of the gate opening. It was hard to make out how many people were approaching. *No time now to call for back up.*

Nolan could hear the sound of someone approaching. Turning on his flashlight, he called out, "Hold it right there. Sheriff's Department." A man was approximately ten feet away. Nolan could tell he was carrying something, and walking towards him. "I've got a gun, now drop whatever you're carrying, and get on your knees."

"Listen, officer; I'm with the Coast Guard, and I needed something from that boat."

Nolan could see that the man was wearing a sleeveless leather vest. "If you're with the Coast Guard then you know that boat and everything on it, is impounded. You are violating a number of laws. Put whatever you're carrying on the ground and get on your knees."

The man ignored the order and continued walking towards him. "I'm not going to tell you again," Nolan shouted. The man was now six feet away. The question of whether he could bring himself to shoot a man bounced around in his head. He fired a warning shot in the air. As he did, he sensed movement behind him. Turning quickly to see what it was, he suddenly felt something hit him in the neck, followed by a sharp pain. He dropped his gun and flashlight and put his hands to his neck. He tried to call out, but all that came out was a guttural spasm. He wobbled on his feet and felt something hit him again. He fell to his knees as whatever it was hit him again. Deputy Nolan was dead before he hit the ground.

"What the fuck, man?" Petr looked down at the deputy, panic in his voice. "I think you killed him."

"If I had waited two more seconds, he would have shot you. You can thank me later. Don't just stand there with your mouth open. Put that box in my Jeep and then come back and help me get rid of this guy."

Reluctantly Petr went back up the hill to where the Jeep was parked. *What the fuck did I get myself into? Maybe I should just take off on my bike, fuck this guy.*

While he was gone, Charles wiped his prints from the angler using a handkerchief. He threw the tool down beside the body. Picking up the cop's flashlight, he walked down to the impound area. He found what he wanted after a brief search and headed back to the body.

Petr was standing by the deputy as if he was saying a prayer. When he saw Charles, "You never said anything about killing a cop."

"As I said, there wasn't much choice."

"What do we do with his car? The guy left it running." Petr was whining now.

"Turn it off."

Petr stood mouth agape, staring at Charles.

"Gadzinga, snap out of it. Pick up that angler while I drag this body to the water." Charles grabbed Deputy Nolan's legs and dragged him the remaining distance to the fence. "We're going to borrow that inflatable and take him out into the Gulf. I'll need you to help me with him, so put the angler down and grab his legs."

Charles found a tarp in an equipment shed. "Here, roll him in this, so he doesn't get blood on everything." They struggled with the man and eventually got Nolan to the raft. Charles went back to the shed and came out carrying a thirty-pound navy anchor.

Once they got the deputy's body onto the raft, Charles ordered, "Row out about fifty feet, while I tie this to him." It took twenty minutes to row the raft out deep enough. Petr and Charles hoisted Deputy Nolan's body into the Gulf and watched it sink.

"What the fuck, you killed a cop. That was nasty."

"Keep your voice down Petr; voices carry across the water. Now let's get the fuck out of here."

As THEY WERE WALKING BACK up the hill, Charles suddenly remembered the angler, "Hey, where did we leave that angler? We can't leave it here."

"It's by the raft."

Charles continued up the hill and got to the Jeep. Climbing inside, he grabbed the box, spun the combination, and extracted $500. He looked up and saw Petr at the top of the hill illuminated by the cruiser's headlights. Charles called out to him, "Turn the car off, leave the keys and lock the door. Oh, and bring the angler and the cop's flashlight."

Once Petr got back to the Jeep, he was still visibly upset. His eyes were wild with fear. "Seriously man, the cops will come looking for that guy."

"Put the angler in the back and get in."

Petr did as instructed, "You know when they find the car, they'll be all over this place like a fat kid on a smarty. You could have just knocked him out. You're a fucking psycho."

Charles gave him a tired look and handed him the $500.

"Fuck man, five hundred ain't going to cut it, not with this shit."

"I would love to sit here and chat about how much damage that deputy's bullet would have done to you, but the sooner we get out of here, the better. As for giving you more money, I am prepared to give you so much more."

"What the hell does that mean?"

"I'm going to let you live," Charles said, pointing the Colt at Petr. Charles watched his eyes go large as he stared down the barrel of the gun. "Now, Gadzinga, I want you to think. You've shown me something tonight. You can follow orders and get a job done. I'll have more work for you. Tomorrow, I'll be by the trailer with your weed. But Petr, listen closely to what I'm saying. We are now linked by what happened here tonight. We have to look out for each other. If you start running your mouth off, or God forbid, go to the cops, I might have to tell them about the murder weapon and whose fingerprints are on it, and on the cop's keys."

Petr slammed his fist against the dash. "You're a fuckhead."

"I don't like being called names. Get out Petr, before I change my mind. Get on your bike and go fuck Lana. You did well tonight."

CHAPTER THIRTY-ONE

Saturday, February 19th, 1983
Gulfport, Mississippi

Charles made himself a full breakfast and watched the news while he drank coffee. There was no update on Jessica Grant, the disappearance of that whore Freda, or anything on the deputy from last night. He looked at his new driver's license. "Keith Jager." He pronounced the last name as if it was spelled with two G's. *I need to get a picture taken with my new hair and maybe some fake glasses. I also have to find a new apartment.* He was still going through his list of things to do when he heard a knock on the door.

He turned down the television and went to the bedroom to get his Colt from under his pillow. *I bet it's that Captain from the Coast Guard.* The knock came again, this time louder. He decided to ignore it, but then he heard a voice in the hall. "Nelson, it's Agnes. Where's the money, Nelson?"

Fuck, Nelson, what's your problem? Another whore you didn't pay? What a ladies' man! He went to the door and checked out the woman through the spy hole. She was middle-aged with brown frizzy hair. She looked familiar, so Charles went to the bedroom and looked at the photo he had seen earlier. *Nelson's ex-wife. By now she'd have noticed the Jeep. The long-lost son routine wasn't going to fly. If I let her in, I'll likely have to kill her.* He put the gun in the waistband of his jeans, behind his back, and took a deep breath. He then opened the door, feigning someone who had just woken up.

"Who are you?" she said, momentarily taken aback, "And where's Nelson?" Her arms were crossed, a threatening look on her face.

"Ship Island," he said, scratching his hair. "He said I could crash here for a few days. Who are you?"

"I'm Agnes Gallant, Nelson's wife," she said in an imperious tone like she was the Queen of Sheba. "What's your name, and how do you know Nelson?"

"Rick...and didn't I just answer that question? I'm a friend of his, and I needed a place to stay for a few days." He let out a deep sigh. "He said I could use his apartment."

"Why would you have his Jeep?"

"Listen, lady, you woke me up, and now you're asking all these questions." His hand slowly reached behind him. "No wonder Nelson dumped you. He lent it to me. Can't very well drive across the Gulf, can you?" Charles began easing the door shut.

She put her foot in the doorway, holding it open. "For your information, Rick, I left Nelson. When's he going to be back? He owes me money."

"I don't know. What I do know Agnes, is you're about to lose a foot."

"There's some cash in a coffee jar in the kitchen. I know where it is. If you let me in, I'll just take that, and get out of your hair."

"No, and you're going to be out of my hair because I'm

shutting the door," Charles said, simultaneously stomping on her foot while slamming the door in her face.

"Fuck you! I'm going to tell Nelson he has an asshole for a friend," Agnes yelled through the door.

If you don't fuck off, you'll be seeing him in hell.

It was a clear, cool day as Charles drove out to the trailer. On the seat beside him was his leather bag containing the cash, the baggies of pot, and the Colt. *I need to find another place to live before any more of Nelson's girlfriends show up.* At the trailer park, he pulled up to a shack with a rental office sign out front. A short, bald man sat behind a desk reading the newspaper when Charles walked into the dusty little room.

"Help you with something?" the man asked without looking up.

"I want to rent a trailer, something clean."

"Yes, indeedy, you came to the right place." The man got up and gave Charles a big smile. "The name's Paul Arnold, I'm the boss, that is, I run the place."

"My name's Keith Jager. Something small, one or two bedrooms."

Paul pulled out a red binder from under the counter. "Most of the trailers are for sale, I've got a beauty that you can get with my special discount, for $8,000."

"Something small, one or two bedrooms is what I said. Don't make me repeat myself. I need it for about 6 months until I can get my boat ready."

"Yes, indeedy." He flipped through the binder, and they looked at pictures of four different trailers. Most were poorly maintained and appeared to be falling apart. He decided on an old Airstream trailer called a Silver Bullet. The rent was cheap, so after a quick inspection, Charles agreed to a six-month lease. It was against type. No one would think to look for Charles Bouvier amongst the lowlifes.

The trailer had a couple of Captain's chairs, a small galley with a couch that turned into a double bed. There was more room in the trailer than he'd had on the boat. Excited, he planned to move his stuff that afternoon.

THE SILVER BULLET was at the opposite end of the trailer park from where Petr lived. When Charles drove over to Petr's, he saw that once again, the bike was not parked in front. Lana was walking into the trailer with a couple of old suitcases when Charles drove up in a cloud of dust. She turned and eyed him suspiciously before putting the bags on the ground and walking towards the Jeep. She was wearing jeans along with a dirty white T-Shirt. Charles saw an expression that was one part anger and two parts hatred.

"You come to give us what you owe us?" she asked as Charles got out of the jeep.

"Are we going braless today, Lana? That for me?"

Lana was about to say something but caught herself. She glared at him as he put the gym bag down and reaching into it, he handed her the weed he'd stolen, followed by an envelope containing the $500. "Did Petr tell you about last night?"

"He just said it was done."

"What's with the suitcases? Are we going on a vacation?"

"Listen, Mister Smith; we don't want any more trouble. We don't want to do any jobs for you. We just want to be left alone."

He chuckled under his breath, "You aren't going

anywhere, Lana." He walked towards her, stopping a few feet away.

"I'd get out of here if I were you. Petr's going to get a dozen of his buddies here to kick your ass."

He caught her by surprise with a hard slap across the face. She fell backward. Her look of defiance melted and was replaced by the familiar look of fear. Charles figured that Petr had shared what had happened with the deputy. "Sounds like you need another lesson," he said, smiling. He debated grabbing her by the hair and dragging her into the trailer, but he didn't want a spectacle in front of his new neighbors. "When you see Petr, tell him I'll be in touch. I might have another piece of business to conduct. Something very lucrative." He turned to walk back to the Jeep. "Best not be going anywhere; I'll be watching."

CHAPTER THIRTY-TWO

Tuesday, March 1st, 1983
Gulfport, Mississippi

Ten nights after the incident with the deputy, Charles walked up to Petr as he was getting off his bike at the trailer. "Hello, Petr," he called out. Petr ignored Charles and started up the steps to the trailer. Charles stood on the edge of the area lit up by the trailer's porch light. The previous evening he'd wanted to talk to Petr, but when he'd approached the trailer, he'd seen that Petr and Lana were entertaining. He watched from the small forest as a dozen members of the Sons of Silence sat around a campfire drinking beer and smoking pot. This had given Charles another idea.

Petr stopped before entering the trailer, without turning around. "What do you want?"

"I have some more work for you, Petr. Do you want to hear about it?" Charles felt the weight of the Colt in his jacket pocket.

"Does it involve killing another cop?" Petr lowered his voice to a whisper.

"Hopefully not. Remember, I did that for you." *Haven't I gone over this enough?*

"Yeah, well, what do you want?" Petr turned to look at Charles.

"A couple of things. But first I'd like to a 'Thank you' for saving your life."

Petr looked up at the night sky as if the heavens could guide him.

"Say it, Petr. Otherwise, I might need to teach you a lesson."

"Thanks," said Petr, his voice full of attitude.

Charles had a déjà vu moment back to his mother, wanting to teach him a lesson. Charles smiled and called out, "Lana, better get out here."

"What the fuck, leave her out of this. I said, thank you." Petr approached Charles.

"Not sincere enough," Charles said. Lana came to the trailer's screen door. "Come here, Lana, Petr has something he wants to say in front of you."

Lana stumbled to where her husband was standing. Charles could tell by her walk and the look on her face that she was stoned. "Okay, Petr, you were going to say something to me. And I suggest some sincerity."

Petr shrugged his shoulders and said thanks again.

"Petr, Petr, Petr, I'm trying hard to like you. You see, if you disappoint me, I'm not going to hurt you. I might still have use for you. But Lana, our little pothead is expendable. So, get down on your knees and say, 'Mr. Smith, thank you for saving my miserable life.'" Just to be sure, Charles pulled out the Colt and pointed it at the man. Petr stared at Charles in disbelief and then looked at Lana, who he knew likely wouldn't remember anything. Charles turned and pointed the Colt at Lana's chest and pulled back the hammer. "Get on your knees," he repeated, looking over at Petr. "One less pothead slut won't bother me."

"Please," Petr slowly knelt in the dirt looking up at Charles. "Please, please, if it hadn't been for you, that deputy would have shot me."

Charles waited ten seconds before pointing the gun at Lana's head. She finally clued in on what was happening and started to whimper. "Would you love her as much with a hole in her forehead?" He held the gun pointed at her for another few seconds. Then, looking over at Petr, "Very good, now get up and tell your woman to go to bed."

Petr got up, hugged his wife, and whispered something to her. When Lana had gone into the trailer, Charles stared at Petr, still holding the gun. "Here's what I want Petr. I happen to have some extra cash. I want to invest in your distribution system."

"I don't follow."

"Have you heard of crack cocaine?" When Petr nodded, Charles said, "Good, it's all the rage in California. I'd like to help you with some seed money."

"We just sell weed."

"I think if you ask around, you'll find that you can make a lot more money with crack. I want to give you $40,000 to start, with more money to follow if you perform. With the extra money, you buy more product, sell more, and you and I split the profit down the middle."

"What makes you think I need a partner?"

"I'm offering you a fair deal, Petr. If you don't want to be my friend anymore, then," he smiled and looked at Lana who was watching from the doorway of the trailer, "No hard feelings."

"Where's the money?"

Charles pulled a paper bag from his leather case and tossed it to him.

CHAPTER THIRTY-THREE

Wednesday, March 9th, 1983
Gulfport, Mississippi

Charles walked into the Coast Guard building and approached a young ensign sitting behind a reception desk. "I'd like to speak to a Captain Rosman."

"Yes sir," the man replied, and pressed a couple of buttons on his phone before speaking into the handset. "Paging Captain Rosman. Captain Rosman to the reception desk."

Charles faded back into a group of tourists before hiding in a phone booth. About three minutes later, a tall, dark-haired man, very neatly dressed, went to the reception area and spoke to the ensign. Charles watched as Captain Rosman looked around before shrugging his shoulders and saying something funny to the ensign.

Charles went to lunch and returned later that afternoon. He was about to give up when his patience was rewarded, and he saw the dark-haired man leave the building. He watched as Rosman got into a tan Subaru and headed east on Beach Road.

THE WALLS and windows were painted black. A strobe light bathed the club in multi-colored lights making the dancers look like they were moving in slow motion. The speakers blared, *It's Raining Men,* by the Weather Girls. There were a dozen people, mostly men, or men dressed as women, sitting at tables. Charles picked a table at the back with a clear view of where Captain Rosman was sitting at the bar.

The place was aptly called the Male Box and was located in the basement of a laundromat. Unlike many in the South, Charles wasn't disgusted by homosexuality. He was, in a way, intrigued by it. In his mind, it wasn't an affront to the word of God. Charles thought that God and all the hicks in Mississippi should mind their own business. It was high time that Mississippi got in sync with the rest of the country. In California, they'd recently ruled that two people of the same sex could marry. But here in Mississippi cops were still kicking down doors of motels looking for homos. Charles figured the blackout windows and the secrecy was to avoid being raided. The jukebox switched to *The Dancing Queen* by Abba. Rosman was sitting at the bar by himself. He was wearing Jordache jeans at least one size too small, and a burgundy net shirt. *He's waiting for someone.* He watched as Rosman repeatedly cycled from looking at his watch, sipping his drink and then glancing at the door.

A heavily inked waitress with short black hair came by and yelled at Charles over the music. "Want something, honey?"

"Sure, how about a Harvey Wallbanger?"

The woman, who sported a nose ring gave him a smile. "One bang against a wall for my little honey."

"Maybe you can offer one to that poor man sitting alone at the bar."

Charles watched as she went to the bar and spoke to Rosman. He gradually turned around and smiled at Charles and held up his drink in salute. Charles gave him a smile and pointed to the empty chair at the table.

Once the waitress brought Charles his drink, Rosman walked over, "Thanks."

"You were looking lonely."

"Have we met before?"

"I'm sure I would remember you." Charles looked up at the man.

Rosman sat down, "I thought I was supposed to meet someone. Maybe I got my dates mixed up."

"It's fate that we meet," Charlie held up his drink to toast. "My name's Keith, and this is Harvey."

Rosman clinked his glass. "I'm Max Rosman," he said, holding up his drink.

"So, who are you, Max, and what are you looking for?"

The question seemed to take Rosman off guard, and he sat back in his chair. After a moment he moved forward with his elbows on the table, "I work for the Coast Guard, where things are supposed to happen by the book. Nothing is supposed to happen by chance. Everything must be in order." He looked over at Charles. "I guessed I'm looking for a little escape."

"'There must be some way out of here, said the joker to the thief. There's too much confusion; I can't get no relief.' Are you a Bob Dylan fan?"

"Yes, cool song, but I prefer the Hendrix version. So, who's the joker, and who's the thief?"

"You're the thief wanting to steal away your sanity from

all the order and discipline. That makes me the joker whose job it is to entertain you," Charles smiled and rested his hand on Rosman's.

After a moment, Rosman pulled his hand away to light a cigarette. He offered the pack to Charles, who waved him off. "Do you know how the drink came to be called a Harvey Wallbanger?"

"I think the waitress has a few ideas."

"It was named after a surfer, who lost a big championship and stopped to drown his sorrows at a local bar. He ordered a screwdriver with a shot of Galliano, and got so totally plastered that he started banging his head against the wall."

"Is that true?" Charles laughed.

"I doubt it. Just something I heard from the men."

Charles nodded and sipped his drink. "What's it like working in the Donald Duck Navy?"

Rosman chuckled, "Most people call us Coasties. I only know one other person who called us that. It was an old guy who liked to camp out on Ship island with his dog. We'd stop by on our patrols and joke with the guy. He'd say here comes the Donald Duck navy and he'd do this little dance."

The best part of waking up. "Sounds like quite the character."

"Kind of lost track of him. I spoke to him briefly on the phone a while back. His dog died, and well, we don't see him anymore. I should look him up; make sure he's okay."

Yeah, you do that, Charles thought, finishing his drink. "Is your family from Gulfport?"

"No, I moved down here in 1978 from New York City. My old man didn't approve of my lifestyle, so I'm not anxious to move back."

"What about friends, anyone special?"

"Not really, least no one you can count on." Rosman smiled, turning around and taking another look at the door. "I've never seen you here before?" He took a long drag from his cigarette and blew the smoke towards the ceiling.

"I'm new to Gulfport. First time here."

"That so? Where did you live before this?" A smile washed across Rosman's face.

So many questions, I remember this from the phone call. "I grew up in New Orleans."

"I love that town." Rosman's expression turned melancholy as if he remembered an earlier time. "Lots of fun. Got to love a parade, huh?"

Charles laughed, "I've always loved Mardi Gras." Rosman had piercing blue eyes. *If I was into men, he'd be my type.*

As if Rosman could read Charles' mind, he commented, "I like your hair."

Charles shrugged and gave him a confused look.

"You dyed it, you can tell it's almost white, but your eyebrows give you away." An uncomfortable silence ensued with Charles wondering if he was taking too much of a risk. Finally, Rosman offered, "Enough about me. What work do you do, Keith?" Rosman took a sip of his drink, "You haven't told me anything about you."

Charles had come up with a convincing cover story, but for some reason, the question stumped him for a few seconds. "My family used to own a store in New Orleans. It was attached to a marina, and we sold small boats, nothing bigger than a Chris-Craft. And of course, marine supplies, that type of thing."

"Sounds like we have the sea in common, Keith. What was the name of the business? I might know it."

"Jager's. That's my family name."

"Never heard of it. Does your family still own it?"

"It was sold recently, so I decided to pull up stakes and try Gulfport." Before Rosman could ask another question, Charles moved his chair so that he was sitting closer. He held up his empty glass and waived the waitress over. When he got her attention, he gestured to their empty glasses.

"Thanks, that very generous of you, Mr. Keith Jager." Rosman lit another cigarette once their waitress returned with the drinks.

"You can thank me later, Max." Charles put his hand under the table on Rosman's thigh.

"All right," Max pulled Charles' hand to his crotch.

Charles eyebrows rose, not bothering to hide his surprise. "Did you want to hang out here, or if you live nearby ...?" Charles gave him a suggestive look.

Max Rosman smiled, butting his cigarette and taking a gulp of his drink, "I just live a few blocks from here, but I'm not sure I have the makings for a Harvey Wallbanger."

"I might have to settle for something else." Charles got up to leave.

It was all Charles could do to keep up with the Subaru as Rosman drove further into Gulfport. *Anxious little fucker. The conversation about Nelson gave me a start and confirmed that this guy is a loose end. I know I'm taking a risk by toying with him. It'd be safer if I just put a bullet in his head. So, why am I doing this?* He watched as the Subaru pulled into a dark laneway half way down 24th avenue. He parked on the street and got out of the Jeep, concluding that getting to know Rosman was part of a game. A way of heightening his pleasure. So far, he'd killed three people he didn't really know. Captain Max Rosman would be a different experience.

The house was a bungalow, set back from the road. As Charles followed Rosman into the house, he could see that the décor was done in an early seventies style with bright colors and cheap modular furniture. "Nice place you have here, Max," Charles lied.

"I like it. Make yourself comfortable in the living room. I'll fix us a drink. Say, how about a glass of wine? I have a bottle of Zinfandel that is just dying to be opened."

"Sounds great; I'd like that." Charles ventured into the living room, which was done in a pastel blue. A rainbow had been painted on the wall above the couch. There was a stereo with a turntable off to the side with a selection of albums sitting on top of huge speakers. Already on the turntable was Wham's *Make it Big* album. he turned the turntable on and soon heard George Michael singing *Wake me up before you go-go*.

"Great choice!" Rosman yelled from the kitchen.

Rosman had an IBM Selectric typewriter on a small desk off the living room. "Are you writing the next great American novel?"

"I wish. I try my hand at poetry sometimes. Nothing special."

"I'd like to read them sometime. Would that be okay with you?"

"Maybe I'll even write one about you."

"That would be great. I noticed there aren't many photographs."

"I have a few in the bedroom. Coast Guard pictures mostly. Beach scenes, the ships I've served on, some of the men I've worked with."

"You like being a Coastie, I can hear it in your voice."

"Best thing I've ever done. My old man wanted me to go into construction. You know that YMCA video with the

Indian chief, the policeman, the construction worker? Well, that construction worker could have been me." Rosman laughed from the kitchen.

"I always liked the cowboy." Charles moved into the kitchen.

"Gee, this cork is a problem," Max grunted. He was struggling with a split cork using an old wooden corkscrew.

"Here, let me give you a hand."

Max was only too happy to let Charles take over, and started to dance seductively while singing along with the music, "*Wake me up before you go go, don't leave me hanging on like a yo-yo.*"

Charles chuckled and managed to get the cork out of the bottle without corking the wine. "I'll get the glasses." Max sashayed to the cupboard. Charles held the wine bottle and poured the wine as Rosman held the glasses. He put the bottle down, leaving Max holding both glasses. Taking one, he made eye contact with Rosman. Max leaned in and kissed Charles on the lips. When the kiss ended, Charles said, "I'd like to see those photographs in your bedroom."

As soon as Max turned to go to the bedroom, Charles put the glass down. He came up behind Rosman and rammed the corkscrew into his neck. Max made a gasping noise, his hand reaching for his throat. Charles, with the benefit of surprise, pulled the corkscrew out and stabbed him again, this time striking Rosman in the eye. A scream tore through the house like shards of breaking glass. Max stumbled, blood pouring down his face as he looked at Charles in horror out of his undamaged eye. Charles went for another swing, but this time Rosman blocked the blow with his forearm. Bent over in pain, Rosman staggered away, wailing in pain. He lurched into the dining room and collided with a table, then pinballed into the buffet before falling to the floor. Charles spied a knife block beside the stove and selected a cleaver. Max was crawling towards the front door when Charles jumped him and plunged the cleaver again and again into his back to the sound of "*But something's bugging me, something ain't right, my best friend told me where you were last night.*"

CHAPTER THIRTY-FOUR

Thursday, April 7th, 1983
Gulfport, Mississippi

There had been no mention of Captain Max Rosman in the news in the weeks that followed. Charles attributed that to two things. First, he'd used Rosman's typewriter to draft a resignation letter to the Coast Guard and slipped it under their front door. Rosman apparently had a family emergency that would require him to relocate up north. Sad, because he loved his job and would miss the hard-working men and women he served with. The second reason was that in the dead of night, he'd dumped Rosman's body into the bayou just east of New Orleans.

THAT EVENING, Charles sat in Boogie's parking lot, waiting for Petr.

Petr came out and urinated on the building, as usual. He was surprised to see Charles step out of the shadows as he began to get on his bike. "Mr. Smith," Petr nodded, getting something from his saddlebags. "I have something for you." He handed Charles an envelope of cash. "There's five grand in here. Your cut."

Charles took the envelope and leafed through the bills before handing it back. "Keep it. I want you to do something else for me."

"What's that?"

"I need some new wheels. It doesn't need to be anything new, just clean. Make it a Suburban. I imagine someone like you might know where to find something like that?"

"I know a guy named Yuri. He runs a place in Gulfport and does good work. Do you need papers?"

"Yeah, my driver's license is under my old name." Charles handed him a piece of paper. "Just use your own address for the ownership. I need everything under this name."

"Keith Jager? I knew Smith wasn't your real name, but Keith Jager?"

"If you can manage it, I want you to deliver the car to me in New Orleans."

CHAPTER THIRTY-FIVE

Friday, April 8th, 1983
Gulfport, Mississippi

The next day Charles was hard at work in his trailer. His map of Gulfport was spread out on the kitchen table, with a blue highlighter indicating the location of the Catholic high schools in and around Gulfport. The one thing he remembered about Jessica was that she had worn a school uniform when she was abducted. He couldn't remember the color of the plaid but thought he might if he was to see it again. There were a handful of Catholic high schools in the Gulfport-Biloxi area, and he prioritized them in proximity to Gulfport. Next, he went through the white pages and used a yellow highlighter to mark the addresses of all the Grants. His plan was to drive to the school and ask if anyone knew Jessica. Before he left, he stopped off at a costume store for more supplies.

CHARLES PARKED the Jeep a couple of blocks from St. John's High School on 17th Street. It was almost 3:30 PM. Hopefully, he would come across students leaving for the day. As he walked, people nodded and wished him a good day.

"Good afternoon, Father," said a pair of spinsters in unison as they power-walked the block.

"Go with Christ, ladies." Charles was carrying a black leather bible and wearing a priest's habit and cross.

A couple of minutes later, he passed a man who was trimming a hedge. "Nice day for a walk, Father."

"Peace be with you, my son."

Charles continued until he got to a long one-story high school. There were some boys on an adjacent field throwing a football. He watched them for a few minutes, remembering his days at De La Salle High School. He'd attended Sally, as it was commonly called, until grade eleven.

Mrs. Kenwick, his homeroom teacher, had told his mother at a 'meet the creature' night that, "Charles has an entitled attitude, very little social skills, and is too lazy to apply himself."

Charles watched as one of the kids ran a pattern, only to drop a ball that had landed in his hands. *Things might have turned out differently had I not tried out for the football team.* Memories flashed back to his high school days. Prior to football season, he had declared to anyone who would listen that he would be the new quarterback and that he was going to lead the team to victory. But after only a few days, Coach Kenwick, the homeroom teacher's husband, had told him he had absolutely no athletic ability. Kenwick suggested that he consider being in charge of the players' equipment. Hurt by the coach's decision, Charles took his disappointment in stride.

Two days before the start of the season, Kenwick fired

him. There'd been complaints about withholding equipment from players Charles didn't like. The dismissal led to a loud, messy confrontation in front of the players, culminating with Charles claiming that the coach was incompetent and the reason the players were underperforming.

Later that fall, things had really started to unravel. A big kid from the football team named Chris Fontenot had started to pick on him. First, there were the insults. "Spoiled little rich kid," or "There goes our quarterback." When Charles ignored the insults, Fontenot started to push him around, daring him to fight. Fontenot wasn't that much bigger, mainly just fatter. He got away with bullying because no one had the guts to stand up to him. He'd stand over Charles, a smirk on his face daring Charles to get up and take a swing at him. Meanwhile, his posse would encircle them and cheer. "Are you going to cry now, little rich boy?"

Fontenot had once said to him, "Listen punk, I don't hate you. I don't feel anything toward you. You aren't worth it. To me, you're just a tool to vent my frustrations and have some fun with. I have you to make me look good. I'm going to beat you every day for the rest of your miserable life. You think I'm superior, don't you Bouvier? Look at you; you're scrawny. You have no friends. When I bully you, I get a surge of power; I can't get any other way. You're like a drug."

Charles had hated himself for being scared. He'd faked the stomach flu for a couple of days while he obsessed about what to do. When he'd returned to school, he'd approached a kid who appeared to be sympathetic and offered to pay him to beat Fontenot up. Rather than just saying no, the kid took Charles' money before telling everyone that he'd hired him to kill Fontenot. Soon graffiti started appearing in the boy's washrooms saying that Charles was a "Killer Faggot."

Mrs. Kenwick found out about what had happened and

came down hard on Charles, suspending him for three days. That was three days of listening to Mother ranting about how he'd never amount to anything.

When the portable schoolhouse had burned down, the fire marshall ruled it was arson. There was a strong indication that an accelerant had been used. The cops showed up at Charles' house, asking questions.

His mother lied and said that Charles had been home with her all evening. After they left, she told him that she knew what he'd done and that she'd smelled the gasoline on him when he'd come home the previous night. "You may think you got away with it, but you didn't. Everyone knows. If you thought you were picked on before, just wait. And don't think I lied to protect you. I lied to the police because of the shame on my good name if people were to hear about my little firebug. I've had enough. I'll speak to your Aunt Edna. You can go live with her in Slidell."

Charles was lifted out of his reverie by a young girl walking in his direction.

"Hello, Father."

"Peace be with you. Do you have a moment to answer a question for me?" The girl looked old enough to be in her senior year. She had dark hair and might have been Mexican.

"Sure, Father."

Charles didn't recognize her maroon plaid skirt. "I heard about a very unfortunate event that happened to a young girl around your age by the name of Jessica Grant. You know her?"

"No, I'm sorry, Father. Maybe they can help you in the office."

Charles smiled at the girl and thanked her for the suggestion. He wanted to avoid going into the school where he might come across nuns and priests likely to see through his disguise. He kept walking towards the school. There was now a steady stream of kids coming towards him. He asked a few other girls if they knew Jessica. None of them did, although one recognized the name because her mother worked for the Coast Guard. He was tempted to ask whether she knew Captain Max Rosman but thought better of it. As he was talking to her, he noticed a nun heading his way. He nodded to her and started to cross the street away from the school.

"Father," the nun called out.

Fuck. He stopped and smiled at the woman. "Good afternoon, Sister."

"Are you Father Jim?"

He thought a moment before replying, "Sure, yes, I'm Father Jim. Why?"

"We were expecting you next week. The diocese told us to expect you. I understand you have a degree in mathematics. Where did you study?"

"All over." Then he added, "At the seminary."

"I've never heard of you, Father Jim. Are you originally from Biloxi?"

"New Orleans. I was at St. David's for the last couple of years."

"Really, that's in a black part of town. How did that work out?"

"Fine, fine. Really fine. God sees no color." He tried to change the subject. "I'm excited about the opportunity to make a difference here. How do you find the kids, Sister...?"

"Emma, Sister Emma May. I teach Grade Nine English. They're mostly well-behaved. Sadly, some won't become scholars."

"Isn't that always the way. We must do what we can. They are all God's critters," he said, then he immediately thought it sounded odd.

Emma seemed to consider what he'd said and then looked at his spiky white hair and smiled. "Would you like to come to the office? I can introduce you around."

"That's okay. Tomorrow's soon enough. I just wanted to locate the school and introduce myself to some of the kids."

"But, there's no school on Saturday."

"Of course, I was thinking Monday, but my mouth said Saturday. It was a pleasure meeting you, Sister Emma." He turned to walk away, adding, "Before I came here, I saw an article about that poor girl who was on a boat with a madman...I think her name was Jessica something. Did she go to school here?"

"It's a blessed miracle that she's alive. I think someone said she attends Mercy Cross."

"Mercy Cross, well thanks, Sis, see you Monday."

Charles hustled back the way he'd come. At one point, he looked back and noticed Sister Emma May continuing to stare in his direction. *What will she do when the real Father Jim shows up?*

CHAPTER THIRTY-SIX

Sunday, April 10th, 1983
Gulfport, Mississippi

Charles was frustrated. He'd spent the previous day watching four different houses in Gulfport - the four from the phone listings that were closest to Mercy Cross. *Four wasted days.* He'd watched as people came and went without any sign of Jessica Grant. One family was colored. *Gone were the days when blacks used to stay in their own neighborhood. What is this world coming to? This is Mississippi. People are supposed to stick with their own.*

Could he have been wrong about Jessica living in Gulfport? He had just assumed that a teenage girl walking the streets at night lived in the neighborhood. But what if she was just visiting a friend? Should he be looking for Grants that live in Biloxi? Maybe I need a new plan.

MONDAY MORNING, 'FATHER JIM' got up early and had a

full breakfast before dressing up in his costume. As he'd done on Friday, Charles parked the Jeep a couple of blocks from the school. It was early, and his plan was to speak to some kids on the way to class. About a block from the school, he merged with a bunch of teenagers heading to school. He spotted a group of girls that looked close to Jennifer's age. They were wearing maroon plaid skirts with white blouses, and Crusaders emblazoned over the pocket.

When he got closer, one of the girls smiled at him and said, "Good Morning, Father."

"Good morning, young ladies. I was wondering if you could help me." Without waiting for a reply, Charles flashed the girls a smile and showed them the photo he'd cut out of the *Herald*. "I'm looking for a student by the name of Jessica Grant. Do you know her?"

The girl who had initially said good morning nodded and was about to say something when one of the other girls put her hand on her arm. "Like, why are you looking for her, Father?" She sounded suspicious.

None of your fucking business. "I've been sent by the Archbishop to offer her some counseling. She's been through a terrible ordeal."

The answer seemed to placate the girl. She shared a quick look with the others before replying, "She hasn't been back to school since like forever. Before all that shit went down. If it was me, I'd be totally bugging out."

"Yeah, like I'd be freaking," shuddered one of the other girls.

"Would you girls know where she lives? I'd really like to pay my respects."

"Um...No. But like, you can check with the school," said the gum chewer, her eyes growing wide. "Seriously, they'd have her address."

"Thanks, girls, I might just do that."

As they were walking away, the girl who originally greeted him turned back and said, "And you can check with Sheri-Lyn Fenn, she's like her bestest friend."

Charles approached a few more teens and showed Jessica's picture. Most had heard of her, but none of them knew her or what class she was in. He briefly considered going to the office, but after the Sister Emma May episode, he didn't want to press his luck.

Later that evening he looked up Fenn in the phone book and found one close to Mercy Cross. He called the number, which was answered by a young boy. "May I please speak to Sheri-Lyn Fenn?"

"What-cha want with her? Are you her 'boyfriend'?"

"No, my name is Father Jim, from the diocese."

"Hold on." Charles heard a clunk as the phone was put down, and the boy's voice yelling. "Sheri, you've really done it now. God's on the phone."

"Ian, who's on the phone?" An older woman's voice, sounding upset.

"It's God. I'm not making it up. He probably heard about her smoking weed with her stupid friends."

"Hello, who is this?" asked a woman. "I'm Mrs. Fenn, Sheri-Lyn's mother."

"I'm sorry to disturb you, Mrs. Fenn. It's Father Jim from the diocese. The Archbishop has asked me to speak to some of the kids about what happened to Jessica Grant and offer some counseling."

"That's very Christian of you, Father. Sheri's outside; I'll get her for you."

"Bless you, Mrs. Fenn."

While he waited, the boy got back on the line. "She smokes that wacky tobacco with her friends. You know, like in *Reefer Madness* in homeroom. But I suppose you already knew that 'cause God knows everything." Charles put the kid's age at seven or eight.

"Yes, God sees everything."

"Everything?"

"Everything."

"Yeah, then what am I doing with my finger right now?"

"Something you shouldn't be doing. God knows, and he will burn your fat ass in hell. You had better pray a little extra tonight and ask for forgiveness."

The phone clunked again, and he heard the boy scream. A younger female voice came on the line. "This is Sheri-Lyn."

"Hi, I'm Father Jim. I'm calling some of Jessica Grant's friends to offer my services, in case you're having problems sleeping, or if you are upset about what happened to her."

"Thank you, Father Jim. I'm okay."

Charles was worried that the girl was just going to hang up, so he blurted out, "Have you seen Jessica since she was rescued?"

"Just once, some people got together, and she came and talked about what happened."

"The newspaper makes the man sound evil."

"I couldn't repeat the words she used to describe him. The tamest thing she called him was a wimp. That he backed right down when she confronted him."

"Thank goodness that she has good friends like you to comfort her. And of course, she has the support of her family."

"She's not getting along with her father right now. He's kind of blaming her for what happened."

"That's too bad. Say, is their number in the book? I'd like to speak to him. Maybe help him see it differently."

"They have an unlisted number. He hates getting calls from people trying to sell him things."

"Oh, I see. Would you have their number? I'll give them a call right away."

Charles felt the girl hesitate before answering, "I don't remember the number off the top of my head. Can you give me your number, Father, and I'll call you back with it?"

"That's alright, Sheri; I'm not at a number where you can call me back. Maybe I can check back with you." Charles quickly said good night before the girl could ask why the Diocese wouldn't have a phone.

Finding Jessica was proving to be more difficult than expected. Another idea started to form.

CHAPTER THIRTY-SEVEN

Wednesday, April 13th, 1983
New Orleans, Louisiana

Charles waited in a phone booth at the Irish Bayou Travel center. It had been a long walk back from where he'd ditched and torched the Nelson's Jeep. He'd driven as far into the bayou as he could before getting stuck. Hopefully, it was far enough in, and no one would notice the flames.

Black clouds darkened the sky; the scent of rain was in the air. The truck stop was a ramshackle building that had seen better days. Despite this, it was busy with cars coming off Highway 11 to refuel before entering New Orleans. He remembered the place from his youth. Hanging out at the truck stop and in the bayou had been a great refuge from Aunt Edna.

As the first drops of rain dotted the phone booth, he pictured his aunt. His soul would forever be haunted by the sound of her dentures clacking as if she had a mouthful of castanets. Although small in stature, Aunt Edna had made up for it with her temper. He hadn't seen her in over three years, but that year and a half he lived with her had caused scars he wouldn't soon forget.

On the day he'd moved in, she'd shown him to a small room the size of a large closet. "*Don't you be thinking I give a fart about you, or that you're welcome here. Your mother has grown sick of the sight of you, and she's paying me so she doesn't have to look at you. This is my house, not yours. You're renting a room. Listen up, as I'm going to explain the rules. I cook when I'm hungry, and if you have a mind to, you can eat in the kitchen when I eat. If you don't like what I'm cooking, there's no need to tell me because I don't care. You're to do your own laundry once a week on Saturday mornings, from 8 to 9 AM. If that time doesn't work for you, then you'll have to wear dirty clothes. You're to keep your room clean. Anything I find on the floor goes in the garbage. You are not to have company, not that you could ever have any friends. Each week you'll be assigned a list of chores. This is a big house, and it needs upkeep.*"

Charles had read her name in the *Herald* recently. He'd been reading a series of articles about what the paper was calling the *Estate of a Serial Killer*. Now that the inquest had ruled that Charles was dead, people were circling like vultures to make claims. The first article had been a recap of his alleged exploits, and the inheritance that came to him when his mother had died. The reporter had insinuated that Charles had something to do with the fire. The next article dealt with the inquest and heart-jarring testimony from Jessica about how the killer had fallen into the Gulf. Likely eaten by a great white, she had speculated. The third article dealt with the families of the missing girls. They'd hired a lawyer to make a claim against the estate, maintaining that any money recovered should rightfully go to them for all of their pain and suffering. *Give me a break. I have not been arrested, nor convicted of anything, and they think they can just take what is mine?*

His attention was drawn to a black Suburban that pulled into the lot. He saw that Lana was driving, with Petr following on his Harley. Charles stepped out of the booth and nodded. Lana parked the truck in front of the general store. As she got out, she tossed him the keys. She was wearing the usual ratty old jeans and a dirty white T-Shirt. "You're looking pretty hot today, Lana," he called out to her as she walked into the truck stop. Without turning around, she gave him the finger.

"It's a 1980, good shape, low mileage. Yuri painted it black for you," Petr said as he approached from behind. "Here are the papers."

Charles gave the Suburban a once over. It looked new, with black leather seats. He nodded to Petr. "Good job, has the VIN been changed?"

Petr nodded, just as a flash of lightning lit up the sky. "There's a little bit of money left over. Yuri gave me a good deal." The wind was blowing trash across the parking lot. The smell of rain was in the air.

"Keep it; I have more work for you." Charles gave Petr an envelope. "If you do good work, then you get another couple of grand...and all you have to do is just keep doing what you're doing."

"Yeah?" Petr fingered the envelope.

"There's a teenage girl by the name of Sheri-Lyn Fenn. Her address is in there. She's already a user. I want you to make friends with her and her crowd. Supply them with as much pot and crack as they want. I'll pay for it out of my share. I don't care if she becomes a pothead or if she ODs, but I do care about one of her friends. There is a picture of the friend in the envelope. Her name is Jessica. You find her for me, and I'll give you the reward. Of course, I want you to leave my name out of it."

Petr held the envelope and gave Charles a questioning look. "And when I find this girl?"

"Leave that to me."

It wasn't long after Petr and Lana took off on the Harley before the clouds opened up. The rain fell first in crazy, chaotic drops making sploshy sounds on the truck's windshield. A few moments later, the wind kicked up, and torrents of diagonal sheets laid assault on the truck. Charles started up the Suburban and pulled away from the truck stop, heading back to Gulfport. He mused about his plan to find Jessica. *Don't worry sweet Jessica; we'll be together soon.*

CHAPTER THIRTY-EIGHT

Wednesday, July 18th, 1984
New Orleans, Louisiana
16 Months later

The sleeping pills wore off early the next morning, and Ben snuck out of the apartment to go for a long walk to clear his head. Two hours later, he sat in a lonely coffee shop trying to think of what he might have missed. *There had to be something. Someone lured Gabriel out to that bar. Why Slidell? Why go to all that trouble? Why use a Croatian name? Was this the work of Charles Bouvier? An associate of Reznikov? I have a lot of questions. For Gabriel's sake, I'd better start getting some answers.*

The early edition of the *Times-Picayune* was delivered as he sat there, and Ben almost spit out his coffee when he read the front-page headline.

Back at the apartment, Chevon was just getting up. "Where were you?" she asked, stretching in bed.

"Just needed to think, so I went for a walk."

"Rachel called late last night after you went to bed to say you should read the paper this morning."

"I got a copy on my walk. The front page is about Hollis Huntley jumping off a building. He was the informant on that bank fraud." Ben sat down on the bed and started taking off his sweatshirt. "I know Huntley, and he wouldn't set foot in a casino, let alone gamble. Someone threw him off that building to stop him from testifying."

"Does this have anything to do with Gabriel's disappearance?" Chevon was worried she already knew the answer.

"I don't know, but I'm calling the DA this morning."

CHAPTER THIRTY-NINE

Wednesday, July 18th, 1984
Gulfport, Mississippi

"Did you get your history homework done last night?" asked Travis Franklin's mother as she prepared his lunch. "I would have helped you with it."

"Just because you're old, doesn't mean you know anything about history." Travis, at age 15, was bored with school. He'd been thinking more and more about what he wanted to do with his life. He was anxious to start his career. American History was definitely not in the plan. On the one hand, he felt drawn to politics and thought about throwing his hat in the ring to be President. *If some third-rate Hollywood actor can do it, then the world is just waiting for me.* The other option was to become a mega-millionaire. He would have to come up with a loony idea like the guy that came up with the pet rock a few years ago. He would patent it and then sit back and watch the money flow.

"There was something in yesterday's *Herald* that

mentioned your friend. The man that runs that detective agency."

"Gabriel?"

His mother nodded. "It was about a guy that he almost caught a couple of years ago. The one that was kidnapping young girls," she said, slicing the crusts off of his PB & J sandwiches just like he'd ordered.

"That dude's deader than a doornail." Travis took a spoonful of his Lucky Charms.

"I wouldn't be so sure about that." She turned around to face him. "Apple or orange?"

"Always orange. Of course, I'm sure. I'm pretty much the big kahuna there."

"Oh, well, then."

"What did the article say?"

"If you're such a kahuna, you probably already know." She put the sandwich and orange into a brown bag.

"It's Mr. Big Kahuna, and humor me, what did it say?"

"Just something about this Mardi Gras Killer having come back to life and throwing rocks in people's windows."

"That doesn't make sense. Where's the paper?"

"I used it already to line Whiskey's litter box."

Whiskey was their orange tabby cat, the spitting image of Bourbon. "Oh, Mom, why'd you do that?" Travis ran down the hall to the laundry room that doubled as the home of Whiskey's litter box.

Travis' mother called after him, "You never read it. Aren't you the one that always says the paper is old news?"

Travis got to the room just in time to see the cat raking the litter box to cover up his business. "Yech! Sorry Whiskey, I need the paper." He picked up the cat and put him in the hall. "Whiskey's already taken a leak on the front page!" Travis whined.

"Lucky for you the article's on page 5. Listen, I don't want to interrupt your important work, but I have to catch a bus. Feel free to clean the litter box while you're playing with it, and don't forget your lunch."

Travis ignored his mother, then heard the front door open and close. The cat had made a mess of the paper. He used two fingers to turn the paper to page 5. The story was under a section detailing police reports from the previous day. It would have been very easy to miss the two paragraphs. The reporter quoted a deputy sheriff who'd responded to an incident in Gulfport the previous day. The homeowner was alleging that Charles Bouvier, better known as the Mardi Gras Killer, had thrown a rock through his window. He also claimed that Charles Bouvier had been sending him postcards. Lastly, it said the killer was now terrorizing a monk. The article went on in the next paragraph to give a brief history of Gabriel Ross' pursuit of the serial killer.

"This is crazy. It doesn't make sense." Travis told Whiskey, who meowed his annoyance at having his business interrupted. As Travis went back to the kitchen, he looked at the wall phone and thought it would only take a minute to call Rachel and mention the article. *It's only 8:20; no one will be there. Maybe I'll just leave her a message.* Travis had known Gabriel from the beginning, when he was just setting up the Eye on You Detective Agency with Ben, and considered himself a key ingredient in their success. It was because of him wearing a wire that they'd been able to crack their first case. He was surprised when Rachel answered his call on the first ring.

"Gabriel?"

"No, Travis."

"Oh. I'm sorry, Travis, I'm a little preoccupied."

"I was calling about a story in the *Herald* today about the Mardi Gras Killer."

Rachel quickly blurted out that Gabriel had been missing since Monday night. They suspected that the Mardi Gras Killer might have abducted him.

"I'll be right there. Don't worry; I'm on it."

CHAPTER FORTY

Wednesday, July 18th, 1984
New Orleans

Ben picked up the phone and dialed the number of Laura Ryan, the District Attorney for Harrison County. Laura was a bright young woman who Ben had dealt with regarding Frank Reznikov's arrest. She struck Ben as capable, ambitious, and professional. While much of the heavy lifting in the Reznikov case had been done by the Mississippi Bureau of Investigation, Frankie had also been indicted for a whole host of offenses in Louisiana. Laura had been able to cut through the interstate bureaucracy to advance the case against Reznikov, Mayor Baxter and Kane Nantois.

"Hi, Laura, it's Ben O'Shea, do you have a couple of minutes?"

"I was wondering when I would hear from you, Ben." Despite Kane Nantois turning state's evidence, Laura felt that Ben's testimony was crucial. She feared that Reznikov's lawyers would be able to discredit Kane's testimony by pointing to the plea deal as well as his long history of criminal offenses. In their last meeting, she'd had strongly suggested that both Ben and Gabriel consider a long vacation, as Reznikov had a reputation of getting to witnesses.

"Have you heard about Hollis Huntley, Laura?" Ben realized she'd been expecting his call.

"Yeah, we just had an emergency meeting about it. Not sure you should believe the business about suicide."

"How damaging is this to the case?"

"In light of what happened with Nantois, pretty devastating."

"What about Nantois?"

"I thought that was what you were calling about."

"No, I was calling about something else."

"He's dead. Someone got to him at Angola. The guards rushed him to the hospital, but he died in the ambulance."

"Dead?" Ben was stunned.

"Stabbed twenty times in the shower."

"I thought he was in solitary."

"He was, this shouldn't have happened. The warden is freaking out and will conduct a full investigation."

"They don't know who did it?"

"Not yet, but let's get real, Ben. We both know that Reznikov ordered the hit. The brotherhood is pretty big in Angola. We'll likely never be able to prove anything, but I wouldn't be surprised if someone paid off a guard to look the other way, just like someone got paid to throw Huntley off that roof."

"What do we do now?"

"I think we still have a good case with your testimony. But in light of this, maybe you and Gabriel should reconsider a nice vacation somewhere."

"It might be too late." Ben told her about Gabriel's disappearance.

"This was Monday night? Nantois was killed the same day."

"I have a bad feeling about this."

"Shit fire and save the matches! He's eliminating witnesses. There goes our case!"

Ben could hear the panic in her voice. "Don't give up hope, Laura. We haven't found a body."

"You probably won't. These assholes are pros. Are the locals on this?"

"Absolutely, the NOPD is pulling out all the stops."

"That's good. Is that what you were calling me about?"

"I was calling to see what my chances would be to get in to talk to Reznikov?"

Laura chuckled sarcastically. "I'd say less than zero. Unless, of course, you have something to trade. His lawyers would never consent to it. Especially given what happened with Huntley and Nantois."

"Damn. I guess I'm not surprised." Ben muttered in frustration.

"Don't be too disappointed about Reznikov. He wouldn't have told you anything, anyway." She added, "Let me know what I can do about Gabriel."

CHAPTER FORTY-ONE

Wednesday, July 18th, 1984
New Orleans, Louisiana

The sound of the wall clock ticking broke the silence. Ben sat across from Jacqueline at the agency. She had a blank expression and a sad stare of hopelessness. "What do they say about missing persons? If you can't solve it in the first 48 hours, the likelihood of ever finding the person drops in half?"

"I think they say that about solving a murder." Ben's answer hung in the air like a cloud. "How's everything at home?" He tried to change the subject.

"Benjamin loves his grandparents. And the owner of the gallery is giving me whatever time I need. How about you, Ben, how did the meeting with Chevon's family go?"

Ben rolled his eyes and smiled. "I'll have a few scars; they went at me pretty heavily. I've got a lot of miles on me, and well, I'm white. Her mother asked me if I wanted some crackers, and her father suggested that in a few years, we could look for retirement homes together. In the end, I think they begrudgingly agreed not to object. As we were leaving," he laughed, "I tried to give her mother a hug. I thought she was going to have a stroke. I'll have to earn my way into that family. The next hurdle is the wedding. I'm going to stay out of that discussion. If it was up to me, we would just go down to the courthouse. Maybe have you and..." he stumbled for a moment before he said, "Gabriel, over for some Chinese food."

Jacqueline caught his hesitation and grasped his hand. "Does Chevon want a big wedding?"

"Not particularly, but I think she wants to make peace with her parents, who want a big wedding and all the hoopla."

Rutledge and Chevon came in with coffee and donuts. "After yesterday, I thought we needed something to help start the day off right." Rutledge put the box of donuts on Ben's desk.

"I didn't agree, but was overruled." Chevon took one of the coffees. "Do you still want me to get Rachel and Arnie on the line for a call?"

"Yes, let's get them on the speakerphone, and we can bring everyone up to date."

A few minutes later Chevon had Rachel, Arnie, Travis, and Star on the speakerphone.

"Good morning, Travis, we can use your help on this," said Ben.

"Rachel was bringing me up to date on what happened and what's being done. Jacqueline, don't worry, I'm on it."

"Thank you, Travis," she replied, appreciating the young man despite his precociousness.

Ben gave a quick recap of what had happened to Hollis Huntley and Kane Nantois, repeating Baylis' caution about going down the rabbit hole. Rutledge, Rachel, and Arnie took turns bringing the others up to date on what they'd discovered the previous day.

"Time is slipping by. I won't lie, I'm worried. Chevon is here to man the phones and can keep everyone up to date. So, folks talk to me, what do we need to do?" Ben asked.

Rutledge was the first to speak. "I want to take another run out to Slidell and talk to that bartender. The blonde convinced me that she didn't spike Gabriel's drink. So, who does that leave? Either something happened in the washroom, or the bartender slipped something in his drink."

"Good idea, I'd offer to go with you, but I have something else in mind."

"What's that, Ben?"

"I want to go visit Baxter. There are too many coincidences. First, why Slidell? Then Gabriel disappears, then Huntley and now Nantois. It might be a longshot, but I have to try. He might not even agree to see me."

Rachel jumped in. "Star and I were talking this morning about Bouvier. Everyone was so positive that he drowned, but he must have been rescued. I thought we could start with the Coast Guard. Maybe they know something about a man washing up on the beach."

"Great. What about you, Arnie?"

"I was reading over the file. The Mardi Gras Killer liked to use the personals column to communicate with the people he used for the abductions. I was going to hit the *Herald's* library and check that out. Next, I expect this guy still has a thing for boats and being on the water. I'll canvas around, take pictures of Gabriel, and Charles Bouvier and see if anyone at the marina saw anything."

Rachel hung up from the conference call with Ben and looked at Arnie and Travis. "He's been missing since Monday night. This is Wednesday! I'm really worried."

"Let's all try to stay positive," Travis stated with a wisdom beyond his years. "Gabriel's been in tough spots. He found this killer once before, and we have Star to help us now." Travis looked over at Star, who was still wearing the tunic. "Can you share any thoughts, brother Star? Anything about this guy that might help?"

"We've talked through pretty much everything. Bouvier has this sick fantasy about young girls with big hair. When he had me on his boat, he made me dress up in weird clothes and insisted that we watch these tapes of Charlie's Angels. He kept on calling me Jill, the actress on the show. I think he's a pussy, always paying someone to abduct the girls. People say he killed all those girls. I'm not so sure - when I fought back, he didn't know what to do."

"So, what do you think happened to all those girls?" asked Arnie.

"I don't know. Maybe he sold them off to some rich sheik or something."

"Any other boats out there that night?" asked Travis. "A boat might have picked him up."

"Not that I saw, but it was dark and raining, and I was having a freak-out at the time."

For a moment, no one said anything. Travis put Bourbon on his lap and asked the feline if he could summon up some magic. As if on cue, the agency door opened, and a young man walked in.

Rachel let out a gasp when she realized that it Don (or Drake or Dan, Mangina or Purplinsky). "Look at what the cat dragged in," she exclaimed, getting up from her seat to greet him.

"You called. I was planning on coming down for a visit anyway. Hello Arnie, hello...er, Father?" Don said awkwardly, looking at Star. He nodded to Travis and gave Bourbon a scratch.

Rachel introduced Travis and Star and explained the monk's outfit. After a moment, she whispered to him, "You know it's been over 3 weeks since you left."

"Don't exaggerate. It's only been two and a half, and besides you told me to leave. Now you leave a message saying how much you love me."

"I did not. What's your name today, hot shot?"

"It's not Don Purplinsky. I'm very sorry that I lied to you, Rachel. I didn't mean to hurt you. Sometimes, because of the job, I have to be careful about my real name. My name is ...," he looked around and said, "Don ... Kittyman." After a quick pause, he looked at her sheepishly and added, "It's German." He continued quietly, "My dad almost drowned when his ship was sunk during the war."

"More bullshit!" Rachel said.

"You said something about your boss being missing...I don't suppose you've called the sheriff?" Don decided it was wise to change the subject.

"Yes, as a matter of fact, we have," Rachel replied, hands on hips. "He was abducted in New Orleans, and Ben O'Shea, Gabriel's partner, has been speaking to them."

"Bring me up to date." Don sat on the corner of Rachel's desk. Between Rachel, Travis, Arnie, and Star they brought Don up to date on Hollis Huntley, the case against Reznikov, and what they'd learned about Charles Bouvier. He remained silent until they finished. "I take it from your reaction that Gabriel doesn't normally take off?"

"No, he doesn't. Do you?" Rachel's arms were crossed.

Don ignored the question. "Okay, back to this killer; what does the local sheriff's department have to say about this?"

Star spoke up, "They blow. My parents went to see the sheriff, plus we had a deputy come to the house yesterday because of the rock thing. They couldn't be less interested. He actually suggested that I sent the postcards to myself to get attention."

Rachel added, "Ben found out the FBI would only be interested if they were invited by the locals, or if another bunch of teenage girls went missing."

"Are there missing girls?"

"No," answered Arnie, "at least not more than the normal bunch of girls that end up sleeping on the beach after a party."

"Do you guys have a plan for today?" Don looked at his watch.

"I was going to check with the Coast Guard and see if they have any records from February 1983 about a man washing up on shore," replied Rachel.

"I'm going to look into marinas and private boat docks," added Arnie. "See if anyone saw anything. It's worked once before. I'll go through the newspaper's archives and see if he's still communicating through the personals."

Don waited a moment before saying, "This is what I'm going to do. I have a buddy with the Coast Guard; depending on how I make out, I'll go pay a visit to the sheriff too."

"I'm coming with you." Rachel grabbed her purse and finished her coffee.

"That's not necessary. I'm a big boy."

"I said, I was coming with you," Rachel replied in a 'Don't mess with me' voice. "Star, maybe you and Travis can mind the store and go over everything again. There's a chalkboard in Gabriel's office, capture everything. See if we missed something."

Don and Rachel walked into the local Coast Guard office. "I'm looking for Lisa McNeil," Don said to a young man dressed in a navy-blue uniform. "Tell her it's Don, an old friend."

When the man left, Rachel turned to him. "Lisa? You said, buddy, now she's an old friend?"

"Long time ago." Don smiled. As they waited for Lisa, he stretched his arms and yawned. "You love me. Don't-cha?"

"No"

"Well, you think I'm hot, don't you?"

I'll concede you have a few attractive qualities. The muscles, the washboard abs, the piercing blue eyes, the dimple, the mischievous smile to name a few. "Not as special as you think you are."

"I knew it."

Rachel was about to light into him again when a tall, attractive woman came to the counter. She wore the navy-blue Coast Guard uniform, which in her case did little to hide her large breasts. The woman appeared to be in her late thirties and had blonde hair tied up in a bun. "Don?"

"Lisa!" Don embraced her.

"How nice to see you, baby. Are you here to tell me that you're moving back?"

"No, I'm afraid not. But I do miss..." Don began to say something before looking back at Rachel. "Is there someplace we can talk?"

Lisa took Don's arm and led him to a private office.

Rachel followed, feeling like an uninvited lost puppy. There were only two chairs in the office, and Rachel, in a scramble reminiscent of musical chairs, clumsily sat down before Don could. "Hi, my name is Rachel Henderson. I work for a private detective agency. Don is here helping me out with a case."

Lisa gave Don a sympathetic look and said there were more chairs in the next office.

While Don went to get another chair, Rachel fixed Lisa with a stare. "Old friends?"

Lisa shrugged. "You could say that I guess."

"Too big an age difference?"

Lisa sat back in her chair and smiled. "Just friends."

"Buddies, as he described."

"What is it that you want?" Lisa crossed her arms.

Don came back into the office carrying a chair. "We could really use your help on a missing person's case that goes back to...," Don said, looking over at Rachel for her to continue, before sitting down.

"The man we are after is a serial killer and fell off a boat on February 11th, 1983. Up until recently, he was presumed to have drowned. But we have come to learn that he's alive."

"Just before Valentine's Day." Lisa winked at Don.

Don smiled and shared a momentary look with Lisa before continuing. "What Ms. Henderson is asking is whether I could take a peek at your legs, errr... I mean logs. For the night, I mean for that night. The night of February 11th, 1983."

Lisa smiled. "Are you still with the MBI up in Jackson?"

"Yes, but let's treat this as an informal request. A friend, doing a favor."

"Give me a minute." Lisa got up and left the office. Rachel watched Don as he stared at the woman's behind as she left.

She reached into her purse and handed him a tissue. "That's for the bullshit that keeps coming out of your mouth."

"Pipe down, I'm just working a contact. She doesn't have to give us anything."

Rachel continued to glare at Don until Lisa returned with a black binder

"Okay, let's have a look-see." Lisa sat behind her desk. She leafed through the binder until she found a sheet for February 11th, 1983. "Is this about the Mardi Gras Killer?" She looked at Don.

"Yes," replied Rachel.

"I don't even need the log. There was a storm that night. The kind that rises up all of a sudden, high winds, swells topping five feet." Lisa read aloud from the log. 'At 21:00 hours, we received a distress call from the Jill, an unregistered cabin cruiser. We dispatched a cutter, and we found the boat adrift about a mile from Ship Island. A 15-year-old female, Jessica Grant was found, hysterical but otherwise unharmed.' The next day I believe the girl met with the local authorities, and my recollection is that she claimed the owner of the Jill had fallen into the Gulf."

She turned the page and continued to read, "We sent out a search team, but nothing turned up." Her eyes narrowed as she looked from Rachel to Don, "Are you saying this guy's alive?"

"Yes." Rachel stretched to try to read the pages in the binder. "He's threatening Jessica and her family. Maybe he wants to get even. Is there any notation of a body, maybe days later, washing up somewhere?"

"Believe me; I would remember that." Lisa thumbed through a few more pages. "There is something weird. A report from Captain Rosman about an old guy, by the name of Nelson Gallant. He liked to fish and camp with his dog on Ship Island. There's a note of a peculiar radio broadcast received mid-day on the 12th from him. The broadcast ended abruptly, and there was the sound of a growling dog in the background. We didn't act on anything because Nelson radioed that all was fine. It also says that the day after the storm, we had a team do a routine check on the island, there was no sign of Nelson, but we found what was left of the dog. Something had done a number on it. It looked like it had been in a fight. Because of that, Captain Rosman followed up the following week and spoke to Mr. Gallant."

"And what did he find out?" asked Rachel, now standing over Lisa, trying to read the writing upside down.

Lisa pulled the binder to her, guarding it. "Nothing, the old man said he didn't see anything."

"What kinds of animals are indigenous to the island?" asked Don.

"There are none. The place is completely deserted, except for tourist season, which starts in late March."

"All this sounds suspicious. A growling dog?" asked Rachel.

"Probably nothing," dismissed Don. "Lisa had a dog," he turned to look at Rachel, "It was vicious. Just like that Doberman at the paint shop, remember?"

Rachel remembered having to outwit the dog when they'd broken into an auto paint shop to get information on a stolen car ring. "Yes, of course, how could I forget?"

"Lisa's dog growled at me all the time. One time it had me trapped in the laundry room."

"Was it a Doberman?" Rachel asked.

Lisa laughed. "Hardly, Pumba's a Miniature Dachshund. But Don's right, she's very protective."

Rachel gave Don a scornful look. "Getting back to what happened on the island, maybe the dog was growling at Bouvier, and the guy killed it. I think we need to speak to this Nelson Gallant."

"Is there anything else that you can remember?" Don gave Lisa a big smile. "Or maybe I could call you later..."

Lisa smiled coyly. "It was great to see you again, Don. Will you be staying in town long?"

"I have one last question," interrupted Rachel. "What happened to the boat?"

"The boat?"

Duh? That's the problem with having your brain in your boobs, thought Rachel. "Yes, the boat you rescued. What was it called?"

Lisa referred to the log for a moment and then flipped to another section of the binder. "It was sold at public auction later that summer."

"I don't suppose the purchaser was named Charles Bouvier?" Rachel asked sarcastically.

"No, it was sold to Mr. Keith Jager."

"Thank you, Lisa." Don stood up. "I think we've taken up enough of your time." He turned to Rachel. "I think we need to go." Turning back to Lisa, he smiled and added, "Seriously, some witnesses remember things later. Maybe I could call you...."

Lisa smiled. "You know the number, baby."

Rachel made a gagging gesture as she got up. Before following Don out of the office, she turned and whispered, "By the way, Lisa, what's Don's last name?"

Lisa looked confused. "It's kind of funny. Tittley, Don Tittley."

CHAPTER FORTY-TWO

Wednesday, July 18th, 1984
Gulfport, Mississippi

Harrison County Detention Centre was located in Gulfport. Ben had been inside the facility numerous times during his career with the Biloxi police. It was an intimidating structure, surrounded by a twelve-foot high fence topped with rolls of barbwire.

On the drive from New Orleans, he thought about how best to handle Baxter. His relationship with the former Mayor had gone off the rails early on when the newly elected Mayor assumed office and found that Ben was unwilling to do his bidding. On his part, Ben took an instant dislike to the man and saw him as someone who could be corrupted. Baxter owed his election win to a strong lobby of land developers with shady pasts. People like Frank Reznikov. Of course, if you were willing to accept the crime and brutality that accompanied the development of a Vegas-type gambling environment, you'd probably say Baxter was a great Mayor.

It was 11:30 when Ben parked his truck in the visitor lot.

He got out and felt the heat bouncing off the asphalt, creating the illusion of wavering images. He went through the security screen and said he was there to see Baxter. Thankfully many of the guards recognized him as a police detective, so they ushered him into a waiting area while someone went to get the prisoner. Fifteen minutes later, a guard came up to him and said Baxter was waiting in the interview room. As he was led down the corridor, the guard asked if he wanted to have the prisoner handcuffed.

"No, I think I can handle it."

"Don't beat him too badly." The guard winked and unlocked the door to the meeting room.

When Ben walked into the room, Baxter was already seated. He had lost weight, a lot of it. He sneered at Ben as he pulled out a chair and sat across from him.

"Come to say you're sorry for selling me out?" Baxter had a smirk on his face. His orange hair was cut short — no doubt by the prison barber.

"No."

"Then, what do you want? By all rights, I shouldn't have agreed to meet with you without my lawyer."

"Why did you?"

"Curiosity."

"You've lost weight. Don't they serve Big Macs?"

"Fuck off, O'Shea. Once everything comes out, I'll be vindicated. Biggly, believe me. People will see how you trumped up these charges; you'll be the one sitting in here."

'Have you heard about Huntley?"

"That he can't fly? Not surprising that he'd take the easy way out. He was born without a spine."

"Did you have anything to do with his death?"

"Of course not, and if the papers say otherwise, it's all fake news."

"How are the showers in here? I hear they can be kind of rapey," Ben said with mock concern.

"Fuck off again. You know, that's rich coming from a faggot like you. Just look at you. Is that shirt peach colored? It doesn't go with the plaid pants. You're a badly dressed clown."

"Fuck off, Baxter."

Baxter chuckled, happy he was up on fuck off points. "Actually, I hear congratulations are in order. I'm told you're engaged to be married. I hear it's to a charcoal briquette," he laughed. "Can't get a white girl?"

Ben took a deep breath and told himself to ignore the comment. "From what I understand, Opey, can I call you Opey?" Not waiting for an answer, he continued. "The prosecutor has a pretty solid case against you. They don't need Hollis, they have all his records, and guess what, he made notes of your conversations. But it's not that bad. You can look forward to 15, maybe 20 years at some minimum-security prison full of little bum bandits."

Baxter stood up. "You should become a farmer. You already have all the bullshit."

He was about to call for the guard when Ben added, "Speaking of farms, when they add kidnapping to the charges, that'll spell Parchment Farms." Ben was referring to the State's maximum-security prison. "Maybe you should save your charcoal briquette comment for your new cellmate. I don't know if you caught the article last week in the *Herald*. The State of Mississippi just passed an amendment stating that all scumbags convicted of kidnapping as of July 1st, get what they call lethal injection." Ben started to gyrate and flop around as if he had received an injection. He watched Baxter's expression closely as the man sat back down again.

"What are you talking about, O'Shea?" Baxter's forehead creased.

"We have reason to believe you paid some thugs to abduct Gabriel Ross."

"Ah, someone stole your midget." Baxter feigned concern. When Ben nodded, Baxter continued, "I don't know what you're talking about. Really, O'Shea, you came down here to ask me if I kidnapped your little buddy? Why would I do that?"

"Revenge. It was Gabriel that figured out you told Nantois where to find Friesen. That's murder one." Ben was referring to Baxter's accomplice at the bank, who had later turned on him.

Baxter laughed briefly. "More bullshit. That Nantois kid did that on his own. He was crazy. The prison phone lines are pretty good in here, so you may not have heard, I guess Nantois slipped or something in the shower and stabbed himself twenty times." He started laughing, which went on for almost a minute. "No, O'Shea, once again, you're proving how lousy a detective you are. You should go home to your briquette." As he stood up, he sneered, "Do her parents like you?"

Something snapped in Ben. Maybe it was because Chevon's parents had put him through the wringer, and now he was getting it from the other side. Or maybe, it was as simple as he didn't like the guy. He propelled himself out of the chair and used the momentum to slam his fist into Baxter's face.

CHAPTER FORTY-THREE

Wednesday, July 18th, 1984
Gulfport, Mississippi

The sheriff's office was located on Larkin Smith Drive in Gulfport. As they got out of the car, Don said, "Let me handle this. Cops know how to talk to other cops."

"Sure thing, Detective Tittley." Rachel laughed. "You are something. Oh no! I hope we don't come across a wiener dog."

Don ignored her and went into the building. He flashed his MBI badge to the deputy and asked to speak to the sheriff.

"On vacation," said the deputy, a man sporting a brush cut on his boxy head. "He'll be back next week."

"Maybe you can help us." Rachel elbowed past Don. "We're looking for information on a man named Nelson Gallant."

The man looked from Rachel to Don. "Who might that be?"

Rachel jabbered a summary of what they'd learned from Lisa.

"Slow down, Ma'am. See this nametag? It says Deputy

Sheriff Weber, not mind reader. Now start over, but this time, don't make me give you a speeding ticket." He laughed at his own joke and gave Don a conspiratorial look.

Rachel ran through everything again, including the killer falling overboard, and ending with Nelson Gallant being a possible witness. The deputy sighed deeply. "Would this have anything to do with the Mardi Gras Killer?"

"Good, you're familiar with the case?"

Once again, Deputy Weber pointed to his name tag and nodded his head. "I make a point of staying up to date. This is the same "Killer" that throws rocks through people's windows, and sends postcards?"

"He's alive and terrorizing a family in Gulfport. We have to speak to this Nelson Gallant; he may have information." Rachel wondered for the first time if it would have been better to let Don do the talking.

The deputy looked over at Don. "Anything to add?"

"No, I think Miss Henderson summarized it pretty well. We'd appreciate any help you can give us, Deputy Weber."

The deputy pulled a long form from under the counter and pulled a pen from his shirt pocket. He made a show of clicking it while smiling at Rachel. "Have to fill in the paperwork if you want me to look into it. Now if you're the complainant, I'll need to see a driver's license."

Rachel fished out her wallet and showed him the license.

"You'll have to take it out of the wallet."

"Is this really necessary? There's some urgency here."

"I like to say to Timmy, he's my son, we're potty training, and well, the job's not done until you finish the paperwork."

"We're potty training? I would have thought by your age you'd have that covered," replied Rachel quickly.

"Oh, that's a good one." Deputy Weber chuckled and looked over at Don. "She's quite the piece of work." He turned back to Rachel. "Now can I have your date of birth?" It took fifteen painful minutes for the deputy to complete his form. "Now that's done, let see what we have on Nelson Gallant." He pulled a phone book out from under the counter and started looking for Gallant in the white pages. "Ah, here it is. Nelson Gallant, 1059 Lamey Bridge Road in D'Iberville. That was pretty easy."

Rachel looked at Don, wondering why he hadn't suggested just looking up the number. "Can you call the number for us?"

The deputy walked over to a desk and picked up a phone. A few moments later, he hung up. "Line's no longer in service. Let me try something else." He looked up another number in a book on his desk and dialed again. Rachel whispered to Don that she had seen Deputy Weber on television and that Star had said he was useless.

"This is Deputy Sheriff Weber from the Harrison County Sheriff's office, I was trying to reach Nelson Gallant, but the phone company says the number's no longer in service." Rachel and Don watched as the deputy listened for a few minutes. He kept saying, "Oh, I see," every minute or so.

After the fifth, "Oh, I see," Rachel wanted to go over and slap him. Finally, the deputy broke the pattern and said, "You don't say?" Followed by another "You don't say," a few moments later. At last, he said, "What did you say her name was?" He listened for a few more minutes before hanging up and coming back to the counter.

"Okay folks, you'll be happy that Deputy Weber is on the job. When I couldn't reach the person of interest, I called the emergency number for that building and spoke to the superintendent. He said this Gallant character skipped out on the rent. The superintendent was upset because he didn't bother cleaning the apartment, and left a lot of his stuff. You wonder what gets into people these days, skipping out on rent, not paying for gas, groceries. A while ago, I even had a report of a phony priest."

"Deputy Weber," Rachel interrupted. "What else did the superintendent have to say?"

The deputy looked down at a name he'd written on a piece of paper. "Probably unrelated, but he said that Gallant had a neighbor on the same floor, who also skipped out the same day. Freda Furlong. They're likely an item and hatched the scheme together."

Rachel shared a look with Don. "That sounds weird."

Don shrugged and said to the deputy, "Can you access the vehicle licensing system and tell me whether Gallant or Furlong have a car?"

"We aren't computerized here. But I can call the Department of Motor Vehicles." He headed back to the desk and picked up the phone again.

Don and Rachel sat on a wooden bench in the waiting area. "So, tell me, Detective Tittley, what do your fine detective instincts tell you?"

"Funny, Rachel. I told you my name. It's Don Kittyman. German? Remember? Dad almost drowned?" Rachel's face reflected her exasperation. "Rachel, you seem upset."

"Not at all. I'm quite calm. Even though I've punched you in the head three times in my mind."

Don moved down the bench a few feet, giving her a questioning look. "Leaving their stuff behind makes me think they left in a hurry. Could be they saw something that scared them."

Deputy Weber came back to the counter minutes later. "Once again, Weber comes through. There is no motor vehicle registered to Freda Furlong. There is, however, a green AMC Jeep Laredo registered to a Nelson Gallant with that address. You know, I always saw myself owning a Jeep."

"Can you put one of those APBs on it?" asked Rachel.

"Stands for *All Points Bulletin,*" corrected the deputy, "Normally that type of thing would need to be authorized by the sheriff. But seeing as he's on vacation, I guess that makes me the top dog."

"Thank you for your help, Deputy Weber," said Don. "Before we leave you, there is one other matter. We were speaking to the FBI up in Jackson; they'd set up a task force originally to help catch this killer. For them to get involved again, they said they would need the local police to request assistance."

"The sheriff handles those requests, and he's on vacation."

"What happened to "top dog?" Rachel used air quotes.

Deputy Weber once again pointed to his name tag. "It says deputy, not sheriff."

As THEY WALKED out of the building, Rachel said, "We should check if Nelson has any relatives who might know something about his disappearance."

"Longshot." Don shook his head as he held the door open for her.

"Freda Furlong too."

"Really long shot."

"Why don't I look into the Gallant angle, and you take Furlong."

"Really, really long shot."

"Listen, Tittley, you think lots of things are longer than they are."

CHAPTER FORTY-FOUR

Wednesday, July 18th, 1984
Gulfport, Mississippi

Lunch didn't go well. Don stopped for pizza, and they got into an argument in the restaurant. "We'll have a medium pepperoni." Don ordered for Rachel and himself.

"No, we'll have the vegetarian."

"Double pepperoni."

"No, vegetarian, with 'extra' veggies."

"What? You mean, like, with broccoli and shit?" asked Don in a shocked tone.

"Yes, among other things," Rachel spoke to the waitress who had been ping-ponging her attention back and forth between them. "We'll have extra broccoli."

"No, I have to draw the line there. As the man in the relationship, I reserve the right to have pepperoni. I come from a long line of meat eaters." He turned to the waitress and said in a deep voice, "Triple pepperoni, hold the broccoli."

"Don, when was the last time you ate a vegetable?" asked Rachel.

"I had some candy corn last night," he answered dismissively.

The great pizza war continued for some time until the waitress, her eyes rolling, suggested they each order a small pizza with whatever toppings they wanted. When the food came, they ate in awkward silence.

Don finished his pizza. "I'm up for a promotion to Senior Investigator."

"Oh, wow, Senior Investigator?" Rachel's eyebrows went up.

"It comes with a sizable increase in salary and responsibility. I wasn't even looking for the opportunity. The higher-ups came to me. Out of fifty agents, it's down to a woman and me." Don humble-bragged.

Rachel immediately started cheering for the woman. "You don't say? I'm impressed." She leaned forward and put a piece of cauliflower on his plate. In response, he used his napkin to pick up the cauliflower and deposit it in her water glass.

"That was pretty childish, almost Senior Investigator Tittley."

He smiled and nodded at her. "Let's split the bill."

"I've got to get back to the agency; we need to start calling the relatives. Are you coming?"

"I said it was a long shot. A real waste of time. I think you should follow my lead on this."

"Fine, you call the Furlongs, and I'll work on the Gallants."

CHAPTER FORTY-FIVE

Wednesday, July 18th, 1984
Slidell, Louisiana

It was going to be another scorcher, with temperatures expected in the low nineties. The muggy heat pressed in on Rutledge. Since his retirement, he was more conscious of the heat. Sweat trickled down his neck as he walked down Main Street, heading to the bar. He was surprised to find that the Hideout's doors were open at 11:00.

"I'd like to speak to the owner." Rutledge flashed his former NOPD identification at the twenty-something blonde girl who was at the bar. He couldn't help but notice that he was the only black man in the place. Freddie Fender was on the jukebox singing about *Wasted Days and Wasted Nights.*

"He's busy in the office. Can I tell him what this is about?"

Rutledge looked towards the doorway and almost on cue, two NOPD uniforms walked in. It was almost like the whole bar took a collective gasp. Rutledge turned back to the girl,

"Tell him, if he ain't out here in two minutes, we'll start checking IDs. You guys opened early and are serving alcohol to at least four people who don't look old enough to have gone through puberty."

The girl understood the threat and disappeared into the back room. A minute later a beefy guy with a ponytail came out, eyeing Rutledge suspiciously.

"You the cop?"

"Yesterday you met with a couple looking into an abduction case. The individual was in this bar the evening before and has not been seen since. Now, if you want, we can have this conversation here or downtown? What's it going to be?"

"I answered their questions yesterday. They asked about some blonde who I've never seen before. The guy they were asking about got drunk and staggered out of here. I offered to call the guy a cab. I can't be responsible for people who can't hold their liquor."

"What's your name?" Rutledge asked, pulling out his notebook.

"Sokolov."

Rutledge looked him in the eyes. "Full name and address."

"Mickey Sokolov and I live on Oak in town here. Why do you want that?"

"I need to contact your parole officer. Judging from that prison tattoo on your neck, I'd say you're violating your parole conditions. Add to that; you're serving alcohol to minors. I'm pretty sure I can get this place closed down by the end of the day."

"What the fuck do you want?"

"Listen, Sokolov. This might be a critical moment in your useless life. That woman from the other night is willing to testify that you spiked the man's drink. On top of all the other shit, you're pretty much done. We have reason to believe the man was kidnapped. Spiking his drink would make you an accessory."

Sokolov took a deep breath and looked around the bar. "Come back to the office, and we can talk in private." Rutledge followed him to a small office that had piles of paper all over the place. Sokolov pointed to a cracked and stained leather couch and sat down in a chair behind the desk. "You can see I have a lot of work to do. If you agree to go away, I'll tell you something. But I'm not going to testify, so this is off the record."

"Go on." Rutledge continued to stand.

"I was approached by a man who said that he wanted to teach a guy a lesson. The guy had hit on his girlfriend or something. He said all I needed to do was slip something into his cocktail. So, I did."

"Why would you do that?"

"The man said it was worth a few bucks, and guaranteed nothing bad would happen. He never said he was going to hurt the guy. It was supposed to be a lesson."

"You're pretty stupid, Mickey. What did this guy look like?"

"Skinny, straggly hair, tats up and down the arms."

"Would you recognize him if you saw him again?"

"No."

Rutledge showed him the wedding picture. "Is this the guy?"

"Listen, I don't want to get involved."

As Rutledge was turning to leave, he stopped and showed another picture to Sokolov. "Ever see this guy in here?"

He took a moment with the picture of Charles Bouvier. It

seemed like he was going to say something and then thought better of it. "Nah. Listen, man, am I in the clear on this?"

"If this man is hurt in any way, I'll be back with my handcuffs."

CHAPTER FORTY-SIX

Wednesday, July 18th, 1984
New Orleans, Louisiana

"I just picked up a message from Rachel. She and her boyfriend from the MBI have a lead," Chevon spoke up as Ben walked into the office.

"Good, makes up for wasting the morning with Baxter."

"You don't think Baxter is part of this?"

Ben wavered, still having an internal debate. "He denied any involvement. Of course, he's a professional liar, but this time, I actually believe him." Ben slumped in a chair in front of Chevon's desk. "So, she's back with that Mangina guy?"

"Last I had heard it was Purplinsky."

Ben waved that off like he was shooing a fly. "What's the lead?"

Chevon told him about what Rachel and Don had discovered from the Coast Guard, and their subsequent visit to the Sheriff's Department.

"Freda Furlong? I bet you they're shacked up somewhere. So, what does Purplinsky think happened?"

"He believes the fisherman and Freda might have seen the killer and recognized him."

They were interrupted by Jaqueline walking in the front door. "How did you make out, Ben?"

He told her about his meeting with Baxter, and Chevon filled her in on Rachel's news.

"What's the next step?" Jacqueline looked back and forth between Ben and Chevon.

"I don't know." Ben hadn't gotten a chance to finish his thought when the door opened again, and Rutledge walked in.

"It's hotter than Louisiana asphalt. Have we found Gabriel yet?"

"No, I wasted the morning talking to Mayor Baxter only to decide that he wasn't responsible. What about you?"

"The Hideout bartender did it." Rutledge told everyone what he'd learned.

"That's good work, Rutledge," Jacqueline said. "Now how do we use it to find Gabriel?" No one said anything. "Please, it's almost 2 PM. There has to be something we can do."

"I understand, but let's not get down on ourselves," said Ben. "We've come a long way to figuring this out. The answer must be right here. Chevon, can you call Rachel and Arnie, we need their brain power."

After a few minutes, Chevon said, "I had to leave a message with the answering service."

Rutledge took charge. "Let's go over what we've discovered. Maybe something might jump out at us. One, this was a setup. The bartender confirmed that. We know the people behind it, Lana Gadzinga and her husband. We know she's an ex-con. Two, based on your interview today, we can eliminate Baxter as the guy behind all this. That leaves Frankie

Reznikov. The death of both Kane Nantois and the banker might suggest that Reznikov is eliminating witnesses."

"But why would he abduct Gabriel?" asked Jacqueline.

"Let me be blunt," said Rutledge. "We don't know what happened, but we have to consider that something bad might have taken place and they've disposed of the body. As for why Reznikov would do it, it's the oldest reason in the book. Revenge. He wants his business associates to know that he can take care of business even from a jail cell. That way, no one will muscle into his territory."

Jacqueline fought the notion, refusing to accept it. "I still think it's a pretty big coincidence that Bouvier just happens to walk on stage now."

"He walked on stage eighteen months ago, we just didn't know it," countered Rutledge.

"First off," Jacqueline explained. "We know that Bouvier is back and has an ax to grind. We know he likes using people to do his abductions. Let's say, this fisherman finds him washed up on the beach on Ship Island. He nurses him back to life, but then suddenly realizes who he is. There's a fight and Bouvier kills the guy. He then steals the man's boat comes back to Biloxi and assumes his identity."

"That's a pretty good theory, Jackie," said Ben. "It all fits, except the Coast Guard called Gallant a week later, and he confirmed everything was fine."

"Listen, why don't we divide and conquer," suggested Rutledge. "You folks follow up on the marinas, I want to take another look at Gadzinga, somebody has to know these people. Maybe I'll take his picture downtown to some of the neighborhood bars and see if someone knows him."

The phone rang. It was Rachel calling back, and Chevon put her on speakerphone. "Sorry I missed your call. Arnie and Star are out checking marinas from this end. I'm here with

Travis and Detective Tittley, better known as Don Mangina, Don Purplinski, Don Kittyburg..."

Everyone started chuckling. When the laughter died down, Ben said, "Whatever your name is Don, I'm grateful for your help on this. We heard your message earlier about the Coast Guard and the sheriff's office. What's your next step?"

"Thanks, Ben, by the way, my name is Don Kittyburg, it's an old German name. We have an APB on Nelson's 1979 green Jeep Laredo, and after that, I er...we're just going to start looking for family members of Nelson Gallant and Freda Furlong."

"That sounds like a good idea."

Before Ben could hang up, Travis spoke up. "Star and I have been reviewing the case and mapped everything on the chalkboard, and I think we've come up with something."

"What's that, Travis?" asked Jacqueline.

"Follow the money."

"Explain," Ben demanded.

"It's simple. I was thinking about career choices earlier this morning and how I planned to become a millionaire. This Bouvier guy comes from a wealthy family. I'm sure all his money must be tied up in the estate, so what's he doing for money?"

"Good question," replied Ben.

"But how do we pursue this?" Jacqueline sounded like a broken record.

"Remember our client, Rod Smith, the lawyer?" asked Rachel. "Why don't we call him and see if he can tell us anything about Bouvier's estate?"

CHAPTER FORTY-SEVEN

Wednesday, July 18, 1984
Gulfport, Mississippi

Later that afternoon Arnie and Star were drinking coffee, standing at the entrance of the Port Cadet Marina. They flashed pictures of Charles Bouvier to anyone either coming or going to the marina. Star wore a pair of Rachel's jeans, a pink T-Shirt and an "I love Biloxi" cap. Arnie had gone over to a craft booth and bought her a cheap necklace with a star pendant to complete the outfit.

Star almost cried when he gave it to her. "I promise, I'll never take it off."

"How are your folks?" Arnie deflected her gratitude.

"They're okay. Mom's back from visiting her family. They haven't gotten more cards or calls."

"That's good. Have you been in touch with your friends to tell them you're back?"

"My best friend, Sheri-Lyn, has turned into a pothead. I don't fit in with that crowd anymore."

"That's too bad; it's good that you found something at the

camp to help you. How's living at Rachel's?" Arnie asked in between sips of his coffee.

"It's cool, kind of like having a big sister. I hope I'm not going to crowd her style."

"I'm sure you won't."

"Do you notice that whenever Don's around, there's this sexual tension?"

Arnie laughed at the thought. "Earlier this year, I told an amorous woman named Bernice that I was already in a live-in relationship with someone named Bourbon. There was a confrontation, and I had to ask the girl I was dating to play along and introduce herself as Bourbon."

Star started to giggle, "Isn't Bourbon your cat?"

"Uhuh."

"Did that work out?"

"Yes, only because the woman I was dating was a fantastic liar."

"Anyone that could pull that off must really be in love with you."

"She says she is, but you know ...that lying thing."

Star abruptly asked, "You were going to check the personals?"

"Nothing but the normal weirdos."

They were interrupted by the sight of a deputy coming out of the marina building. "Speaking of freakazoids don't look now, but here comes Deputy Dumbo," Star whispered under her breath.

Deputy Weber said good morning and stopped mid-tracks to point at Star. "I have a mind like a steel trap. I never forget a face." After a minute of searching the sky, "I give up."

"Jessica Grant, you came to my parent's house." When he still looked confused, she added, "The rock through the window?"

"You're not wearing the tunic. Threw me off. I remember now, the vandalism case."

Star rolled her eyes. "That's right. This is Arnie, remember?"

"Sure," Deputy Weber said, shaking Arnie's hand. "What brings you two down to the marina on such a fine day?" He saw the stack of photos Arnie was holding.

Arnie handed a copy to the deputy. "This is Charles Bouvier, better known as the Mardi Gras Killer."

Weber nodded his head. "I know that. The dead guy you said threw the rock through the window."

"He did a lot more than that, Deputy." Arnie glanced at Star. "You said you would speak to the sheriff about helping us find him before he hurts anyone."

"Right, I said that, and no, I haven't. He's away until next week."

"Okay then Deputy Weber, it was nice seeing you again." Star grabbed Arnie's arm.

The deputy stepped in front of them, blocking their way, "Say, since you're kind of in the business, in a junior way, let me ask your opinion on a case." He pulled a picture of a man out of the breast pocket of his uniform. "This man, Deputy Nolan, went missing. He was a fellow cop out on a routine patrol when he disappeared. We found his cruiser abandoned, doors locked, key in the ignition, only thing missing was his flashlight."

"Haven't seen him, but I'll keep an eye out." offered Arnie. "When did this happen?"

"Over a year ago," replied the deputy.

"And you're just starting to look for him now?" Star was incredulous. "That explains a lot."

The deputy ignored the comment. "A diving school

pulled Nolan's body out of the Gulf yesterday. It was weighed down with an anchor."

Arnie flashed a look at Star. "Where did you find the cruiser?"

Deputy Weber referred to his notebook. "Over on 26th."

"When was his last check-in?" Arnie asked.

"Precisely at 11:04 PM. An all-clear after checking the Coast Guard Building."

"And the car was found on the street, not in the parking lot?"

"Yep, no sign of a struggle."

"He might have gone to check something out. It was night time, so he took his flashlight, and he saw something he wasn't supposed to see," said Arnie. "Isn't the police marine impound area there?"

"That's exactly what I was thinking."

CHAPTER FORTY-EIGHT

Wednesday, July 18, 1984
Gulfport, Mississippi

Captain Rosman, that was the name, Rachel thought. She picked up the phone and dialed the number for the Coast Guard. When the line was answered, she asked for Captain Rosman. There was a pause on the line before a young man, who introduced himself as Ensign Bennett, asked who was calling.

"My name is Rachel Henderson; I was in earlier speaking to Lisa McNeil."

"Alright, hold on Ma'am." She was expecting to be connected to a man and was surprised when Lisa answered the phone.

"I'm sorry, Miss Henderson, maybe I should have told you, but Captain Rosman is no longer with the Coast Guard."

"Too bad. I wanted to confirm a few details about his call with Nelson Gallant."

"I wish I could help you, but he left kind of suddenly. We wanted to arrange a retirement party for him, but before we knew it, he was gone. We were quite surprised. He appeared to enjoy his job."

"When did he leave?"

"I believe it was March or April last year."

"Did he talk to you about his decision?"

"I wasn't his superior officer, but I'm told a typed letter showed up one day saying he had to leave for a family matter and wouldn't be returning. He thanked us for everything and wished us well."

"What about a girlfriend? Would she know how to reach him?"

Lisa's voice dropped a couple of notches. "Captain Rosman was a little light in the loafers if you know what I mean."

"Gay?"

"I think his family is someplace up north, New Jersey."

"Would you be willing to share his last known address with us?"

"Us? Is Don there?" Lisa's voice perked up noticeably.

"He's gone out," Rachel lied, "But I'll be sure to tell Detective Tittley how helpful you've been."

There was an awkward moment of silence as Rachel considered Rosman's retirement in light of everything else that happened. *Could something have happened on the call that made the Captain suspicious?*

Her thoughts were interrupted by Lisa. "I shouldn't be doing this, but for Don, it's # 612, 24th Avenue in Gulfport. It's right off the strip."

Arnie and Star filled Rachel in on what Deputy Weber had told them when they got back to the Agency.

"But what ties this to Bouvier?" Rachel asked.

"I don't know, other than we know he's a killer and it fits the timeline," replied Arnie. "He went missing in February last year. Weber said the coroner's looking at the remains of Deputy Nolan's body, but it's been in the water for about as long."

"And," Star said excitedly, "The divers found his body on the bottom with an anchor tied around his legs."

"Let's say Bouvier did it. Why?"

"Maybe Deputy Nolan saw something." Arnie patted Bourbon.

Rachel told them about Captain Rosman and his sudden retirement. "Now there's a link between him and the Gallant fellow who also disappeared. There's also Freda Furlong,"

"Maybe we should get those divers to keep looking," suggested Star.

Captain Rosman's old home was a brick bungalow with a beautiful oak tree shading the property. A rusty, gray Magic Wagon sat in the driveway. "I'm kind of nervous about this, Rachel. What if the killer lives here?" Star was biting her nails.

"I doubt that. This may be a dead end, but I would like to find this Rosman so we can ask about that call to Nelson Gallant. Don't worry; let me ask the questions."

The front door was opened by a young woman holding a toddler by his shirt collar. "Are you two selling something? I already have a vacuum, don't need any magazines." Then she turned to look at Star, "And Girl Guide cookies make me fat." From inside the house came the shriek of a baby.

"I'm sorry for the intrusion, my name is Rachel Henderson, and this is my associate Jessica Grant. We work with a private detective, and we're looking into the disappearance of the man who used to live here. His name is Captain Max Rosman."

"Oh him, I heard he was in New York or something. If you come across him, I have a bunch of his things in my garage. The landlord said I could keep the furniture, but I packed away his clothes on account of my no-good husband leaving us," the woman answered, just as her toddler struggled to escape.

"Cute kid," said Star, "What's her name?"

"It's a boy, and his name's Luke. My ex was a big Star Wars fan. It was that or Chewie."

"Rosman left without his stuff?" asked Rachel.

"Right down to the half-used tube of toothpaste."

Rachel flashed a glance at Star thinking, *People leaving suddenly without their stuff is becoming an epidemic.* "Did he get any mail after he left?."

"Sure, bills, magazines; I contacted the utilities and told them I wasn't planning on paying for anything."

"Did you keep the bills?" Rachel turned to Star and added, "Maybe we might be able to find them through the phone company."

"You want them; you can have them. I have a box." The woman handed her toddler to Star. "You hold Skywalker here, and I'll get them."

"Hey, little guy!" Star said enthusiastically, crouching down to his height and removing her cap. The kid seemed fascinated by Star's bald head and stopped fussing.

"You like kids, don't you?" asked Rachel.

"Always have, this guy is a real cutie."

The woman came back carrying a shoebox. "There's one other thing I should tell you. A month after I moved in, I got a postcard from New York City addressed to him. It was from someone named Bruce. It was kind of gay, you know, with little hearts over the I's?"

"Did you keep the card?" Star handed Luke back to his mother.

"I'm afraid not. I remember the picture on the front was of a parade. People were wearing costumes. I thought it was a little early for Halloween. I didn't pay that much attention because it wasn't for me."

"Do you remember what it said on the back?"

"Well I guess I was a little nosy, it was something like, 'Enjoyed our weekend, looking forward to you moving here. We'll have a blast! Lotsa love Bruce'. Something like that. There was an address in Manhattan, I think."

"Would you happen to remember if the card was post-marked from New York City?" asked Star.

The woman gave her a confused look. "No, I don't remember anything like that. I'm amazed I remembered as much as I did."

"What about phone calls after he left?" asked Rachel.

The woman shook her head. "I had the number changed right away. You might check with the lady next door. She's the neighborhood busybody."

"Okay, we'll do that. If possible, can we take a quick look at the clothes he left behind?"

"Help yourself; I've been thinking of hauling it all down to the Sally Ann."

"Good question about the postmark, Star," Rachel said as they looked through three boxes of clothes. Most of it was blue Coast Guard uniforms. "What do you think about the postcard?"

"Fucktar...I mean Bouvier likes sending postcards. The ones my parents got were postmarked from different towns, but all had Mardi Gras shit on the front. The one this lady received had a parade on it. I think he sent that card to Rosman's address to make people think he was still alive."

"I think you should consider being a detective." Rachel pulled out a leather jockstrap and held it up for Star to see.

Star giggled and pulled out a leather Captain's hat. She began singing, "*It's fun to stay at the Y.M.C.A.*"

Rachel was going through pockets of the clothing and found a used pack of matches from a place called the Male Box. She tossed it to Star. "Maybe we should check that place out. Sounds like a place a person who's 'light in the loafers' might go. For now, let's go talk to the old lady next door; she's been watching us from her porch since we got here."

They walked up to the porch and to Rachel's surprise, Star took charge of the questioning. "Afternoon Ma'am, my name's Jessica Grant, and this is my associate Rachel Henderson. We work for the Eye on You Detective Agency, and we're looking into the disappearance of the man who used to live next door."

"You mean the homo?" asked the old woman sitting on the porch. Despite the hot weather, she was bundled under a quilt.

"His name is Rosman, I believe." Star ignored the comment.

"He's a tutti-frutti. If he disappeared, then he probably got Aids or something. Maybe he's in a clinic."

"How do you know he's gay?" Rachel sat on the swing with the older woman.

The woman gave Rachel a look that suggested it was obvious. "He made no secret of it, dear. I've never seen him with a woman. Besides, he was always so neat. That's how you can tell. My late husband was such a slob, but he was a real sex hound if you know what I mean. Now, this guy was quite the sight in his little sailor suit; all fancy-schmancy. An attractive young man like that, he should be with one of you two. You know, I used to be the belle of the ball myself when I was your age. Best you use it before you lose it, I like to say. I wanted to fix him up with my granddaughter, and he said thanks, but no thanks. What did Mrs. Hefner tell you?"

"You saw us talking to Mrs. Hefner?" asked Star.

"These eyes might be old, but they don't miss much. Not that I have much truck with nosy neighbors. Now, Hefner, she's a might better off without that fatso husband of hers. He leaves his young wife with a baby literally sucking on her tit."

Rachel jumped in. "Getting back to Rosman, did you ever see him with anyone special?"

"You mean like another pansy boy?"

Rachel shrugged.

"No, as I said, I keep to my own. He had visitors, and I know he went out late at night. Probably off to some sex orgy or some such thing. Not that I know about that kind of stuff. Back in the day if a boy had a crook in his unit, he'd keep it to himself. Next thing you know, they'll be out flaunting their stuff in a parade."

CHAPTER FORTY-NINE

Wednesday, July 8th, 1984
Irish Bayou, Louisiana

Ben got out of his car after pulling up behind the NOPD Jeep on the shoulder of Highway 10. "Thanks for the call, Don," he called out to the heavy-set officer who was leaning against the Jeep smoking a cigarette. "You said there was something out here I should see?"

"I got an APB on a green 1979 Jeep Laredo. It was put out earlier today by a Harrison County deputy. He told me it had something to do with an investigation being done by the Eye on You Detective Agency. That's your outfit, right?"

"Yep." Ben used a handkerchief to wipe the sweat from his brow. He knew Don McRae through Rutledge, and from last spring's shoot out in New Orleans. Rutledge liked to say you could tell how hot it was by the size of the sweat stain under Don's arms.

"The deputy said this has something to do with the Mardi Gras Killer or as he put it, a killer who died and somehow came back to life and started sending out postcards and throwing rocks in people's windows. Not sure what that's all about, but I figured you might be interested in having a look-see."

"When did you find it?"

"A few months ago, some fishermen found it. From the look of things, I'd say it was abandoned over a year ago. I figured some kids stole it and ditched it in the bayou. They torched it, probably to cover up their prints."

"Doesn't sound like kids. How far in is it?" Ben saw a trail leading into a forested area.

"Quite a ways. The path's not great, that's why I suggested we meet and take the Jeep. We can drive a piece, but then we'll have to hoof it the rest of the way." Don looked down at Ben's Italian loafers. "Not going to be pretty."

"Did you run the plates?" Ben wished he had a pair of rubber boots like the officer.

"They must have removed them. Probably in the swamp. And before you ask, the fire made most of the serial numbers unreadable."

"Let's go," said Ben, swatting a mosquito that was dive-bombing him.

THE TRAIL WAS OVERGROWN with vegetation that scraped the Jeep's windows as they drove. They lost daylight after about five minutes, and Don had to put on the headlights. The trail took them around stagnant black pools with cypress trees standing tall in the shallow water. Flotsam like rubber tires, a rusty bicycle, and a steamer trunk, bobbed on the surface.

"People are using the bayou as their personal garbage dump." Don shook his head. "What does this have to do with Gabriel Ross disappearing?"

"The theory is that the killer was rescued by a fisherman who was camping on Ship Island. He owned a Jeep and hasn't been seen in over a year. Maybe the killer did the fisherman, and stole his Jeep."

The vehicle hit an unusually deep hole, and Don fought hard to keep the Jeep from veering into the marsh.

"Go slow, Don; I don't want to get stuck out here."

"Not sure what would kill you first, the mosquitoes or the gators. How did you make out with that Gadzinga woman?"

"She's definitely involved, but we went out to her last known address and found she'd skipped. Rutledge was going to ask you to get her picture on the wire and see if anyone knows her."

"Sure, tell him to get me the stuff. How's Rutledge doing?"

"It's only the third day, but so far so good. He's a good man."

"From what I know, since his wife left him, he's pretty much alone. I hate to think of what would have happened to him if you hadn't given him this chance." They drove for another few minutes until the trail abruptly ended. Don turned off the Jeep and turned to Ben. "It's about a ten-minute walk further up. Watch where you step; there are lots of cottonmouths."

"I don't do snakes." Ben got out of the vehicle and immediately started waving his arms in front of his face.

"Keep moving. It probably doesn't help, but they'll eat you alive if you just stand there."

Ben made a few tentative steps forward only to find that his shoes were sinking in the muck. He struggled to catch up to Don and heard a sucking sound as he lifted his feet out of the mud. At one point he looked back and saw that his footprints were gone, already filled in by water. There was a symphony of sounds coming from the swamp; Frogs with their deep-throated croak, mixed with crickets, and birds that sounded like they were laughing at him. He heard a splash and wondered what kind of animal had just slithered into the water. "Are there really gators in this swamp?" he asked.

"Yep, did you know there are more gators in Louisiana than in any other state? Also, keep in mind, they like to come out and lay on land. A while back, I heard tell of a boy who got his arm ripped right off by a gator. Kids like to play out here. So, this kid goes into the water to fetch a ball when the gator got him. He had no idea the gator was even there. It made kind of a ticking noise before it clamped down on his arm. Of course, once a gator clamps its jaws on you, nothing's going to get him to release. As soon as it got ahold of the boy, it started to roll and dragged him under the water. The other kids were screaming and throwing stones. They pulled their friend out of the swamp, but not before he lost most of his arm."

Ben longed for a machete, not just to beat back any alligators but also to take out his frustrations on the vines and thick vegetation that were blocking their path. A hundred mosquito bites later, they came to a small clearing where they found the burned-out carcass of a green Jeep Laredo. Vegetation had blanketed the vehicle. Looking in the Jeep, Ben saw that the seats had burned down to the metal, and a family of cottonmouths had found a home in the back.

"Do you think this is the Jeep?" asked Don.

"My gut says yes, but I wish we could be certain." A snake slithered from under the seat, revealing a black cylindrical object. Ben turned and pointed at the object. "See that in there?"

"No, I don't see anything."

"Right there, right where that big fucking snake was."

"It must be a baby snake."

"I think it's a flashlight."

"Nah, baby snake."

"With writing on its side?" asked Ben.

"Good point, are you going to reach in and get it?"

Ben looked at Don, who just shook his head. Ben pulled a pair of plastic gloves from his pocket, went to a nearby tree and picked up a stick off the ground. He leaned in and maneuvered the cylinder to the front of the Jeep. As he was about to reach for it, the snake hissed and struck out possessively at him. Ben jumped and fell backward into some muck.

"Fuck, grab a stick, Don, keep that snake off of me while I grab the flashlight." It took a few tries before Ben had the flashlight. It was miraculously in good shape despite the fire. He wiped away some of the grime and found a partial inscription *'Pr erty of Harr on Co ty P li D ar ment'. "The body of a* deputy was found off the coast in Gulfport. The only thing missing was his flashlight, Finding it in Nelson's jeep would suggest that Nelson's killer is likely the guy who killed the deputy." He put the flashlight in an evidence bag. "Maybe we should look around in case he dumped something else."

CHAPTER FIFTY

Wednesday, July 8th, 1984
Gulfport Mississippi

When Rachel and Star returned to the agency, they found Arnie and Travis talking to a well-dressed black man. Arnie introduced him as Rodney Smith.

"Nice to see you again, Mr. Smith," Rachel shook the man's hand. "This is another associate who recently joined us, Star...Grant." Star awkwardly shook Smith's outstretched hand.

"Wonderful to see you again, Rachel. I remember all the great work you did on my case. Motten owes his freedom to you. I'm sure if he was here and sober enough, he'd say thank you. Well, maybe not."

"It was a team effort. By the way, where's Don?" Rachel looked at Arnie.

"Said he need to check on an old buddy," said Arnie, adding, "Rod was just about to brief Travis and I on the Bouvier Estate, did you gals want to sit in?"

WHEN THEY WERE all sitting in Gabriel's office, Smith took charge. "Arnie told me what's been going on. I am very sorry. Everyone must be beside themselves with worry over Gabriel. Please tell Mrs. Ross that I will keep her husband in my prayers. When I got the call, I dropped everything and pulled together what information I could on the estate of Charles Bouvier."

"Thank you, Mr. Smith," replied Rachel.

"Please call me Rod. There has been quite a bit in the *Herald* about this case. It had a number of unique issues. I'm not sure how much everyone knows about the laws of the State of Mississippi on this matter, so I'll cover the basics first. When a person disappears and is suspected of having died, there's usually a lengthy waiting period; in Mississippi, it's seven years before a declaration of death can be made. This is obviously to see if they resurface. In the Charles Bouvier case, because there was an eyewitness, a Jessica Grant, who testified to the man falling into the Gulf, and since no body was recovered, the court granted what is called Death in Absentia. I should back up a bit, as this didn't just happen. There was a petition to the court for the ruling, presumably because the heir wanted to expedite the settling of the estate. The estate itself was worth well over a million dollars."

Star wondered if she should disclose that she was the eyewitness, but stayed silent.

"Mr. Bouvier died intestate, which just means that there was no will presented, so again under Mississippi law, a person's estate would flow to their heirs based on a pre-existing formula. In Bouvier's case, he wasn't married, had no children or siblings, and both his parents had predeceased him. The court issued an order establishing the only heir as his mother's sister, Edna LeGrand, who lives in a place called Slidell, Louisiana."

At the mention of Slidell, Rachel shared a look with Arnie.

"So Rod, you're saying that Bouvier's aunt inherited a million dollar estate in May of 1983?" asked Travis.

"I'm rounding off. To be exact, it was closer to $1.3 million, less legal fees."

"How did they know there weren't other heirs?" asked Rachel.

"They have to follow a process that calls for interested parties to present themselves and their interest in the estate. Now, this is where it gets interesting. The families of the missing girls hired a lawyer to make a claim against the estate and to block the petition made by the aunt. Now, remember what I said at the beginning. There is usually a seven-year waiting period before a Death in Absentia can be declared. To this day, the bodies of all the other girls have not been found. No one knows for sure that the girls are dead."

"So the families get nothing?" Star sounded incredulous.

"Correct."

"Here's the million-dollar question," asked Arnie. "If the estate has been paid out and later it's determined that the man is alive, then what?"

"Great question. Before the aunt got any money, she would have had to buy what is called a refunding bond."

Rachel looked over at Arnie and said, "We'd better tell Ben about this."

CHAPTER FIFTY-ONE

Wednesday, July 8th, 1984
New Orleans, Louisiana

Ben returned from the bayou and told Rutledge what he'd found. "I get the feeling that the flashlight might be important. It ties the Jeep to Gulfport. Any luck with your informants?"

"Yeah, mostly all bad, though. No one recognizes this Gadzinga woman; no one has heard anything about an abduction; no one recognizes the husband's picture. One doped-up informant said he thought he recognized Lana's picture, but couldn't remember her name. He wasn't sure if she was a stripper, a prostitute, or his second cousin. He did, however, say that he knew a guy, who knew a guy, who knew a girl named Lana, or Anna or maybe Brianna, who hangs out with some guy who rides with the Sons. He said that they're heavy into the crack cocaine scene."

"That sounds promising. How can we follow up?"

"A guy who knows a guy, who might know a girl...not sure I'd describe it as promising."

"At this point, Gabriel has been missing for almost two days. I'll take whatever leads you can get me."

Rutledge rolled his eyes and took a deep breath. "Listen, Ben, Gabriel's not missing. Let's face the facts. Reznikov is getting rid of loose ends. Gabriel is dead; we just haven't found his body yet. They probably dumped him in that same bayou."

Ben felt an urge to punch the man. Instead, he flung his stapler against the wall. "Listen, Rutledge," he yelled, "You might be right. But until a body is found, I won't be giving up hope and neither will you. Is that clear?"

Rutledge was taken aback by the outburst. "I'm sorry, Ben, I'll go back out and see if I can come up with something more."

The phone rang, and Ben picked up. "It's Rachel," he mouthed to Rutledge.

Ben listened for a minute and then put his hand over the receiver and whispered to Rutledge, "We've got a lead." Ben told Rachel that he was with Rutledge and he was going to put the phone on speaker. Rachel repeated what Star and Arnie had discovered from Deputy Weber, and what they'd learned from the lawyer.

"What are you thinking, Rachel?" asked Ben.

"Gabriel disappeared while in Slidell. The fact that this woman is Bouvier's relative, lives in Slidell, and inherited his money, is too much to be a coincidence. Maybe that's where Bouvier is living."

"It's the best lead we've had so far. Jacqueline asked me why Slidell? Maybe this explains the connection."

Ben hung up from Rachel with a promise to call her back as soon as he'd checked out Bouvier's Aunt Edna LeGrand.

Rutledge was already on the other phone to his contacts at

the telephone company. After a couple of minutes, he shook his head, "No active listings."

"Maybe she doesn't have a phone," suggested Ben. "Rachel also said that a deputy was pulled out of the Gulf. He had been weighted down with an anchor. He disappeared about 15 months ago. His cruiser was abandoned in Gulfport, the only thing missing was his flashlight."

"That cinches it. That must have been the fisherman's Jeep. The person who killed the fisherman likely killed the deputy too."

"We better call the local sheriff, just in case Bouvier is living with his aunt."

"I saw a movie once where a son kills his old mother and continues to live in this creepy house wearing a wig and her clothes so that everyone would think she was still alive."

"That's *Psycho*."

"Yeah, I know, really weird.'

"No, I mean, the movie was called *Psycho*."

"No, I think it was called something else."

"And the killer stabs a woman in the shower?"

"Yeah, that's it." Rutledge snapped his fingers.

Ben picked up the phone and dialed the number for Sheriff Hardie. He was surprised to find the sheriff still at work.

"Oh, hi Ben, I meant to call you. How goes the hunt for your friend?"

"I'm grasping at straws. He's been missing for two days now."

"I'm sorry the search of empty warehouses didn't pan out."

"That's all right; I appreciate the help. We have a lead that you may be able to help with."

"What's that, Ben?"

"Do you know an Edna LeGrand?"

"There was an Edna LeGrand who lived out on Highway 10 coming into town. What would she have to do with this?"

"What can you tell me about her?"

"Not much, I'm afraid. Long-time resident. As I recall, an old spinster, she lived by herself in a big house on a hill. People in small towns like to talk, and because Edna didn't have much truck with people, they liked to talk about her. Now let's see, I heard she was cheap, likely because she never donated to fundraisers. I heard she was a witch and performed sacrifices, presumably because she never went to church. I heard she had a hundred cats and ate cat food. I heard she was related to Howard Hughes and was a millionaire. I heard she was almost crippled with arthritis and wore a black witch's hat. That's about it."

"Did you ever meet her?"

"I make it a point of meeting everyone who might vote for me. I remember knocking on her door once. I was running for Sheriff, and I wanted to put a sign on her property. There's lots of traffic that pass by her place. She wouldn't even open the door. Just told me to go away."

"Earlier, you said she lived in Slidell. Did she move away?"

"Last year, apparently her arthritis got so bad, she needed to go to one of those long-term care places."

"Somewhere local?"

"No, I'm thinking Texas. I got a card from her. She moved to a nursing home in Texas. It kind of struck me as odd because she didn't seem particularly friendly, then out of the blue, this card shows up addressed to me. Anyway, she wrote that the arthritis was so bad she had to get one of the other residents to write out the card."

"Do you remember what else the card said?"

"I think she just wanted someone to have her new address. The old house is still vacant. A shame, a property like that must be worth something to a developer."

"I don't suppose you kept the card?"

"No, but now that we're talking about it, there was one other thing. I thought it was a nice gesture on her part, so I wrote to her. The letter came back, no such person. I think at that point; I just threw everything away."

"One more thing, Sheriff, are you sure she lived alone?"

"I think so, well just a minute. Ralph, he's the janitor, is around here somewhere, and he knows just about everything about Slidell. I'll call you back."

A few moments later, the phone rang again. Even though all Ben could hear was crying, he knew somehow that it was Jacqueline.

"Jackie? Are you alright?"

"He's dead."

"Jackie, ...did you find something?" Ben's voice cracked.

"No, but by now, he would have to be. Rutledge said so."

Ben looked over at Rutledge and wished he had another stapler. "Jackie, where are you?".

"I'm out at a South Shore Marina. It's been a long, frustrating day. I'm scared, Ben."

"Listen, Jackie, stay put; give me a half an hour, and I'll come to get you. Rachel just gave me a lead that sounds promising. I'm not giving up, and neither should you."

Ben hung up the phone and Rutledge quietly retrieved the broken stapler, sheepishly putting it back on his desk.

Sheriff Hardie called back and spoke to Ben. "I thought so. Ralph said that the old lady pretty much lived by herself. He thinks there was a boy living with her for a while. Not her boy, maybe a relative. The kid went to the local Catholic school, Pope John Paul the Second. This was back in the mid-seventies. He's not sure, but he thinks the kid's name was Christian or Christopher. Presumably LeGrand. If you want to check it out, let me know. Father Wilborg is the principal; we golf together. I can give him a call tomorrow morning if you're interested. He's been there a while; he might remember something."

"Any chance you can call him tonight?" asked Ben. "We're up against the clock on this."

There was a pause on the line before the sheriff asked, "Are you going to tell me what Edna LeGrand has to do with Gabriel's disappearance?"

"I will, but it's a long story...."

CHAPTER FIFTY-TWO

Wednesday, July 8th, 1984
Gulfport, Mississippi

Rachel took charge of mobilizing the team. She gave Travis and Star a list of people named Furlong and another list named Gallant from the phone directory. The goal was to find a family connection and see if they could shed some light as to where Freda and Nelson might have gone.

Don returned from visiting his "buddy" and was clearly in a funk over lunch. He had found some string and was teasing Bourbon when Rachel approached. "Okay, I know you're obsessed with pussy, but maybe you can give it a rest and come with me."

"Where?"

"There's only one Jager in the phonebook. That's the name Lisa gave us for the man who bought Bouvier's cruiser. I want to go see him and ask if he just happens to be related to a crazed psychopath. In case he is, I'd like you and your gun to back me up."

The drive to 1440 Mill Road in Gulfport was an exercise in one-up-man-ship. It started with Don commenting on her AMC Pacer. "This car has no pick-up. It wouldn't be any good if you had to get somewhere fast."

"I like it; it's good on gas."

"You would."

"What does that mean?"

"Nothing, just that it would be a good city car for a girl. Do your shopping, meet your girlfriends for lunch, get your nails done...easy to park."

Rachel ignored the condescending comment and turned onto Mill Road. The homes were enormous. "These mansions sure make my apartment look like a dollhouse."

"Yeah, your place is kind of small. "

"Is this where you tell me how big your apartment is?"

"No, no. It's maybe a little bit bigger than yours. Just forget it. Two bedrooms, eat-in kitchen, sunken living room..."

"Bully for you, Detective Tittley."

"I can afford it. Once I get that big promotion."

Rachel ignored him and drove down the street looking for number 1440. She was mildly upset at the thought of Don making more money than her. She finally turned into a circular driveway in front of a majestic, two-story home. "So, this is how the other half lives."

"If you like a big house with a tiny yard." Don looked up at the house.

"This place has to be worth a million."

"I wouldn't take it if you gave it to me."

"Really? I didn't realize until now, just how stupid you are," shot back Rachel, getting out of the car. "Are you coming? I might need you in case he has a wiener dog."

"Let me handle this," replied Don, running to catch up.

"Fine, Detective Tittley, dazzle me with your skills."

Don was about to use the door knocker when the door was opened by a white man wearing glasses, golf attire, and holding a crystal tumbler of what looked like bourbon. Based on the salt-and-pepper hair, Rachel guessed his age at fifty.

"Yes?" He looked at them over the top of his eyeglasses. The man had a weather-beaten complexion with skin like the apple that had been sitting on her coffee table for two months.

Rachel looked over at Don expectantly before speaking up. "Are you Joe Jager?"

The man nodded. "It's pronounced Yeah-gar." He looked from Don to Rachel before giving her a smile. "And to what do I owe this pleasure?" Not waiting for a response, he continued, "No, let me guess. Husband and wife real estate team. It's a beautiful home. Designed it myself, and no, I'm not interested in selling."

"Not quite," said Rachel. "My name is Rachel Henderson, and I'm an investigator at the Eye on You Detective Agency, and this is Don Tittley, he's an almost Senior Investigator with the Mississippi Bureau of Investigation."

Don flashed a foul look at Rachel and showed his MBI badge. "Could we come in and ask you a few questions?"

The man took a sip of his drink and gestured for them to come in. "It's kind of late, do detectives always work so late?"

"We're on a special case," replied Rachel.

"Whatever she said about me is a lie." Joe Jager offered.

"A lie? Who is 'she'?" Rachel stepped into a large foyer.

"Whichever one of my ex-wives hired you. Can I fix you a drink, maybe some spiked lemonade?"

"If you promise not to spike it, I'll have some lemonade." Rachel looked up and admired the fancy plastered ceilings.

Don said he'd have one too and Jager escorted them to a

well-lit patio that bordered a large kidney shaped pool. "Have a seat. I'll get those drinks."

While he was gone, Rachel stood up to take in the view. She could see from the lights that the property extended down to a river. Illuminated by floodlights, was a cabin cruiser. "Hey, check this out. That must be his dock and his boat. Do you think? No, couldn't be. But maybe just in case, we should take a walk down there and check it out."

"You said Bouvier was in his late twenties."

Rachel was about to respond when Jager came back carrying a tray with a pitcher and a couple of glasses. "Now, which one of them hired you, and for what?"

"Which one? How many wives have you had?" asked Don.

"Five at last count. Are you married, Don?"

"Uh no, too busy for that kind of thing."

"Take my advice; they don't show their bitchiness until you marry them."

Don gave Rachel a knowing look.

"My guess is Denise, my third. She's the queen in the bitch parade."

Don clinked his glass with Jager's.

"The last one sued me for divorce, citing alcoholism as the grounds." Jager punctuated this by pouring his remaining bourbon into his lemonade glass.

"We're not here because of your ex-wives. It's another matter," broke in Rachel.

"Let me guess, if it wasn't one of my ex-wives, then it was my ex-business partner. Who, as it turns out, is plowing the cornfields with Denise anyway."

"What kind of business are you in, Mr. Jager?" Don took a sip of his drink.

"I am a part owner in Jägermeister, the liqueur. It's a family business that started in the old country."

"I tried it once in college. Can't say I liked it very much," said Don.

"It's unbearable stuff." Jager cringed. "I send a bottle to my ex-wives every Christmas. I hope they choke."

"Do you have a large family around these parts?" asked Rachel.

"Most of my real family, not the phony-baloney ones belonging to the ex's, live near New Orleans."

"We're looking for Keith Jager." For the first time, Rachel detected something other than a smile.

"What's this in regards to?"

"Fair question," replied Rachel. "A man named Keith Jager purchased a cabin cruiser at a public auction. It's a 1975 Chris-Craft, very similar to the boat you have docked down by the water."

Jager took a moment to respond. "That's my boat. I can show you the registration and the bill of sale where I bought it. As for Keith Jager, I had a nephew by that name, but he, unfortunately, passed away many years ago."

"I'm sorry to hear that. How did he die?" Rachel took a sip of her lemonade.

"He was the victim of a hit-and-run when he was seventeen."

"What can you tell us about your nephew?" asked Don.

"Not much. He was my sister's son. The Tammany Parish Sheriff said he was riding his bike on his way to school when a car hit him. Probably a drunk driver who didn't have the decency to stop."

"You said Tammany Parish. Where exactly did your cousin live?" asked Rachel.

"A small town east of New Orleans called Slidell."

Rachel got back to the agency and found Star hanging up from her last call. Rachel filled Star and Travis in on their conversation with Joe Jager and then asked how they'd made out with their calls.

"Where's Don?" asked Star.

"He said he had to go look up another old buddy."

There was an awkward silence, broken by Travis. "I was able to get ahold of most people. The Furlongs are a big family; a couple knew Freda really well." Travis picked up a pad from his desk. "Let's see; they described her as a hosebag, a slut, a tart, and a whore. No one knew Nelson Gallant, nor had anyone heard from Freda in over a year, which isn't unusual apparently. My last call was really freaky," he said, laughing. "I spoke to a crazy woman by the name of Dixie Furlong. I think she might have been half in the bag, but she claimed to be Freda's twin sister."

"Dixie Furlong?" Rachel interrupted. "I think Ben interviewed her a few months ago. She's a ...lady of the night."

"Right off the bat, she told me that her sister was dead. When I asked her how she knew this, she said she could feel it, plus she'd had a dream. In the dream, she was at Burger King in the washroom washing her face. When she stood up, she saw her sister behind her in the mirror. She was carrying her head in her hands."

"Yikes!" Rachel commented.

"That's kind of what I said, she turned around, and Freda's head spoke, 'It takes two hands to hold a whopper.' I said that was funny, and then Dixie kind of cackled sarcastically and said, 'Right, I almost laughed my head off.'"

"She sounds like quite the character," Star said. "Mine were not so dramatic. I was able to contact a half dozen people named Gallant; most weren't related to Nelson. I did find someone who recognized the name and gave me a women's number in D'Iberville. It turns out she's Nelson's ex-wife and had changed her name. She said she gave up banging on his door for her alimony. She told me that the last time, the door was opened by a man who looked in his late twenties. She described him as having Billy Idol hair - white and all spiky and shit. He said he was a friend of Nelson's and that he was hanging out at the apartment while Nelson was camping on Ship Island. She said she didn't like him and that he was rude to her. I pressed her on the date, and she couldn't be sure, but thought maybe February."

CHAPTER FIFTY-THREE

Wednesday, July 8th, 1984
New Orleans, Louisiana

Father Wilborg was expecting Ben's call and answered right away. "I'm sorry to be calling so late, Father Wilborg. My name is Ben O'Shea, and I'm working with Sheriff Hardie on a missing person's case. I'm hoping you might remember a student who went to your school in the mid-seventies."

"Sheriff Hardie said there was some urgency to the matter; how can I help you, Mr. O'Shea?"

"Do you remember Christopher LeGrand? Or it might have been Christian LeGrand."

Father Wilborg repeated the name before saying he couldn't remember a student with that name. "Now we're a pretty big school, and I'm getting a little long in the tooth, but the noggin still works pretty well. To be safe, I suggest you stop by the school tomorrow. We're on summer break, but I can meet you, and we can go through the yearbooks."

"Thank you, Father; I appreciate that. Before you go, do you remember a student by the name of Charles Bouvier?"

There was a long pause on the line. Ben prompted, "Father, are you still there?"

"Is that what this is about? I only wish I could forget him."

"We have reason to believe that he may have abducted someone."

"The newspapers said he drowned."

"That's what everyone thought, but somehow he survived. What do you remember of those days?"

"Survived?" Father Wilborg repeated to himself. "He was a troubled child. We're taught that we're all God's children, but God should take a mulligan on him. Of course, we had no idea that he'd go on to do what he did, but looking back, there were early indications that he was disturbed."

"Disturbed how, Father?"

"He came to us from a school in New Orleans. He wasn't well-liked there. Kids can be cruel; they called him a spoiled little rich kid. As he reached puberty, he became frustrated and often acted out in class. The principal suspended him for trying to hurt another kid. While suspended, one of the school portables burned down. His mother swore to the police that Charles had been home with her. Nothing could ever be proven, but it was decided that for everyone's sake, he should change schools. He spent his senior year with us. When the same pattern of behavior started here, we tried to get in touch with Mrs. Bouvier, but she never returned the call."

"Do you remember any specifics about his behavior?"

"I know he was frustrated. From what I was told, he came on too strong and frightened people. Particularly the girls. My best memory of his behavior was during a school mass I performed for a classmate of his who had died in a tragic accident. Charles laughed throughout the service."

"Did he finish the year?"

"No, one day, he just stopped coming."

CHAPTER FIFTY-FOUR

Wednesday, July 8th, 1984
New Orleans, Louisiana

"How is this a big lead? It just confirms what we already know," said Jacqueline when Ben told her about his conversations with Sheriff Hardie and Father Wilborg. "We already knew Charles Bouvier was crazy and had a messed-up life." They were sitting in Ben's truck. Her eyes were red from crying. "What are we going to do, Ben?"

"We know that his Aunt Edna inherited his money. I think the postcard that Hardie got in the mail was a trick to get people to think she was still alive and living in Texas."

Jacqueline paused for a moment, "Let's say I give you that. The old lady is probably at the bottom of Lake Pontchartrain. How does that help us?"

"The money."

"The money?"

"A million is a lot of money. If I'm right, old Aunt Edna is dead, and Charles found a way to reclaim his inheritance. Not sure how all that works; you can't just go to a bank and cash a million dollar check. I think he has an account somewhere."

Jacqueline was quiet for a minute, staring out the window. Raindrops started to fall on the windshield.

CHAPTER FIFTY-FIVE

Saturday, June 25th, 1983
Slidell, Louisiana

Charles got out of the truck and climbed the steps to the old house. The rain had lightened up and had turned into a fine mist as he climbed the front steps. He knocked a few times before trying the doorknob and finding it locked. *She's in there. She never goes anywhere.* He walked back to the truck and leaned on the horn until he saw the front door open. An old lady using a cane stepped onto the porch.

"Stop that. What do you want?"

"It's Charles, Aunt Edna." Charles tried to read her mind. *Does she know it's me?*

She turned her head sideways so that she was looking at him while still hunched over. "You steal that truck?"

"In a manner of speaking."

"Figured so. Papers said you were dead." He noticed that she didn't have her dentures in and was gumming her words.

"Shouldn't believe everything you read in the papers."

"I read about what you did to those girls."

"Like I said about newspapers. Can I come in and visit for a while?"

"No, you mean nothing to me, never did. Should have stayed dead. Go away, or I'll ring the sheriff."

Charles approached the front steps. "You won't. You're too cheap for a phone, remember?"

"I have a gun."

"You don't."

She moved quickly and had the door half closed behind her before Charles ran up the steps and stopped her. He gave her a light shove, and she flew backward, falling heavily to the wooden floor in the hallway. He laughed at her. "Now Aunt Edna, is that any way to treat your last living relative?"

She gave out a cry of pain, "I think my hip is broken."

"Ah well, you shouldn't have tried to close the door on me. Listen, I'd love to stay and chat, but since you don't sound interested in a visit, I'll just take my money and go."

Edna shook her head and started to cry. "I gave it to the church."

"You didn't. Quit all the lying, Aunt Edna."

"I need an ambulance."

Charles reached down and grabbed what little hair she had. She let out a wail of pain as he dragged her into the living room. He sat down on the couch, said in a compassionate tone, "I'll be happy to fetch an ambulance for you, but before I do, I know about the petition to the court, and I know that you got a check. That was my money, and I need it. So where is it?"

"Please, Charles, I'm in pain."

"So am I. You never believed in banks, so I figure you somehow finagled a big pile of cash and have it all hidden somewhere. Unless you want me to hurt you, even more, you'd better start talking."

It took ten minutes before Aunt Edna cracked and told him to check the oven. Charles went into the kitchen only to find she'd lied. When he came back to the living room, she'd crawled a couple of feet towards the door. He kicked her viciously in the ribs and was about to kick her again when she spat out blood and said, "You were always a mean little bastard. Get me a glass of water, and I'll tell you."

Charles went to the kitchen and came back with a glass of water. He watched as she drank, the blood in her mouth turning the water red.

"I put the money in a couple of suitcases in my bedroom closet."

Charles went to check and discovered she'd lied once again. This time when he went back to the living room, she'd crawled almost to the hallway. He stomped on her fingers, bringing on another scream.

The screaming eventually turned into whimpering, and she grasped her chest. "My heart..."

"Is that right?"

He knelt down and looked into her dull, sunken eyes. "You know I'll eventually find it. I'm going to go room by room taking this place apart. Make things easier on yourself, and I'll stop hurting you."

"It's in the bank. I have some cash in a trunk in the basement."

"I'm getting tired of this, Aunt Edna. You're pathetic. You want me to run off like a dog just so you can crawl a couple of more inches. If you're lying to me again, I'm going to put you in that trunk." He ran down the stairs to the basement and searched until he found an old trunk hidden under some blankets. Expecting once again to be disappointed, he tried to open the trunk but found it locked with an old padlock. He used a rusty hammer from a workbench and hammered repeatedly to break the lock. When he lifted the lid, staring back at him were neatly stacked bundles of Benjamin Franklins.

Charles dragged the trunk over to the stairs. It took him a number of tries, but he was finally able to drag it up to the main floor. "Okay, you old crone, I found it." He went back to the living room. She was where he'd left her, except her prune-like face was contorted with pain and frozen in death.

CHAPTER FIFTY-SIX

Monday, July 20th, 1983
Gulfport, Mississippi

It's been more than a month since I gave Petr the job of finding Jessica. So far all I've received from him was an assurance that he was working on it. How hard could it be to find one girl with all the information I've given him? Charles waited in the trees for Petr to get home. When he finally heard the motorcycle, he pulled out his gun. He approached Petr as he was getting off his bike.

Petr seemed to know what Charles wanted and without being asked said, "I found the parents' address. They live at 4750, 60th Street in Gulfport. But don't blow your load yet. The girl had a falling out with her old man and moved out."

"Finally, some progress. Have you been watching the house?"

"Don't worry, I have eyes on it. Sheri-Lyn is trying to get me the name and address of the friend she's living with. I'll know more next week. I'm the guest of honor at a rave this weekend. I'm hoping this heartthrob of yours is going to be there."

"Where's the party?"

Petr took a deep breath before responding. "No, it's my show. I don't need you showing up and acting like a psycho."

Father Jim rapped on the screen door of the small bungalow. He clutched his bible, trying to get into the role. After his second knock, the door was opened by a middle-aged woman with gray hair. She gave Charles a confused look. "Can I help you with something, Father?"

"I'm Father Jim from the Catholic Arch Diocese. You must be Mrs. Grant?"

"Yes, I'm Gloria Grant, but there must be some mistake, we're not practicing Catholics."

"I understand. Is Mr. Grant home?"

"Yes, he's just finishing reading the newspaper in the kitchen. Come in, Father." She turned and called out to her husband that they had a visitor.

A few moments later a tall man wearing soiled denim overalls came out of the kitchen and stopped in his tracks when he saw Charles.

"Would you like some tea, Father? I was just brewing a pot," offered Mrs. Grant.

"That would be lovely." Charles removed his Nikes and took a look around at the home. He was about to compliment them when he saw a picture of Jessica Grant on the phone table. The picture set his heart racing. She was standing in front of her parents. She looked in her early teens, her hair a beautiful golden color. Her expression was mischievous, as if she was telling the cameraman that she didn't want to be photographed with her fuddy-duddy parents.

The woman followed Charles' gaze, "That's my daughter Jessica. Isn't she beautiful?"

"Yes, you're blessed to have such a breathtaking child."

Mrs. Grant ushered him into a living room and went to get the tea. Mr. Grant followed Charles into the room, eying him suspiciously. "What's this all about?" he asked when the priest sat on the sofa. When Charles didn't answer right away, he added. "We ain't holy rollers, you know."

"Your wife told me, yet your daughter attended a Catholic School?"

"Yeah well, we used to be, but there's just too much hypocritical, double-talking bullshit. We haven't been to church in years.""That's too bad, Mr. Grant. I'm sorry you've lost your faith. It might have helped you through your ordeal."

"I ain't interested in a sermon."

"I was very concerned when I heard what happened to Jessica. There is so much evil in the world today, we need to protect the young from Satan. If it would help, I can read some Bible with you."

Mr. Grant rolled his eyes and looked up at the ceiling. "Gloria, is that tea ready?" As if on cue, she came in carrying a tray containing a pot of tea along with some peanut butter cookies.

"Oh, thank you, Mrs. Grant. Can I call you, Gloria?"

"Of course, Father Jim," she answered while pouring the tea.

"Now, you're sitting down. You got your tea. You got your little cookies. Get to the point. What do you want?" Mr. Grant ignored his wife's reproachful look.

Charles ignored the question and looked at Gloria. "I can

see where your daughter got her beauty." Mrs. Grant blushed at the comment.

"You don't look like any priest I've ever seen." Mr. Grant shook his head. "They teach you to spike your hair at the seminary?"

Charles smiled at him. "Can I call you Frank?"

"Can I call you child molester?"

Charles turned away and looked at Gloria."I understand that Jessica doesn't live with you anymore."

"That's true, Father. Her ordeal has been very hard on everyone. She's currently living with friends." Charles detected a quiver in Gloria Grant's voice. Frank gave Charles a sour look and shook his head.

"Sometimes, friends can help a soul find the way forward."

"Christ, what the fuck does that even mean?" asked Frank.

Charles stared at Frank. "Maybe if you went to church every once in a while, God might give you more wisdom." He turned back to Gloria, "The friends that have sheltered poor Jessica, are they local?"

"Never seen a priest wearing Nikes."

Charles flashed a quick look at Frank. "It's so I can outrun the devil." *If I had brought my angler, I'd rip out your throat.* "It's all right, Gloria, Mr. Grant is just careful. The archbishop has asked me to pay a visit and offer counsel to you and to your daughter. To help you return to the path of God."

"Path of God, my ass."

"Frank, please you're rude," said Gloria. "Try one of the cookies, Father, I baked them myself."

"I will. They look delightful." Charles could see out of the corner of his eye that Mr. Grant was mimicking him. He took a cookie and shoved it in his mouth, looking at Mr. Grant with a satisfied expression. Turning back to Gloria, "Now, where did you say Jessica was staying?"

"I...er, we don't know. It's kind of embarrassing. I think you'll understand that she found it a little hard to live here." She looked over at her husband.

Charles gave Mr. Grant a look and a nod that signaled that he'd figured about as much. "It is a shame that all of this has driven a wedge in the family. I think I can help. You must be able to get word to her. Maybe we can arrange a family meeting."

"I'm friends with some of the mothers. I can ask them to get a message to her."

There was a moment of silence as Charles waited to see if Gloria would offer anything else. *That's just not fucking good enough.*

Frank broke the silence and stood up, "Well that's it then, thanks for stopping by..."

CHAPTER FIFTY-SEVEN

Monday, August 3rd, 1983
Gulfport, Mississippi

Almost a month after Charles disposed of Aunt Edna, he read in the *Herald* that in conjunction with the Federal Customs Department, the Harrison County Sheriff was going to have a public auction of an inventory of repossessed and impounded property. In the advance listing, he saw a 1975 Chris-Craft Catalina. He'd been back to the impound a couple of times to check on the Jill. With money coming in from Petr's drug dealing, he had plenty of cash to upgrade and get a newer, bigger, and faster boat. But there was something about the Jill. He wanted to have her back.

He was surprised that the Jill would be included in the auction, given that his estate had been settled. Everything he owned, he thought, should have belonged to Edna. Unless of course, she said she didn't want it. The auction was being held in a large hangar near the Coast Guard building.

Petr was given a program upon entering and paid a token fee to be able to bid. There had to be over a hundred and fifty people in the room to bid on a bunch of sports cars, trucks, jewelry, boats and musical instruments. Pictures of the boats were displayed on easels with a full description of vital information. He noticed that the Jill had been freshly painted and the name of the boat removed.

Charles hadn't expected so many people. He grabbed a chair near the front beside a short, squat man wearing a beret. The man wore a windbreaker and boat shoes, so Charles figured that he was there to bid on the boats. As Charles sat down, the short, middle-aged man nodded to him.

"Good morning," said Charles. "Bigger crowd than I expected."

The man leaned in close to Charles, whispering with garlic breath, "Always is, lots of people looking for a deal," he added, crossing his arms over his considerable girth.

"You're not here for a bargain then?" Charles looked at the man.

"I'm only interested in one item. That 1975 Chris Craft Catalina. Pardon me; my name is Simon Villemarette," he said, extending a hand comprised of meaty little pig sausages.

Charles shook the hand, "Keith Jager. From the pictures, the boat seems to be in good condition."

"I've been down to the impound yard a couple of times. It might need a bit of work."

"What would a boat like that go for?" Charles nodded at the program.

"There's a reserve of ten grand, but that boat is priceless."

"Priceless?'

"It used to be owned by a man who killed a whole bunch of people."

"What?"

"Yep, he abducted a bunch of teenage girls that happened to look like Farah Fawcett. He'd take them out on the Gulf and do dirty stuff to them before dumping their bodies." Villemarette's eyes lit up with excitement. "A real sicko. Apparently, it's like a museum inside, dedicated to the actress. He even called it the Jill, which was the actress' name in Charlie's Angels. Word is that the guy killed a half dozen girls before he died by falling into the Gulf. Pretty fitting end if you ask me."

"That's quite the story. You appear to know a lot about this. Why would you want a boat with such a horrible past?"

"For the World's Fair, of course, it's coming up next spring, and I'm going to park this baby in the lot and sell tickets to people who want to see the 'Vessel of Death,' 'Satan's Angels,' the 'Naughty Yachty'..."

"The naughty yachty? Is that what you're going to call it?"

"I haven't made up my mind. But mark my words, I'm originally from Memphis, and people pay lots to check out Elvis' plane. I also built a castle east of New Orleans. It's not full size, but it has the ramparts and the watchtower. I figure I'll clean up." After a few moments, Villemarette asked, "What's got your fancy?"

"I'd like a boat. Maybe something smaller."

"There's a nice skiff. Apparently, it was abandoned at a marina in D'Iberville. It's got a 250 Johnson motor. Nice little boat. Number 14 in the program," he whispered as if he was letting Charles in on a big secret.

The auction went quickly, with the auctioneer disposing of the cars and trucks first. He was successful at getting bids close to the stated values in the program. Midway through the auction, number 14 came up.

"The reserve is only $500. Take it from me; it's a steal," whispered Simon. Charles remained impassive. Simon kept on glancing at him throughout the bidding. Finally, when the auctioneer ended the bidding at $900, Simon turned to him, "You really screwed the pooch there."

More boats were auctioned off, Simon continuing to steal looks at Charles, whose expression remained deadpan. "Do yourself a favor pal. Don't be thinking of bidding on the naughty yachty." Finally, the Chris Craft was put up with a reserve bid of $10,000. Charles watched as Simon and a couple of others bid the price up to almost $20,000. When it looked like the bid had stalled, the auctioneer said the high bid was $19,000.00 by the man in the beret. He looked around the room, going once, going twice and then Charles yelled out $25,000. There was a buzz in the room, and everyone was looking at Charles. He heard a woman behind him say, "Billy Idol, I think.I saw him on the Grammys."

"You're an asshole," whispered Simon. When Simon didn't counter, the auctioneer's gavel closed off the bidding.

CHAPTER FIFTY-EIGHT

Monday, August 24th, 1983
Gulfport, Mississippi

It was a chilly night in late August when Charles once again appeared out of the darkness as Petr arrived home.

"I know it's taking longer than you thought, but I have news. Sheri-Lyn told me that Jessica is living in Mobile, Alabama. Apparently, her mother has a sister. I have the address, and I have someone checking for us."

"I'll take the address."

"Figured you would." Petr reached into his vest pocket and passed a piece of paper to Charles. "Give us a week to check it out for you. If she's there, I'll deliver her to you. Just like Dominos."

"I need a banker who will agree to negotiate some personal checks without asking a lot of questions. I'll guarantee the checks will go through without anyone sounding the alarm. In return for making this work, I'm prepared to cut him in for a slice."

"How much are we talking about?

"Each check will be made out to cash and will be $50,000. In all, we're talking about twenty checks, one every few weeks."

"That's some scam. You really are something, Jager. You want to rob some little old lady of her nest egg. We can make the arrangements, but my guy will want at least 10%. Oh, and the bank guy comes out of your share."

"Nice little payday for making a few arrangements. I'm the one taking the risk and providing the guarantee."

"I'll speak to my guy, but he's not the kind of man you can bargain with. Nor is he the kind of person you can mess with."

Charles nodded and handed over a check drawn on the bank of Louisiana. He'd found Edna's account statement and checkbook. "Just so you know what you're dealing with."

CHAPTER FIFTY-NINE

Monday, September 1st, 1983
Gulfport, Mississippi

A week later, Petr met once again with Charles in Boogie's parking lot. "Good news and bad news," he said, lighting up a cigarette. "The boss is fine with the arrangements, and I have a bag of cash for you. The banker wanted 5%, so all in, you get 85% of the check. Pretty sweet deal if you ask me."

"It's expensive."

"Not bad considering it's not even your money."

"And what's the bad news?"

"My guys in Mobile went to that address, and there was no sign of the girl. They did a number on her aunt, but all they could get out of her was that the kid left to go live with some hippie named Steve."

I should have done this myself. "What now?"

"I'll ask Sheri-Lyn if she knows the dude. Don't despair, we'll find her. Meanwhile, just think about all this money."

CHAPTER SIXTY

Wednesday, July 18th, 1984
Slidell, Louisiana

Gabriel awoke with a start. The sky was full of stars, a sight he'd never seen before. Some were twinkling. There was one in particular that shone the brightest. *Must be the North Star.* When he'd first met Jacqueline, they'd look up at the North Star and make wishes. Every so often, they'd see a shooting star. She'd claimed it was a good omen and meant their wishes were going to come true. It had to be an old wives' tale because the following morning, he'd still be only five feet tall. *I wonder if Jacqueline is looking up at this star right now?* He closed his eyes and let himself fall back onto the pillow.

Pillow? I'm lying on a pillow. Where am I? I have a blanket on me. He heard a tick-tock sound and saw a luminescent clock off to his left showing the time as 8:22. It was a pink, Barbie doll clock. He rubbed the sleep from his eyes. The headache was still there, but less blinding than before.

There was a bit of light, courtesy of a nightlight by the bed. It gave off enough light to bathe the room in shadows. He could make out shapes at the back of the room watching him as if they were observing a science experiment.

"Hello," he said tentatively. When no sound came back, he lay back on the pillow and looked up at the night sky. *I'm in a bedroom.* He realized that what he was looking at were glow-in-the-dark stickers. *Where the hell am I? I remember lying in an alley. I remember a man lying on top of me. I was holding onto a building trying to get to the street.* He reached out to his right and felt a lamp on a nightstand. He turned it on, and the room was instantly immersed in light. He looked around at what he'd thought were people and realized they were stuffed animals. There were a couple of life-size dolls, a full-size Chewbacca, and a C3PO.

His feet were up against the footboard of the bed. *A kid's bed?* A little girl's bed. He was lying in a pink Camaro equipped with pink pillows and blankets, all with pictures of Barbie. Gabriel tentatively put one leg out of bed onto the carpet. He looked down and saw that he was wearing a pink nightie. *Maybe I'm in an episode of the Twilight Zone. This must have something to do with driving a pink car. I must be traveling in another dimension.*

He tried to stand up but felt dizzy again. Using the wall to steady himself, he crossed the room to a washroom and looked at himself in the mirror. His green eyes looked like they had shrunken into his eye sockets. His cheeks were gaunt, and his complexion looked like something out of the *Living Dead.* His dark hair had tufts of grass with bits of something disgusting in it. He pushed back the pink curtains covering the window and saw nothing but darkness. There were no street lights, so he figured that he was out in the country. He tried to slide the window open, but it wouldn't budge. Someone had nailed it closed.

The trek to the window had exhausted him. Gabriel sat down on the bed; Ben had once told him that making decisions when tired was like drunk driving through life. He lay back down and closed his eyes again. When he woke up and looked around, he thought, *I'm in some kid's room — a little girl who likes Barbies. Where are my clothes?* There was a desk in the corner of the room. He struggled to make his way to the chair, the room spinning. He sat down on the floor and rested. *How long have I been sleeping?* He went to check his watch, only to find it was missing.

After a few minutes, he used the desk to pull himself up to the chair. There was a couple of textbooks on the desk. He opened an American history book and on the first page, written in flowery script was a name, Heidi Gesche. There was a date below the page, November 14th, 1978. Sitting at the desk, he tried to do the math. If the grade eleven book was dated six years earlier than that would make her almost forty. He then rechecked his calculations and revised his estimate to twenty-two. It didn't fit with the décor of the room, so he repeated his calculations again.

There was a framed photo of a teenage girl face down on the shelf. She was pretty with dark hair cut in a pageboy style. She was smiling for the camera and standing in front of a large weeping willow tree. *Was it face down because someone was ashamed, or because it was too painful to look at her?*

Gabriel began looking through the drawers. There were sketchbooks showing a talented artist. He found a copy of *Teen Magazine* with a very youthful John Travolta on the cover asking the reader about their flirting style. Beside the desk, a milk carton contained classic LPs from that era. Gabriel thumbed through *Abba, Bay City Rollers, The Bee*

Gees, Deep Purple, Michael Jackson. They were neatly organized alphabetically, each with its own dust jacket.

Okay, it's time to find out what the hell is going on. Gabriel marshaled his energy and made it to the door, only to find it locked.

CHAPTER SIXTY-ONE

Wednesday, July 18th, 1984
Slidell, Louisiana

Gabriel sat back on the bed. *Heidi Gesche, I presume this is your room. Why is your door locked? Why are your windows nailed shut? What happened to you? Why does everything in the room seem to be frozen in time?*

Gabriel tried once again to remember what had led to all of this. *There was something, just on the edge of my consciousness. Almost there. Just when I think I have it, it dissolves away like waking from a dream.* He lay his head on the pillow.

"Hey, c'mon! Let me out," Gabriel called, banging loudly on the door. *If someone wanted me dead, then why not just kill me in the alley. And that girl, the blonde, was she part of the deal? I feel like I've been drugged. If I want to get out of here, I need to think. But who would have done this? Baxter, Reznikov? If I couldn't testify there would still be Arnie,*

Rachel, and Ben. And they have Nantois. So why kidnap me? Unless it's to send a message to the others. Maybe I'm being used as leverage.

I'm not even sure how long I've been out because I lost my watch. He walked around the bedroom and looked out the window again. *If I had to, I could break it. I could put that night table right through it. My God, Jacqueline! If this is Tuesday, or even worse, Wednesday, you must be frantic. I bet you've already called the FBI, the Governor, asked for the National Guard. I have to get out of here and get word to everyone that I'm okay. Maybe Ben can help me figure out what happened.* He continued to pace the room and stopped in front of the life-size Chewbacca. *Why here? Why keep me locked in a little girl's room? Why go to the trouble of dressing me in this nightie? I'm going to give them one more chance; then I'm going to smash that window.*

He went to the bedroom door and starting banging his fists against it. "Come on. I need help here. The toilet is overflowing; if you don't let me out of here, there's going to be a mess. I'm going to put Abba on the record player, full blast!" He had just about given up when he heard some shuffling on the other side of the door. *Someone was coming.* He frantically looked around for something to use as a weapon. As he heard the deadbolt turn, he grabbed a toy lightsaber from a shelf.

CHAPTER SIXTY-TWO

Wednesday, July 18th, 1984
Slidell, Louisiana

The door opened slowly, revealing a large woman wearing a print dress holding a toilet plunger. There was an awkward moment as she stared down Gabriel and his lightsaber. Finally, she smiled, "I see you're up. Do you drink coffee?"

Gabriel stared at the lady who looked like she was in her sixties. He nodded slowly, unsure of what was happening.

"There's another washroom down the hall on the right. I will put some coffee on." Gabriel inched past the lady, who was at least a foot taller than him. "I hope you are in better shape than you were on Monday night." The woman had an accent. Her words were clipped, precise.

What the hell is this? I've read stories about older women kidnapping younger men to be sex slaves. In the bathroom, he tried the window and found that like the others, it was nailed shut. He splashed some water on his face and looked at himself in the mirror. He now looked like a zombie with a wet face. The headache had returned and was pounding like a bass drum.

Gabriel left the washroom and followed the smell of coffee to the kitchen.

The woman had her back towards him and was using a ladle to put something into a soup bowl. "Hope you like oatmeal?" she turned around to face him. She had wispy white hair, barely enough to cover her scalp.

He looked around the kitchen and noticed a cuckoo clock showing the time as 8:50. "What am I doing here, and why was the door locked? Why are the windows nailed shut?" He tried to keep his tone non-confrontational but failed. He sat down at the table and put the lightsaber down.

She smiled, "It is okay Mr., 'whatever your name is', I am not a Klingon."

"That's *Star Trek*."

She put a bowl of oatmeal in front of him along with a cup of coffee. "*Star Trek*, *Star Wars*, what is the difference?"

"What am I doing here? Why was the door locked?"

"First, introductions are appropriate, no?" she sat down across from him. "My name is Esther Gesche. As for why you are sitting in my kitchen, eating my oatmeal, I found you on the street. You were bedrunken as we say in the old country. I almost ran over you. I thought you were going to lie down in the middle of the street, so I brought you here."

"And why did you lock me in? Who hired you to kidnap me?"

"I locked you in because you were raving mad. All the way here you were trying to open the car door and walk out of the moving car. You were shouting about pink cars and someone named Wackolyn. I was worried you would hurt yourself."

"Jacqueline," he corrected. "My wife."

"And you are? You had no wallet or identification."

"Gabriel Ross. Someone drugged me," Gabriel said, taking a sip of black coffee and looking around. They were in an old-fashioned farmhouse kitchen. Linen tablecloth, old-fashioned china. "So you're saying, you're just a good samaritan?"

"Yes, samaritan. This is correct. I couldn't leave you there. It was late."

"What day is it?"

"It is Wednesday, July 18. Coincidentally the government raised the drinking age from 18 to 21 yesterday. You are 21, aren't you? It is hard to tell with that nightie." She smiled. Gabriel looked down at his clothes and gave her a doubtful look. "Your clothes were soaking wet and smelled terrible. I laundered them for you."

He finished his coffee and took a tentative bite of oatmeal. "Why were you in Slidell in the middle of the night?"

"Why were you?" she countered.

"I was working. I'm a private detective and was following someone."

"A private detective?" she repeated. "Do you think that this person put something in your drink?"

"Maybe, I don't know. I can't remember everything."

"Ach, nee! And then this person stole your wallet, and left you in that alley?"

"I don't know. Now your turn, why were you out so late at night?"

The woman hesitated for a moment, a look of sadness washing across her face. "I sometimes have a problem sleeping. When my daughter was little, she would cry, and we would take her for a drive until she fell asleep. So now, when I can't sleep, I drive. It relaxes me."

"You said we."

"My husband Erich passed a few years ago."

"I'm sorry, Mrs. Gesche. How did he die?"

It took a few moments for her to find the words. "Heart attack, working in our garden. It is what he enjoyed the most in the world. Except..."

Gabriel allowed the silence to sink in for a few moments before asking, "Except what, Mrs. Gesche, what else did he like?"

"Our daughter," she said, getting up and turning towards the sink.

"Heidi? That's who sleeps in that room?" At the mention of the name, the woman turned to face him. Her eyebrows were raised and mouth open. "I saw her name in her textbooks. Heidi. There's also a picture of her. She is very pretty."

Mrs. Gesche nodded, "She liked Barbies, Star Wars, the things that all kids like these days, I suppose."

She spoke of her daughter in the past tense. The sadness returned to her face.

"I was confused when looking at her stuff and the decorations in the room. I thought she was a teenage girl. But based on the date in her textbook, she would be in her twenties now. Is she away at college?"

"Mr. Ross, perhaps you would like to shower? Then, I can drive you back to town."

"Thank you, Mrs. Gesche, and thank you for last night. Would you have a phone I can use? Jacqueline must be very upset."

CHAPTER SIXTY-THREE

Thursday, July 19th, 1984
Slidell, Louisiana

"Oh my Lord, it's Gabriel!" Chevon answered the phone. "My Lord, Gabriel. It's Gabriel. Are you okay? Where are you? We're all worried sick about you." Without waiting for an answer, she added, "I'll put you on the speakerphone, so everyone can hear."

"Who's there?" Gabriel's voice over the speaker sounded weak.

"It's Ben. I'm glad to hear your voice partner. Jackie is here, too; she's been helping with the search."

"Gabriel, where are you? I'll come and get you." Jacqueline was half crying, half laughing with joy.

"I don't know. This lady, Esther Gesche, she lives in the country. She found me wandering the streets and brought me to her farmhouse. She probably saved my life. Someone drugged me. It might have been a blonde."

"The bartender said she was all over you," Jacqueline said, her tone hardening.

"Well, that's not totally correct," replied Gabriel with a touch of uncertainty.

"How correct is it?"

"Not at all. You know I wouldn't ever...I'm sorry Jacqueline, I don't really remember what happened. You sound upset."

"Very upset."

"I hate that you were worried."

"Very worried."

Ben jumped in. "Rutledge and I interviewed a woman named Brenda. It wasn't her. We discovered that someone paid the bartender to slip something into your drink."

"Why would someone do that?"

"We don't know yet. Rutledge just handed me a note. There's an Esther Gesche who lives off Highway 11. Hang in there, Gabriel; we're coming to get you."

Esther nodded again and said, "Your clothes should be dry. I will take them down off the line, while you shower."

"I would like to be able to repay you for your kindness."

"It was nothing. Go now. Your friends can't see you wearing that nightie. I will put your clothes by the door."

While Gabriel was showering, he thought of the lost expression he'd seen on Esther's face. Something bad had happened to Heidi when she was fifteen. Maybe there'd been an accident, or she'd gotten sick. Once out of the shower, he retrieved his clean clothes and got dressed. He found Esther at the kitchen table, reading the local newspaper.

"Thanks again for everything, Mrs. Gesche."

"Please call me Esther, and it was my good deed for the day. There are many bad things in the world. I try to do something for someone every day. I help out at the local church most days. I do what I can." She stood and went to the window as they heard the sound of a truck coming up the lane. They waited in silence, hearing the sound of car doors slamming. When they heard footsteps on the porch, she went opened the door.

"You must be Mrs. Gesche," Gabriel heard Ben say. He got up and went to the door. As soon as he made eye contact with Jacqueline, his wife pushed past Mrs. Gesche to embrace him.

"Oh my God Gabriel, I have never prayed so much for anything, as I prayed for you."

"Why don't we all sit down in the kitchen?" asked Mrs. Gesche. "I have coffee and some cherry strudel. I am sure you must have questions."

When Jacqueline stopped crying, they sat down around the kitchen table. Gabriel made introductions and started by telling everyone about the meeting with Lana Tadic, and her hiring the agency to surveil her husband, Petr.

"Actually, we found out that her real name is Lana Gadzinga." Ben picked the story up from there, explaining how Rutledge had discovered that Lana had made up the story and that everything she'd said was bogus.

"She said all that just to get me alone so they could drug me? Why?"

"We don't know that yet." Jacquelin took a bite of strudel and complimented Mrs. Gesche.

"And the bartender drugged me? Why would someone pay him to do that?"

"We're not one hundred percent on that either. There might be people who want to get back at you. Apparently, a man paid the bartender to put something in your drink. He said it was because you stole someone's girlfriend," said Ben.

"The woman in the bar gave you a matchbook with her name and number. She wanted you to call her," said Jacqueline.

"I don't remember that."

"We found the matchbook in the alley," explained Ben. "Rutledge and I traced the number and went out to see her. We both felt she was legit. I think it was just a case of a woman wanting to make friends."

"What happened in that bar, Gabriel?" Jacqueline moved her chair closer.

Gabriel let out a sigh and tried to remember. "She bought me a drink; then I bought her one. That's when I noticed that Petr Tadic had left. I tried to stand up, but I felt dizzy. Like everything was out of sync. I was sweating and needed fresh air. I threw the bartender the cash from my wallet and stumbled out of there. I don't remember much after that. There's something about a cat, an alley and then someone hit me. I remember hearing a siren, wondering if they were coming to arrest me for public drunkenness. I fell asleep, or I passed out. When I woke, it was raining. I was really confused. My mind kept bouncing around from one thought to another. I tried to stand up, but it was like I was paralyzed. Nothing made sense. And I was really, really tired. I must have fallen asleep. When I woke up the second time, it was pitch black, and someone was going through my pockets looking at my wallet. He kept saying something to me, but it wasn't registering. I tried to say something, but couldn't."

Ben jumped in, "I believe that person is Jerome Pichette. He's in custody at the Sheriff's Department. He was caught using your Visa card to buy a bottle of bourbon. He said you asked him to because you were too drunk."

"I wasn't able to move my lips, let alone ask for anything."

"He said you gave him your watch as payment for getting the booze."

Gabriel just shook his head. "I was wondering what happened to my watch. At one point, I remember him lying on top of me." Gabriel looked over at Esther. "Maybe you can take it from there."

Esther sat back in her chair before she spoke. "I sometimes like to drive at night. It relaxes me. I saw a boy on the street and almost hit him. He was wandering around in circles like a spinning top. Then he just lay on the ground in the middle of the road. I was scared that someone would run over him. I picked him up. He does not weigh much, so I put him in my truck. He was raving about pink cars. I put him into a spare bedroom and looked in on him. He slept pretty much all day Tuesday and then for most of today. He finally woke up about an hour ago threatening me with a toy lightsaber.

Everyone laughed, then Gabriel said, "Why would someone go to all this trouble? All I can come up with is that Reznikov or Baxter thought that abducting me would send a message to anyone else thinking of testifying."

"Hollis Huntley is dead," said Ben. "Someone threw him off a tall building, and Kane Nantois was stabbed to death in the prison showers."

Gabriel let out a groan. "That's it. They're getting rid of people before they testify against them."

"That's possible. I met with Baxter today, and I don't think he's responsible. As for Reznikov, I think if he was behind it, you'd be dead. He wouldn't mess around with kidnapping."

Jacqueline gave Ben a look before explaining about Jessica Grant and the postcards her parents had been receiving.

"What? Charles Bouvier is alive? That can't be possible."

Gabriel got up from the table and looked back and forth between Ben and Jacqueline.

"It is. We have Rachel and Arnie keeping a close watch on Jessica," replied Jacqueline.

"I can't believe it." Gabriel shook his head. He turned to Esther, "Have you heard about the Mardi Gras Killer?"

"Yes, in the newspapers."

"We have to find him," said Gabriel. "Wil Graham helped last time, remember Ben?"

"I remember. Wil has retired and is off traveling the world, but I did speak to Dr. Baylis. He said that Charles Bouvier always used other people to make the abductions. He said he'd try to get the new director involved, but they'd need to be invited by the locals, and according to Rachel they don't seem to be very interested because there are no girls missing."

Gabriel looked at Esther and saw the sad look return to her face, her eyes tearing up. "Esther, are you alright?"

"You asked about my Heidi; she disappeared 4 years ago. At first, we thought someone had taken her."

Jacqueline got up and put an arm around the woman. "Esther, my husband is very good at his job. He finds people."

"I don't have money to pay for a detective." Esther wiped her eyes with a tissue.

Gabriel got up, and together with Jacqueline, they led her back to the table. "Don't worry about that, Esther. I'll work this on my own time. What can you tell us about Heidi?"

CHAPTER SIXTY-FOUR

Wednesday, July 18th, 1984
Slidell, Louisiana

"Heidi was a very good student at the local high school. Erich, my late husband, had his hours cut at the insurance company, and money was always tight. There is an all-night convenience store just on the outskirts of town. She put her name in for a job. They needed people to work night shifts and weekends. Some in the town, and in our church, felt it was wrong to have people work all hours of the night and on the Sabbath. We tried to talk Heidi out of it. There was a big argument. Erich and Heidi," Esther rolled her eyes and shook her head. "They were both so stubborn. Me too, I guess. She wanted to go to college, and she knew it was beyond our means."

Esther stood up and went to the window before continuing. "I'd drive her to work, and Erich would pick her up at the end of her shift. One night when he got to the store, he found it empty. He knew right away that something was wrong. The lights were on, the front door unlocked, but there was no staff. He called the sheriff, who contacted the owner of the store. The man came down right away and waited with Erich."

"Did they have her working alone?" asked Jacqueline.

"There was a man, a boy, really, not much older than Heidi. He was supposed to be working with her. He arrived at the store with his infant son when the sheriff was there. He said his wife was working, and the sitter had called in sick."

"He'd left Heidi alone in the store?" asked Ben.

"He said it was less than an hour, but Erich didn't believe him."

"What kind of investigation did the sheriff conduct?" asked Gabriel.

"He came out and asked us if Heidi was the type to run away. He asked whether she was a loose girl. This made Erich angry. I said no, she was very driven to make a good life for herself. I heard that the sheriff talked to the people at her school, to Heidi's friends, the pastor at the church."

"Did Heidi have lots of friends?" Gabriel asked.

"I suppose. She was a normal child. She went to dances, played volleyball. She was not a troubled teen."

"Did she have a boyfriend?" asked Ben.

"No. She was a pretty girl, but we did not want her to get involved in that nonsense."

Gabriel thought about Heidi's room and how it had seemed frozen in time. *Were they the ones clinging to her childhood?* "Tell me about Erich."

"Erich and I came from Germany after the Berlin crisis in 1961. We settled in Slidell because he had family. The Croatian side of his family was living in New Orleans. Erich was a God-fearing man who worked hard to provide for his family. He was trained as a bookkeeper but didn't enjoy the work. He always wanted a big family, but we were not able to have more than Heidi. He was so proud of her, but some people have problems expressing their emotions. Heidi's disappearance hurt us. Erich blamed himself and was never the same. He hounded the sheriff up until the day he had his heart attack out in the garden."

"You said at first you thought she was abducted, what changed your mind?" asked Ben.

Esther got up from the table and went to a shelf above the stove and returned with an envelope. The envelope was addressed to Mrs. Esther Gesche and was postmarked from New Orleans with no return address. "A month after Erich passed, I received this," she said, handing the envelope to Ben.

Inside was a pink sheet of paper which Ben read out loud. "'Mom, I'm sorry. Thinking of you.". He commented, "There's no signature or explanation. It's written in blue ink, and the handwriting is flowery." He returned the letter to Esther. "Is this Heidi's handwriting?"

"I don't know. Somedays, I think yes other days ...I don't know. I want to believe that she is alive." Ben waited for Mrs. Gesche to continue. "When the sheriff saw the letter, he said that it went with what he believed all along. Heidi had run away."

"If she ran away, she likely wasn't alone. Did the sheriff have any theories?"

"Before the letter came, everyone, including the sheriff, thought something bad had happened. Other employees started receiving phone calls at the store, threatening them, suggesting that they might end up like Heidi. The sheriff put a tap on the store's phone, but nothing ever came of it. When Erich asked about the wiretaps, he was told they were just crackpots who didn't like having a store open those hours."

"We'd like to take a look in her bedroom again if you don't mind."

"Go ahead, you know where it is."

"This is where I woke up." Gabriel pointed to the Barbie bed.

"Now I know what to get you for your birthday," said Jacqueline.

"I don't know, this whole pink thing seems to be following you." Ben picked up the Barbie nightie and winked at Gabriel.

"Hardy-har-har, check this out, here's a picture of Heidi." Gabriel showed them the photograph.

"Beautiful girl," said Jacqueline.

Ben was looking through the sketchbook. "She's a pretty good artist."

Gabriel noticed a sketch of a boy and pointed to it. It showed a young man posing for a portrait. He had dark hair and an impish grin. Despite how good the sketch was, someone had put a big X across the face. He stared at it for a few moments before asking Ben if he recognized the picture.

"I remember seeing a picture in the papers when they were covering the Mardi Gras killer, are you thinking that this is an early sketch of Charles Bouvier?"

Gabriel shrugged his shoulders, looking again at the drawing in Ben's hands. "I wonder if Mrs. Gesche would be able to recognize it."

As soon as he said this, Mrs. Gesche walked into the bedroom and looked at the photo that Jacqueline was holding. "That was taken when she was in Grade 10."

"Can we borrow this?" Gabriel took the photo from Jacqueline.

"Of course. When I came in, you were saying something about a sketch?"

Ben, who was still holding the sketch pad, showed her the drawing of the boy. When she shook her head, Ben asked if they could borrow the sketchpad as well.

Mrs. Gesche nodded. "As long as you return everything to me. It is all that I have."

CHAPTER SIXTY-FIVE

Friday, July 20th, 1984
New Orleans, Louisiana

Ben dropped Gabriel and Jacqueline in downtown Slidell so they could retrieve his VW Bug. Jacqueline drove the car home while Gabriel slept on the way. "That poor woman," she said when Gabriel woke up. "Do you think Heidi was taken by the Mardi Gras Killer?"

"Anything is possible, but after seeing that picture, she wasn't his type."

"Maybe this was before his fixation on blondes." Jacqueline looked over at Gabriel, who was resting his head on the side window.

"Do you think she's dead?"

"I don't know. I'm not sure a letter with a few words proves anything. I guess it gives her hope."

"I saw a postcard. One that Bouvier sent to Jessica - it had eight children all wearing creepy Mardi Gras outfits. On the back, he wrote something about Jessica joining the group."

"There were only six girls abducted."

"Which might mean there could be a couple of others."

"It's great to be home," Gabriel sighed as Jacqueline pulled into their laneway. "Aren't we going to get Benjamin?"

"It's late, let's get you into bed, and I'll pick him up in the morning."

"I'm too tired to argue."

"I wonder what happened?" asked Jacqueline as she helped her husband to the door. "I hate to think of what might have happened had Mrs. Gesche not brought you home."

"I don't know. Maybe they were interrupted."

"What's to stop them from trying again? Bouvier is offering money for them to abduct you."

"I'll stay away from blonde women in bars," Gabriel answered as they opened the front door.

"Seriously, Gabriel!" Jacqueline exclaimed, following him in. "What are you going to do to make sure they don't try it again?"

"I don't know. I'm still a little fuzzy. I hadn't considered that they would try again."

"Maybe it's time for you to take a trip? Like I did after Boone Cooper tried to bury me alive."

"Jacqueline, think this through. If we're right about all this, then this lunatic wants to hurt me. He wants to exact his revenge. If I left, he might figure out the best way to hurt me is to come after you or Benjamin. No, what I have to do now is find him."

"So how are you going to do that?"

"I don't know, let me sleep on it. But I promise I'll get him this time."

CHAPTER SIXTY-SIX

Friday, July 20th, 1984
Slidell, Louisiana

Gabriel slept in the following day and woke up feeling much better. His late-night promise to his wife still rang in his mind, and over the objections of both Jacqueline and Benjamin, he headed out to meet Ben at the sheriff's office in Slidell.

Sheriff Hardie came out of his office when he heard Ben's voice at the reception desk. "Ben O'Shea," he extended his hand. "How did you make out with Father Wilborg?" Hardie asked, before noticing a short man stepping out from behind Ben.

"Sheriff Hardie, I'd like to introduce my partner, Gabriel Ross."

The sheriff and Gabriel shook hands, and Ben said, "We

have quite the story to tell you, can we go somewhere and talk?"

Ben and Gabriel followed the tall sheriff into his office. "I wanted to thank you for your help, Sheriff," said Gabriel once they were all seated.

"What can you tell me?" asked Hardie.

Ben and Gabriel took turns, filling him in on the abduction, and the rescue by Esther Gesche.

"I know Esther. She is a fine woman and has been through a lot in her life. It won't take long for the word to get out about this. She's a hero."

"I owe her my life."

"Should I be sending a deputy to pick up the bartender?"

"I suppose, but I'd be inclined to wait on that," said Ben. "My associate Rutledge was pretty hard on him. He claims not to know who was behind it. We'd like to watch him for a day or two, just in case."

"What about Jerome? Should I be charging him with attempted fraud, or cutting him loose?"

"It's your call, Sheriff. Gabriel would like to get his wallet and watch back, though."

"Sure. That's no problem. I'm not sure how Jerome will feel about being released. He's been enjoying the hospitality." Hardie got up and left the office, returning a few minutes later with Gabriel's property.

"There's one thing you could help me with," said Ben. "It involves something that happened here four years ago."

"Heidi Gesche." Sheriff Hardie resumed his seat.

Ben nodded. "Mrs. Gesche told us a little bit, but I wanted your take."

Hardie took a moment to organize his thoughts. "Folks around here are not likely ever going to forget it. Heidi was 16 and a smart kid. I took a personal interest in the case and spoke to a lot of people. But," he said regretfully, "it looked like she ran away. Heidi had a tough relationship with her father."

Gabriel recalled Star running off to a commune because of her father.

Ben interrupted his thoughts. "Originally you thought she was abducted, right?"

"I thought that for a while. Mainly on account of the phone calls. There were some prank calls after Heidi disappeared. We traced the calls back to payphones around town. I listened to them, and it was the same voice on all the calls. Because the caller used the word Sabbath, I brought a collection of ministers, rabbis, and priests, to the station to listen to the recordings. The priest over at *Our Lady of Perpetual Help* recognized the man's voice."

"We took a drive out and talked to him. His name is Dechesne. Of course, he denied making the calls. It turned out he had an alibi for the night of the disappearance. He drove a truck and was out of town. I still think he made the calls though. On the way back from visiting him, the priest said something that put things in perspective for me."

"What was that?" asked Ben.

"He said that what motivates good people to make calls like that is their belief that they are doing God's work. But abducting a young girl and doing whatever to her, is a whole different motivation. A totally different person."

Ben nodded, "Did you ever have anything solid?"

"We looked at one of the store employees where Heidi worked. I imagine Esther told you that. Eric Gesche was adamant that this boy that worked at the store knew more than he was saying. The kid, his name is Hendricks, ended up moving to Harvey. We checked out the story with his wife and babysitter. Hendricks might have been away longer than he said, but there was nothing in his past to suggest that he was capable of this. We had him in, did a polygraph on him, and he passed, so I had to let him go."

There was a pause in the conversation. Hardie asked, "How did you make out with Father Wilborg?"

"He doesn't remember the LeGrand boy, but he definitely remembers Charles Bouvier and his time in Slidell. Since we know that Edna LeGrand inherited Bouvier's estate, I'm going to say that the boy your caretaker remembers living with LeGrand was Charles Bouvier."

"You don't think that The Mardi Gras Killer had anything to do with Heidi's disappearance?"

Ben shrugged his shoulders.

"This was four years ago. At that time, there was no talk about the Mardi Gras Killer."

Gabriel pulled Heidi's sketchbook out of his briefcase and asked the Sheriff if he recognized any of the drawings.

Hardie went through each page before shaking his head and saying, "Nothing stands out, but that doesn't necessarily mean anything. Is there a reason this picture has a big X through it?"

"We wondered the same thing," said Gabriel, "Mrs. Gesche didn't know."

Hardie got up and went to a file cabinet, pulling out a thick manila folder. "I still keep the file handy." He sat down at his desk and started looking through the folder. After a couple of minutes, he looked up. "One of Heidi's friends told me that Esther and Eric Gesche wouldn't permit their daughter to date anyone, but she thought Heidi had a crush on an older boy."

"Did you ever show this sketch to Heidi's friend? See if she recognized the person?"

The sheriff let out a sigh and shook his head. "I don't

remember seeing this. The picture you see in the newspapers of Charles Bouvier is an early high school yearbook photo. I suppose it could be him. Let me run it by my janitor; see if he recognizes it."

"Good. When I was on the job, I used to get a gut feeling about a case. Did you ever think that it was someone from outside the community?" Ben asked.

"Of course, that was the consensus opinion amongst the deputies and most of the town. It's easier in a small town to think that it couldn't be one of their own. For me though, I always thought the creep was from here."

"Why's that?"

"You probably didn't realize it, but every window in Mrs. Gesche's home is nailed shut. Erich did that because Heidi woke up one night and found someone trying to get into her bedroom. She screamed, and her father came running. Whoever it was got away through the cornfields."

"When was this?" Ben leaned forward.

"Three weeks before she disappeared."

Ben shared a look with Gabriel. "One other thing, one of our associates in Gulfport interviewed a man yesterday about this case. His name is Joe Jager. He mentioned that his nephew died while riding his bike to school."

Hardie got up and pulled another file before sitting down. "I remember. Keith Jager. Our investigation concluded it was a hit and run. Probably a drunk driver."

"Any potential suspects?"

"No witnesses. The body wasn't found for two days. Whoever hit him must have been going pretty fast. We found the body a good ten feet from the road."

CHAPTER SIXTY-SEVEN

Friday, July 20th, 1984
Slidell, Louisiana

On the way back to the agency, Ben asked Gabriel whether he'd gotten any sleep the night before.

"This has been a whirlwind, and I was still feeling the effects last night. Jacqueline gave me something to help me sleep."

Ben nodded. "Travis Franklin read something in the newspaper about the Mardi Gras Killer, and when he found out that you were missing, he dropped everything and came to the agency to help. He's the one that suggested we follow the money."

Gabriel nodded as if he understood, but then asked, "What money?"

Ben told Gabriel about Travis' idea, as well as the subsequent meeting with Rod Smith. "Aunt Edna inherited over a million dollars. The theory is that if we find Aunt Edna and the money, we'll find Bouvier."

"I get it. You said she lived in Slidell. Did she move?"

"She disappeared shortly after getting the money." Ben explained about Sheriff Hardie receiving a card from Texas. "My thought is that somehow Bouvier reclaimed his money, got rid of his aunt, and sent the card to make the sheriff believe that she'd moved away. Rachel said he used the same trick when a Coast Guard Captain suddenly disappeared."

Gabriel shook his head, wondering if the killer had written the letter to Esther. "Is there any doubt that if Esther Gesche hadn't have come along, I'd be dead?"

When Ben and Gabriel walked into the agency, they found Rutledge finishing a meeting with a woman at his desk. When she'd left, Gabriel told him, "If that's an infidelity case, you'd better take it."

"I owe you one. She works at an insurance company and saw your interview. She was just in to check out our services." As the three men sat down, Rutledge continued. "On my way in this morning, I stopped by Aunt Edna's. The place is empty, and the mail has started to pile up."

"Anything interesting?" asked Ben.

"She has one of those letter-drops in the door, but I could see all the mail through the slot."

"If she inherited that much money, she would have received a check and have to deal with a bank," said Ben. "We need to go to the banks and find who she deals with. We might need to get the sheriff to get a court order. There can't be that many banks in Slidell."

"There's at least a couple of dozen. If you include the S&Ls and credit unions," replied Rutledge. Ben groaned, but Rutledge said, "I might be able to narrow down the search." Gabriel and Ben waited for the black man to continue.

"When I was there this morning, I thought I smelled something bad coming from the house." Rutledge gave an exaggerated wink. "I thought what if Bouvier's in there, or if the old lady was in there and hurt somehow...or maybe dead? I suppose I should have called the cops, but geez what if she needed an ambulance? So I picked the lock on the door and had a quick look. I happened to notice that she had mail from the Bank of Louisiana on Pontchartrain."

Ben and Rutledge thought the situation at the bank called for ex-cops with bogus identification, so Gabriel stayed back and called Rachel. She answered on the second ring, "Jacqueline called last night and filled us in. Gabriel, I'm so happy that that woman picked you up. We were all worried."

"Thanks for all you've done, Rachel. I'm okay. Well, my head is still a little stuffy. Ben and Rutledge are following up on a lead, so I hope we'll get this guy soon."

"Until we do, Star is going to stay with me. She's out with Arnie today. They went to visit her parents to bring them up to date."

"Ben told me about Keith Jager. That was good detective work."

"Thanks, boss, I've learned from the best."

"So, you're back together with Mangina?"

"Let me check the time. Apparently, the name is Kittyburg, but he was playing with Bourbon when he came up with that one. I'm not sure of anything with him. After we met with Jager, Don threw a little hissy fit about me taking the lead in questioning people. He left again in a huff."

"Maybe it just wasn't meant to be."

Ben and Rutledge flashed their expired credentials at a middle-aged woman and asked to speak to the bank manager. After a short wait, they were greeted by a tall, dark-haired man.

"Hello, my name is Boris Fedorov. I understand you're from police. How can we be of assistance?"

"Is there somewhere private we can go to discuss this? It involves Edna LeGrand. One of your customers."

"Come into office. I should tell you, I am embarrassed to say that I do not know this woman. I know she has account but not much more. I believe the account was opened while I was at meeting. We've been trying to get in touch with her, but apparently, she has no phone and hasn't answered any of our letters."

They followed Fedorov into a spacious office. Once everyone was sitting down, Ben asked for a glass of water. Fedorov left the office, and Rutledge went to work attaching a listening device to the phone. A few minutes later, Fedorov returned with the water and asked how he could help.

"I believe Mrs. LeGrand and the bank might have been the victims of fraud," replied Rutledge.

Fedorov's expression didn't change. "Please explain."

"We were hoping, Mr. Fedorov, that you would agree to let us see the activity on her account. We know that she received a very large check."

"You have court order?"

"No, but we can get one for you. If you would like to call Sheriff Hardie, he's aware of this. We're working against the clock to minimize the amount of the fraud," replied Ben.

They could almost hear the wheels turning. "Let me get a copy of statement." Fedorov left the room again, returning a few minutes later. "The account was opened last summer with deposit of one million dollars. A withdrawal of $200,000 was made. Over next few months ,she cashed checks on the account. Balance is little over $300,000."

"Could we see these checks?" asked Rutledge.

"Gentlemen, we always compare the signatures against the documents signed at account opening."

"We'd still like to see them," Rutledge repeated.

There was a moment of silence punctuated by a staring contest. "I'm sorry, I don't understand gentleman, has Mrs. LeGrand filed a complaint?"

Rutledge looked at his watch and turned to Ben. "Maybe we should go see Sheriff Hardie and get that court order."

"That will not be necessary gentlemen, I will get you some checks, and you will see that the signatures are fine. But before that, maybe I call my customer and ask permission? Can you wait outside?"

When they sat down in the waiting area, Rutledge leaned over and whispered, "That's a lot of checks."

After about five minutes, Fedorov waved them back to the office and said he'd been unable to reach Mrs. LeGrand. He then put five checks and a signed account agreement on the desk.

Ben and Rutledge compared the signatures. The signature on the checks was very shaky but appeared to match the signature card. Rutledge took the checks and the signature card and turned them upside down on the desk. "This is an old trick to spot forgeries," he said, leaning forward. After a few minutes, he sat back. "Not bad forgeries, but you can tell by the loop in the 'L' and the shape of the 'D.' These were signed by a different person." The smile faded from Fedorov's face.

Ben spoke up for the first time, "Mr. Fedorov, these checks are made out to cash, isn't that unusual?"

Boris ignored Ben's question and picked up a check. "This looks fine, but since you are concerned, I will notify our security people. They will no doubt want to speak to you and the customer. As for your question, it might simply mean the customer wanted cash."

CHAPTER SIXTY-EIGHT

Friday, July 20th, 1984
New Orleans, Louisiana

Ben and Rutledge walked back into the agency and found Don McRae, the NOPD policeman, waiting for them. Gabriel was chatting with him over coffee.

"Glad you're here, Ben. Gabriel was just filling me in on his ordeal. Any progress on finding this guy?"

"We're working it. We just got a good lead at the bank." Ben filled Don and Gabriel in on what they'd learned.

Don paused before staring seriously at Ben. "I have something I think you should see. We'll have to take a short drive." He looked down at Ben's shoes. "I don't suppose you brought your rubber boots today?"

"The bayou again?" Ben frowned.

"Yep."

"I had to throw those Italian loafers out last time."

Ben and Gabriel left Rutledge to man the Agency as they followed McRae's Jeep to the Irish Bayou. A couple of police cruisers and a medical examiner van were parked along the side of the road.

"This should be interesting. I've never been to the bayou." Gabriel got out of the truck.

Ben laughed. "It might be interesting if it wasn't for the mud, the snakes, and mosquitoes the size of vampires bats." He gestured that they should get in Don's Jeep. "The less we have to walk in the mud, the better."

As they drove together into the bayou, Ben asked, "What did you find, Don?"

"I couldn't begin to describe it, Ben; you guys will have to check it out for yourself."

The trail led to a small pond with stagnant, brackish water. Partial trunks of cypress trees sat in the bog, their branches reaching upwards out of the swamp like hands. There were a couple of uniformed cops pulling debris from the swamp. Gabriel smelled the earthy-wet smell of the bayou when they got out of the Jeep and were immediately swarmed by giant dive-bombing mosquitoes.

Don led them to where a man with a long, straggly gray beard was looking at something in a steamer trunk. Don whispered that he was the County Medical Examiner. Ben nodded the M.E. while brushing flies from his face.

"Last time we were here, Ben," said Don, "You asked about what else might have been dumped here. I've had a team of volunteers looking. One of them almost had a coronary when they fished this trunk out and looked inside."

Ben looked at the open trunk and was immediately repulsed. Inside was a mangled corpse of an old lady. The expression on her face was one of horror, with her head turned to an unnatural angle. Her legs had also been broken to fit her into the trunk. Gabriel, peeking from behind Ben, took a look and started to gag. "Aunt Edna," said Ben under his breath.

"Do you know this woman?" The M.E. stood up and made a note on a clipboard.

"Not really, but there's an old woman, Edna LeGrand, she's a person of interest. I'd say we found her," said Ben. "Any markings on the trunk?"

The M.E. shook his head and then gestured to Gabriel to come nearer. "Come here, young man. I want to show you something." Gabriel reluctantly approached. "You see the lines around the mouth? She wore dentures, but you can tell by the lines she wasn't wearing them when she died." Ben thought Gabriel was going to throw up and handed him a handkerchief. "You see what I mean?" asked the coroner.

"No, I don't see anything." Gabriel, spoke from behind the handkerchief, not looking.

The bearded M.E. shook his head and looked at Ben. "I don't know why they have these 'bring your kid to work days.'"

"Do you have any idea how long she's been in the trunk?" Ben swatted a fly away from his face.

The M.E. gave Ben a tired look, "I reckon for about as long as she's been dead."

"Well, of course, but can you pinpoint when she died?"

The M.E. looked down at his clipboard and seemed to be making a calculation. A couple of flies had flown into his beard and were slowly crawling around. "Months, maybe a year, we'll be able to be more precise when we get her to the morgue. There's been some decomposition, but the body is in remarkably good condition. You see, the trunk acted like a coffin. Notice the look of horror on her face? The acidic nature of the water that crept into the trunk helped to preserve much of the body."

Don dropped Gabriel and Ben off at their vehicle. "So let's assume that the body in the trunk is who you think it is, what's your next step?"

"If it is Edna LeGrand, she been writing a lot of checks," replied Ben.

CHAPTER SIXTY-NINE

Friday, July 20th, 1984
Gulfport, Mississippi

Back at the Agency, Ben and Gabriel offered to get coffee. When they returned, Ben asked Rutledge if he'd listened to it. He explained to Gabriel, "Rutledge bugged the banker's phone. I had the receiver attached to a recorder in my truck."

"You called it," said Rutledge. "He made two calls, one when we were waiting outside his office and another about ten seconds after we left. You'll want to listen to them yourself." Gabriel and Ben sat down across from Rutledge's desk, and Ben nodded for him to play the tape.

"This is Boris; we have problem." They could hear a jukebox playing country rock in the background.

"Yeah, what?" Another man said.

"Policemen come to office asking questions about checks."

"Who were these policemen?"

"I don't know, one black, one white." There was a minute

or so of dialogue in a foreign language, followed by some nervous laughter.

They resumed speaking in English, and the other man asked, "Did they have a court order?" The voice sounded foreign, the tone demanding.

"No paper. They say checks are phony. You said, no one make trouble."

"Are they still there?"

"Waiting area."

"Show them the checks. Maybe they'll go away." The call ended, and Rutledge paused the tape.

"Sounds Russian," Gabriel said.

"The bank manager we met with was Boris Fedorov. Can't get more Russian than that." Ben recounted what they'd learned by looking at the bank statement.

"Wait until you hear the second call." Rutledge pressed play once again.

"We still have problem. Black cop says check no good. I told him they were fine, that I would contact our security people and speak to customer."

"So, they left?"

"Yes."

"You did good, Boris," said the other voice. "If they come back, you don't know anything."

"I don't know anything." Fedorov sounded indignant. Like he should know something.

"Listen, Boris, stay in the dark. You were paid to negotiate those checks. If they come back with a court order, tell them that you can't find anything. Maybe you had a fire in the back room. Got it?"

Rutledge stopped the recording. "If we'd gotten a court order then we could use the tape to sweat Boris. He might be willing to give up whoever is behind all this."

"That might have worked," agreed Ben. "But even if we got the court order, he likely wouldn't cooperate. I'm sure he knows what the Russian mob does to cooperating witnesses."

"Can we trace the call through the phone company, find out who he called?" asked Gabriel.

"Already done," said Rutledge. "It pays to have connections. It's a pay phone at a local bar down on the strip called Boogie's. I think it's a country and western bar with a tough crowd."

"Why don't I check it out tonight? See if I recognize the guy from the wedding picture," offered Gabriel.

"That didn't work out so well last time, remember?" asked Ben. "I'll go, but I'll wear a wire, and I want backup in case something happens."

CHAPTER SEVENTY

Saturday, July 21st, 1984
Gulfport, Mississippi

Boogie's was a dump and smelled like urine. Following Rutledge's advice, Ben dressed in jeans and a red western shirt with a string tie in order to blend in. He felt a little self-conscious when he noticed that everyone was wearing leather biker gear and watching him. Creedence's *Born on the Bayou* was on the jukebox, and it made Ben think of the earlier, gruesome discovery of Aunt Edna. *What kind of hatred would drive a person to do that?*

The bartender was named Moe and looked like someone's sketchy grandfather. Because of Gabriel's experience, Ben declined the offer of a glass and took a swig of Budweiser from his bottle. "So, Moe, is there a payphone? I think I need to call the old lady," he said, looking around.

"It's by the can, help yourself, Tex."

Cops have a very distinctive walk. Shoulders back, head held high, a purposeful, confident stride. Ben decided to take his beer with him and dance to the music as he made his way across the room. He made it halfway before the catcalls started.

"Shake it, dude!"

"You dance like a chicken, Tex!"

The payphone was next to a window that looked out on the parking lot. Ben could see Gabriel and Rutledge sitting in the VW. He picked up the phone and pretended to be making a call. "Gabriel, if you're listening, flash your headlights." Rutledge had attached a listening device to Ben's tie.

He watched as his partner flashed the headlights. "I just made a fool of myself in front of a bunch of bikers. Rutledge, this is definitely not a country and western bar. There's no sign of Gadzinga, but it's still pretty early. The bartender said that the place fills up just before eleven. Flash your lights again, if the others are in place."

Once again, the headlights came on. "No sign of any Russians, so I'm going to see what I can find out. If I recognize Gadzinga, I'll follow him out."

"Want another, cowboy?" asked Moe. Ben nodded, having once again danced his way back to the bar. "You get ahold of the little lady?"

"Yeah, she's at home with her mother. That's why I'm here."

Moe laughed, "Right on, Tex. Figured you for a tourist. Never quite seen those dance moves around these parts."

"I've lived on the coast for a while now. Well, ever since I married the ole ball and chain." Ben took a swig of beer.

"What kind of work do you do, Tex?"

"The name's Ben by the way." They shook hands. "A lot of this and a little of that."

"That so? Well if I see anyone looking for a little of this and a lot of that, I'll send them your way."

"No, it's a lot of this and a little of that," Ben laughed. "Say, Moe, do you own this place? Is your last name Boogie?"

"Nah, I just sling beer. Don't rightly know who the owner is."

"Who do you get your paychecks from?"

"A guy named Sue, just like the song." Moe looked over at a group playing poker at a table and calling for another round.

"Really? That's cool, never met a guy named Sue."

"It's a nickname. I think the guy's name is too hard to pronounce ... something like Suloveskyanovovov..." Moe said trailing the ovs for another few seconds. "Say, Ben, how did you pick this bar to get away from your mother-in-law?"

"A friend told me to look up a guy named Petr. He said he might be able to hook me up..."

The smile faded from Moe's face. "I have to get some Buds to those guys before they go crazy." Moe popped the lids and carried four beers to the tables. Ben resisted looking over his shoulder but watched in the mirror behind the bar. Moe was deep in conversation with a heavy-set biker who was looking over at Ben. The man was sitting with four others who looked like members of ZZ Top.

Ben said under his breath, hoping Gabriel could hear, "Stand by, I may have just overstayed my welcome."

A FEW MINUTES EARLIER, Rutledge had been shaking his head dismissively. "This ain't no fucking surveillance car. We might as well have strung Christmas lights and a neon sign. Why the fuck is it pink?"

"Long story," replied Gabriel, fiddling with the receiver trying to get a signal.

"We got nothing but time, so give it up."

Gabriel told him about the visit to Huedunit Painting on a previous case, and how it had been a cover for a chop shop. Pink was the first color Rachel had come up with when the manager had pressed her.

Rutledge once again shook his head and rolled down the window. "Should have taken my car."

"Your car looks more like a cop car than most cop cars. Think about it this way. No one will think we're on a stake-out." They heard Ben's voice asking for a pay phone. The next sound they heard were catcalls and someone yelling about a dancing chicken.

A few minutes later, they heard Ben ask Gabriel to flash his lights and then asking if the others were in place. Once again Gabriel flashed his lights, looking over at Arnie's van which was parked on Beach Boulevard. Star and Rachel were with Arnie, ready to follow anyone leaving Boogie's that looked like Gadzinga.

A COUPLE of minutes later the biker Moe had been talking to came up and put his arm around Ben's shoulders. "I hear you're looking for something."

"Yeah, a guy named Petr. Sorry, I don't remember his last name."

"It's Petr, Mind-Your-Own-Fuckin'-Business."

"Unusual last name." Ben took another swig of his beer.

"What do you want with Petr?" The man's grip on Ben's shoulder tightened.

Ben gripped his beer, preparing to use it as a weapon. "Maybe something to take the edge off."

"You sound like a cop. You dance like a cop. You dress like a cop. Did someone tell you to wear this outfit, or are you just an idiot?"

"Whoa," Ben shrugged his shoulder, trying to loosen the biker's grip. "I'm no cop."

"I don't know. First, you ask about Sue, and then about Petr. I smell pig."

"Maybe we better bust in there. Sounds like his cover is blown," Rutledge said, looking over at Gabriel.

"Let's give him another minute. Ben is pretty quick on his feet."

Six Harleys roared into the gravel parking lot. The bikes came to a stop just outside the front door. Both Rutledge and Gabriel recognized one of the men getting off his Harley as Petr Gadzinga. "Hold on, things are about to get interesting." Gabriel pulled out his .38.

"What do you think is going on in there, Arnie?" asked Star from the backseat.

"I figure Ben is trying to blend in, and find the Russian voice that was on the other end of that call." Arnie's eyes were glued to the bar.

"Maybe I should go ask Gabriel, they can hear what's going on," said Rachel.

Rachel was about to open the door when Star reached out and grabbed her arm. "Here come some motorcycles."

THE FRONT DOOR of Boogie's opened, and another bunch of bikers entered. In the group was Gadzinga. Ben recognized him from the wedding photo.

"Well, you're in luck Ben, the not-a-pig, Petr just walked in." The biker waived Petr over.

As Petr neared the bar, he looked at Ben's outfit and sneered. He pointed at Ben's stomach. "Who the fuck is Pauncho?"

The heavy-set biker started to laugh. "I think he's a cop. He says he was told to look you up. Looking for something to take the edge off." Ben looked around the bar; everyone was watching them.

"Who told you to look me up?"

"I'm not a cop." Ben madly scrambled to come up with a good biker name...Popeye, Handlebar, Gears, Shovelhead... and spit out "Keith, Keith Jager." A look of surprise washed across Petr's face. Ben continued, "You know Keith."

Petr stared at Ben for what seemed like an eternity. Ben must have discovered the magic words, as Petr nodded to his biker friend before turning back to Ben and smiling. "Yeah, I fuckin know him. What do you want?"

"Just a dime." Ben hoped he was using the up to date drug-buying terms.

"Sue doesn't like me dealing in his bar. Come outside." Ben breathed a sigh of relief and followed Petr out to his bike.

When they were outside the front door, Petr turned around. "How do you know Keith?"

"I run into him every once and a while. I used to do some work for him."

"That so? What did you say your last name was?"

"Goodman. Benny Goodman."

They walked out to the parking lot where a row of Harley's was parked. Petr stopped suddenly as he noticed something. "What the fuck?"

"Shit! Get down, they're coming out," whispered Gabriel. Rutledge was a big man and could barely fit in the car, let alone be able to duck under the dash. Gabriel ended up below the dash with Rutledge sprawled across him. Gabriel turned off the receiver and held his breath. Moments later, they could hear footsteps approaching the car and a voice saying, "What the fuck?"

CHAPTER SEVENTY-ONE

Saturday, July 7th, 1984
Gulfport, Mississippi

A couple of weeks earlier...

Charles sat in his truck, brooding over his situation. He had nothing to complain about. As far as he knew, no one was looking for Charles Bouvier. Money was rolling in from the check scam and from the drug sales. He had his boat back; it had been retrofitted, and over the past few months he'd used it to explore the Gulf waters. But still, there was something missing. He wanted Jessica.

Last year when the summer of '83 had turned into the fall, Charles had sweetened the reward to five grand as long as she was found before Mardi Gras. When fall gave way to winter, he'd raised the reward to eight thousand if she was found before the World's Fair.

It was now July, and Charles was growing more frustrated by the day. Petr had started asking him stupid questions. "Why it is so important to find Jessica? What did she ever do to you? Are you planning on hurting her? Maybe it's time you forget about her?" The questions made him suspicious.

Charles watched as the front door of the bar opened, and Petr did his normal thing on the side of the building. He then got on his motorcycle and roared off into Gulfport. Charles followed as Petr led him through town, making a couple of stops, and then going to an apartment building in Pass Christian. Charles parked down the street and wondered if Petr was making a delivery.

Forty minutes later, Charles was getting restless. *What's he doing in there? Maybe he found Jessica, and for some reason, he's been keeping the information for himself.* The more he thought about it, the more agitated he became, and the surer he was that Petr wasn't being honest. After another ten minutes, he got out of the Suburban and walked to where the motorcycle was parked under a streetlight. Petr had taken the saddlebags with him. *Maybe I should fuck up his precious bike. Slash a tire.* He looked up at the apartment building, imagining Jessica and Petr in a passionate embrace. He changed his mind. It wasn't the bike he wanted to fuck with.

When Petr was leaving left the apartment building a half hour later, he wasn't thinking about Keith Jager, or how he was going to find Jessica Grant. He was thinking about the blowjob he'd just gotten from Sheri-Lyn. He knew she had fallen big time for him. She probably thought the free drugs were just part of the deal. It had all happened naturally. When her parents had started asking questions like, "What's happening with your grades?' 'Who are you hanging out with?" 'Why are you out so late at night?', Petr had been happy to jump in with a solution. He knew of an apartment she could get for next to nothing.

It was all coming out of psycho's share, and Sheri-Lyn had already proven her worth by getting Jessica's parent's address. But since getting him the address of the aunt in Mobile, she had proven to be pretty useless. Plus, she had become more and more dependent upon him. 'Will I see you tomorrow? Can you stay a little longer? I love you." Petr almost felt sorry for her. Once he found Jessica, he'd quietly leave Sheri-Lyn to her crack pipe. It didn't bother him that he would be leaving her crippled with an addiction, an emotional wreck estranged from her family. Sheri-Lyn was just a job.

THE FOLLOWING DAY, Charles returned to the apartment building and stopped in the lobby, looking for familiar names on the mailboxes. He found the name S.L. Fenn beside apartment eight. The frequency and duration of Petr's visits added more fuel to his suspicions that Gadzinga was holding out on him.

CHAPTER SEVENTY-TWO

Saturday, July 14th, 1984
Gulfport, Mississippi

A week later, disguised as Father Jim again, Charles decided it was time to confront Sheri-Lyn himself. Maybe Jessica was living with her in the apartment. Maybe it was all a part of some love triangle. Images of the three of them poisoned his mind. He was prepared to do whatever he had to. When he approached Sheri-Lyn's apartment, he found the front door open and the apartment empty.

He followed a paint smell to a bedroom where an older man was using a roller to paint the ceiling. Charles knocked to get the man's attention. "Excuse me. I was looking for Sheri-Lyn Fenn. Does she not live here?"

"Used to, Father." The painter stopped work and wiped his hands on a rag. "It's a shame about what happened to her."

"I thought something was wrong when she wasn't at mass. I stopped by to offer my help."

"I'd say you're just a wee bit late on that one, Father. Sheri's a very troubled girl. She was looking worse and worse until her family found her near dead on the floor. The doctor said she almost died from an overdose. She told her parents her boyfriend had dumped her. I'm told she's in some kind of drug rehab program in Hattiesburg."

"Maybe it's all for the best. God works in mysterious ways."

"That he does Father."

CHAPTER SEVENTY-THREE

Saturday, July 21st, 1984
Gulfport, Mississippi

"I told Gabriel it was a mistake to take the Bug and park it so close to the bar," Arnie said to Rachel as they watched what was happening in the parking lot.

"God, Arnie, that guy is going see them hiding in the Bug!"

"We have to do something, Arnie," urged Star.

Arnie took a moment to think things through before starting the van. "Hold on folks; it might get a little rough." His plan wasn't fully thought through, but if the motorcycle guy went any further, he was going to drive his van into the parking lot acting like a drunk driver.

"Have you ever seen anything like that, Goodman? What kind of crazy asshole would do that to their car?" Peter was standing about a dozen yards from the Bug, and Ben could see that the windows were rolled down. Petr started to walk towards the VW.

What if they're hiding under the dash? "Fuck if I know," Ben replied. "Maybe one of your pals is a fag."

Petr turned around and looked at Ben. "Nobody in Boogie's would drive this. Is it yours?"

"Nah, that's my ride." Ben pointed out his yellow and red truck. He wished he had taken Chevon's advice and had it painted.

Petr took in the F150, and he shook his head. "What the hell is going on, you a homo?"

"Just got it, and haven't had it painted yet."

"You should take it down to Yuri's. He runs a place called Huedunit on the waterfront. He'll fix you up. Tell him Petr sent you." Petr lost interest in the VW and went to a black Harley, reaching into a saddle bag. He threw Ben a baggie. "That'll be $20 bucks. That's the friend-of-Jager price. You tell that psycho I did right by you." After Ben handed him the cash, he said, "Now, we should fuck up this fag's car. Maybe I'll take a piss through the window." Petr was laughing as he started towards the car.

"Yeah, that'd be cool, but I have to bolt. You should get some soap and do the guy's windows."

Petr paused again before turning around and saying, "Good idea, Pauncho."

"I'm heading out now. I'll mention it to Keith when I see him. Get some soap from the washroom and do it right." Ben walked over to his truck, passing right by the VW. He could see that Rutledge was lying on top of Gabriel, who was scrunched under the dash. When he got in the truck, he saw Petr walk back into the bar. As he left the parking lot moments later, he saw the VW start up and follow quickly behind him.

CHAPTER SEVENTY-FOUR

Saturday, July 21st, 1984
Gulfport, Mississippi

Travis answered the phone immediately, thinking it might be Gabriel.

"Yello, is ...Rachel there?" asked a slurred voice he didn't recognize.

"Rachel Henderson is on assignment. This is Travis Franklin; can I help you?"

"Travisssssssss, my man. I know you. 'Member it's me, Don Kitty. Kittyburger." A stench of booze seemed to be coming over the phone line.

"Had a bit to drink, Don?"

"Just a teeny-weeny bit. Listen, Travis, very impotent. You have to get a massage to Rachel, right...like now. Okay? Can you do that little buddy?"

"Yeah sure, Don, what's the message?"

"There's a 1975 cwift cwast...," Travis heard what he thought was a belch over the line. "Registered in Lousana. It's called the Jessica. The Jessica, get it?" Don started laughing hysterically.

"There's a 1975 Chris Craft registered in Louisiana called the Jessica."

"Bingo dingo, and listen. Listen very, very, very cawfully. The reservation, no re-gis-tra-tion was filed in a place called Belle Chaz. That's Frenchie for" ...another belch...."chasing hot chicks, I think."

"Anything else, Don?"

"Just tell her I'm ...sorry. I've been a wiener lately. Tell her ...tell her...I love her. Like really, no shit here. Tell her, I want to show my ...love to her." Travis heard the sound of kissing on the phone; it went on for a disturbing ten seconds. "Can you pass that on little buddy?"

"Sure, Don. You can count on me."

"Like, everything, okay? Don't leave anything out. I love her. Tell her that. Tell her I pwomiss to eat my bocklee."

"Oh, that was so fucking close!" Star breathed out as they watched Gadzinga go back into Boogie's. Moments later they watched as first Ben, and then Gabriel and Rutledge left the parking lot.

"There's a pay phone over there," Rachel gestured as she got out of the van. "I'm going to check in with Travis while we wait on the guy to come back out. I'll keep watch, and if Petr starts to leave, I'll come right back."

Travis answered her call, and Rachel explained what

had happened at the bar. "Is anything happening from your end?"

"You could say that. Some guy named Don called. He said to tell you that a boat named the Jessica was registered in Belle Chasse, Louisiana."

"Really? Did he say anything else?

"He said a bunch of other stuff."

"What stuff?"

"Sucky stuff, he might have been drunk because he kept going on about how much he loves you and how sorry he is. It was all pretty gross, so I hung up."

"DID you notice that the man Ben was talking to had a Sons of Silence vest?" asked Star. "I hear they're really bad news. They're heavy into the drug business. A friend of mine, well she was a friend, now she's in rehab, got hooked on crack. She's like a total mess now. That could have been me had I not met Steve and spent the past year at the camp."

"You're lucky, Star." They watched as a man came out of Boogie's carrying a bar of soap. He was followed by a couple of other bikers. Arnie and Star watched as he looked around for the pink VW Bug. He seemed confused and then angry that it had disappeared.

"I bet you, I can tell you what he is saying," said Star. "Seriously, I can read lips." She deepened her voice. "Like dudes, it was right here; I was going to mess it up. You know, soap the windows." They watched as the man walked over to where the VW Bug had been parked and pointed down. "Right fucking here, I tell you...painted fag pink." The other guys waived their hands at him and started heading back into the bar. "Seriously, dudes, it was right here."

Once the others had gone back into the bar, Gadzinga went over again to where the VW had been parked and pulled his zipper down. "Jesus, he's peeing," said Star. She deepened her voice again, "How do you like that, fag boy. You want some of this? That'll teach you to show your homo car around." Arnie burst out laughing just as Rachel opened the side door. Their laughter was short-lived as Petr went over to his black Harley and started it up.

BEN DROVE to an all-night coffee shop where they had pre-arranged to meet and settled in to wait for Gabriel and Rutledge to arrive.

They pulled up beside his truck, and Rutledge called out to Ben. "That was close. I thought that guy was going to piss all over me!"

"Thank goodness you suggested that he get some soap," said Gabriel. "Otherwise, I was ready to say that Rutledge was giving me a blowjob."

Ben laughed. "With that car, he'd have gone for it. Now we just hang back and wait for Arnie to tail Gadzinga."

"I think we should switch spots with the girls. Maybe you can drop us off and then one of us can take them home," suggested Rutledge.

"Sure. Leave the VW here, Gabriel. We'll take the truck."

When they got to Beach Blvd, they found Arnie's van had disappeared.

CHAPTER SEVENTY-FIVE

Saturday, July 21st, 1984
Gulfport, Mississippi

The porch light was on when Charles drove his Suburban up to Petr's trailer. There was no sign of Gadzinga's motorcycle. *That's okay; maybe I'll visit Lana and have myself a TV dinner. Maybe she'd like to hear about Sheri-Lyn.* His heart raced in anticipation as he knocked on the screen door. The *Tonight Show* was on TV, so Lana had to be in there. The screen door was locked, and he sprung his switchblade. He got the door open, entered, and saw the door to the bathroom was closed. He heard the shower running.

Charles looked around. The dishes hadn't been done in a week. He selected a Hungry Man Salisbury Steak dinner from the freezer, leaving the unopened package on the stove. Grabbing a beer from the fridge, he turned off the lights and the TV and sat in the easy chair. He doused a dish towel with some chloroform, just to help Lana get in the mood.

Lana came out of the washroom wearing a silk bathrobe and drying her hair with a towel. She stopped for a second when she realized that the trailer was dark and that the television was no longer on. "Don't tell me the fucking power is off again." She turned around and saw the light was still on in the bathroom."What the fuck?" Lana noticed the Hungry Man dinner sitting on the stove, and a shiver ran down her spine. After a moment of hesitation, she bolted towards the screen door.

Her moment of hesitancy had given Charles the opportunity he needed. He reached out just in time and grabbed Lana by her wet hair, using his superior strength to pull her back into the trailer. She held onto the screen door and refused to let go. When he tried to wrap his left arm around her, she elbowed him in the chest. The blow stunned him for a moment.

"You bitch!" Charles didn't release his grip. He tried to grab the chloroform towel, but it was out of reach. He changed tactics, slamming her head into the wall beside the door. He repeated this another couple of times before he sensed the fight go out of her. "Now, Lana, I just want my hungry man dinner."

Lana stomped on his foot, causing Charles to yelp. She resumed her struggle to get away.

Finally, in a fit of rage, Charles rammed his switchblade repeatedly into her back.

CHAPTER SEVENTY-SIX

Sunday, July 22nd', 1984
Gulfport, Mississippi

Arnie followed Petr Gadzinga's Harley to the eastern end of Gulfport, almost to Long Beach. He watched as the motorcycle turned left into a trailer park. He could still see the taillights stop in front of a trailer. Arnie turned off the headlights and parked near a group of pines. A porch light was on, and they watched a man disappear into the trailer.

"Quite the dump!" commented Star. "Okay, what do we do now?"

"Think he's in for the night, Arnie?" asked Rachel.

"Looks that way, but let's stick around and make sure."

Rachel rolled down her window and took in the fresh air. The chirping of crickets filled the night. She told the others about Don and the boat registration.

"I think Belle Chasse marina is about ninety minutes away." Arnie kept his eyes on the front door of the trailer.

"I wonder what Gabriel and the others are doing?" asked Star.

"The plan was to call Travis at the agency. If we could get to a payphone, we could tell them where we are."

"There might be a rental office or a convenience store with one," suggested Star. "I can go look. I kind of have to go pee anyway."

"Can you hold on for a bit?. If the porch light goes out, we'll all leave," replied Rachel.

"No, I can't hold it." Star opened the back door. "I'll just sneak into those trees. Be back, pronto."

"Do you think Bouvier lives here too?" Rachel asked, turning to ask Arnie.

"From what I read, he's a spoiled little rich kid. Someone like him wouldn't be caught dead in this dump."

"Let's assume Gadzinga lives here, then what?"

"The idea is to watch him and see if he leads us to Bouvier. Say, did you hear something?"

"Probably a squirrel or a raccoon."

They waited in silence for a few more minutes before Rachel opened her door. "I'm just going to check on Star." Arnie could hear Rachel quietly calling out. All of a sudden, she ran back to the van. "Arnie, I found Star's Biloxi hat, but there's no sign of her."

Arnie got out of the van, and they scoured the woods looking for Star.

Charles had taken Lana's body and dumped it behind the trailer. He hadn't meant to kill her. She'd left him no other choice. *Just as well, she was a distraction.* He was returning from the back of the trailer when he noticed a dark-colored van parked beside the copse of trees. Charles hid in the bushes and watched.

There was something familiar about the van. *The same van had been parked in front of Jessica's house. What connection could this have to Petr?* The side door of the van opened, and he saw a girl get out. There was something familiar about the way she moved. Charles circled around to get a closer look.

"THE VAN'S GONE, and so is Gadzinga's bike," said Gabriel as they pulled up across from Boogie's. I bet you Petr's driving around looking for the VW, and Arnie is following him."

"Let's do the same." Ben put the truck in gear and turned down one of the side streets.

After about ten minutes of searching, they gave up and drove back to the Agency. They walked in and found Travis sitting at Rachel's desk with the phone to his ear. He hung up immediately.

"Have you heard from Arnie?" asked Gabriel.

"Jesus, I was looking for you guys. I just hung up from Jacqueline. She's freaking out. Arnie called about five minutes ago. They followed the guy to the Hidden Acres trailer park. They were watching Gadzinga's trailer when Star went into the woods to take a leak. Now Rachel and Arnie can't find her. They searched and found Star's Biloxi hat, so they think someone grabbed her. Arnie was going to bust in on Gadzinga, but I told him that I would find you guys and check first."

Ben shared a look with Gabriel. "Shitfuck! Travis, if Arnie calls back, tell him to hang tight, we're on our way."

CHAPTER SEVENTY-SEVEN

Sunday, July 22nd, 1984
Gulfport, Mississippi

When Ben and the others arrived at Gadzinga's trailer, Arnie and Rachel were standing beside his van, having just returned from the camp office.

Ben looked at Rachel; her face said everything. "Where's Gadzinga?"

Rachel nodded to the trailer, "He rode up, went in, and never came out."

"Rutledge, you circle behind the trailer, just in case there's a back door. I'm going to go talk to him." Ben got within six feet of the trailer and thought he saw movement at the front door. "Hey Gadzinga, come on out. It's Benny Goodman. Remember me?"

There was no sound for about ten seconds. Finally, a voice came from the window, "Ah fuck, you're a cop. You going to arrest me for a goddam dime bag?"

"Listen, Petr, I'm not a cop. I'm not here to arrest you. Can you come out? I just want to talk to you."

Gadzinga came to the screen door holding a beer. "Who's that with you, the little guy?" Ben turned around and saw that Gabriel had come up behind him.

"He's a friend of mine. He's not a cop, either."

"Have him stand under the porch light." Once he did, "Jesus, I know that guy."

"That's right. You paid a bartender to slip something in his drink. You were going to kidnap him."

"Not exactly, but it doesn't matter; we were interrupted. The cops were on the street, and when we went back, there was someone lying on top of him." There was a pause for a minute before Petr added, "Is that why you're here? You pissed because he had a bad trip?"

"Is Lana in there, Petr?" Gabriel spoke up.

"Lana? She's out with her girlfriends. What do you want with her?"

"The man who paid you to drug me," said Gabriel, coming closer, "is Keith Jager. He's a serial killer. We need to find him. It's important."

"Listen, shrimp, you don't know what you're talking about."

"I know you know Keith Jager," said Ben. "We need to find him."

"I know him...he's a fuckin psycho, but he's not interested in you. He's obsessed with finding this blonde chick."

"You're saying that Jager didn't pay you to abduct me?" Gabriel's voice was incredulous.

"No flies on you, little man."

"If Jager didn't pay you, who did?"

"I've already said enough. You guys better clear out before I decide to finish what I started and see if I can still get the money I was promised."

Rutledge emerged from behind the trailer and walked over to Ben, speaking softly to him.

"What the fuck is going on here?" asked Petr. "Who the fuck is that?"

"Listen to me Petr, Lana didn't go out with her friends. I suspect your pal Keith was here earlier. Her body's behind the trailer."

Petr's face went white, and he raced outside and around to the back of the trailer. When they caught up to him, they found Petr on his knees crying beside Lana's body, which was lying in a heap of garbage. Lana was dressed in a bathrobe and clutching a TV dinner.

"I'm sorry, Petr," said Ben.

"That fucker! The TV dinner was a message . She said I shouldn't have anything to do with him."

No one said anything for a long moment. Finally Ben put his hand on Petr's shoulder. "What matters now Petr, is that she didn't die in vain. We have to get this guy before he hurts anyone else. How do you get in touch with Jager?"

"I don't. The fucker just shows up when he wants something."

BEN, Gabriel, and Rutledge returned to the van. Ben told Arnie and Rachel what they'd discovered behind the trailer.

"How long has she been there?" asked Rachel.

"Her body's still warm, so maybe an hour, ninety minutes tops," replied Rutledge.

"Gadzinga was with Ben at Boogie's at that time," said Arnie.

There was silence for a few minutes. Rachel was the first to say what was on everyone's mind. "He's got Star, and at least an hour head start on us." Her face mirrored the panic they all felt. She told the others what Don had said about the Chris Craft being registered in Belle Chasse.

Ben looked over at Gabriel before responding. "I think Petr was telling the truth about not knowing where Bouvier is. Arnie, why don't you and Rachel head down to the marina. If he's there, don't approach him, let Travis know."

"What are you going to do?" asked Rachel.

"I'm going to play a hunch."

CHAPTER SEVENTY-EIGHT

Sunday, July 22nd, 1984
New Orleans, Louisiana

Star groggily awoke to find herself with a size ten headache. She tried to move her hands, but they were tied together. Her last recollection was being at a trailer park with Arnie and Rachel. She'd left the van to pee and had a vague memory of someone coming up behind her.

I'm in the back of a moving car. The car went under a street light momentarily, casting a brief glow. *I think we're on a highway.* She felt the vehicle speed ahead. Someone she didn't recognize was driving. *Is it that Petr guy we were following?* She was about to call out to him when she suddenly remembered how Nelson's ex-wife had described his killer as looking like Billy Idol. Silent panic gripped her. *Okay, okay girl, calm down, and you'll get out of this. This guy is a wimp, remember.* Her instincts told her to stay quiet and wait for her chance.

THIS MUST BE *some kind of divine intervention,* thought Charles. *I was right about Petr, lying to me all this time. After all these months trying to find her, and she falls right in my lap.* He thought he heard something in the back seat.

He adjusted the rearview mirror, "Why'd you cut your hair, Jill?"

After a couple of moments, Star spoke. "Because it reminded me of you. Every time I looked at myself in the mirror, I'd blow chunks at the thought of you. Now could I get a glass of water, fucktard?"

"Jill, you forget that I don't like that name."

"Fucktard, fucktard, fucktard," she repeated, trying to provoke him.

"We have a lot of catching up to do. I've changed my look too. I think you'll like it. Much more youthful. But tell me why you really cut your hair?" When she didn't answer, Charles continued speaking to her reflection in the mirror. "Maybe I'll give you some water, but I need you to tell me... why did you cut your hair?"

"Fuck, you're like a broken record. I wanted to be someone else. Don't you ever wish you were someone else, fucktard?"

"It's Charles."

"Answer the question, Charles. Do you ever wish you were like a normal person? Not a deranged psycho living a make-believe fantasy based on a crappy TV show that was so bad they canceled it?"

"I am a different person Jessica, I'm not the guy you met before. I don't have the same ...interests."

"So, who are you, Charles?"

"I'm fun, someone you'd like. That is if you got to know me. Wait until you see where I'm taking you, my queen." He laughed while eyeing her in the rearview mirror. "You'll be so happy."

"I would never be happy with a loser like you."

"I had hoped our time away from each other would have warmed your heart. It's still not too late. We could go somewhere, be alone together, tie the knot. I have some money and can provide for you. We could have a great life. I have my boat back. It's been totally retrofitted and painted. I named her Jessica after you. I even registered her this time. Kind of like a marriage license. I've often thought it would be fun to live on an island somewhere in the Caribbean. I think you'd like Cuba. Oh, and I have a surprise for you."

When Star didn't answer, he continued, "I've worked hard to keep myself young and in good shape for you. I know I'm not perfect. I met your parents. I think your mother liked me. Your dad, well...let's not talk about him. Your mom might say I'm a little old for you. But once she realizes how much you love me, she'll accept it. I bet she would like a granddaughter. I want lots of kids. Maybe not right away, but once we get settled. Lots and lots of girls with blonde hair."

Hearing that Charles had met her parents pushed Star to her limit. "I'd never be happy with a fucktard like you. You're a loser, a pathetic loser." An icy silence fell over the truck. Star thought she'd crossed a line.

After everything I've done for her. "Ungrateful bitch," Charles spoke to the rearview mirror. *All the plans I made for us to be together, this is the thanks I get.* "You don't deserve me. Don't be thinking I give a fart about you. I'm sick of the sight of you, you ungrateful bitch." *I've been kidding myself, thinking that she'd ever love me. Somewhere deep inside, I always knew it wasn't going to work out. It never does. I could tell as soon I saw she'd cut her hair.*

CHAPTER SEVENTY-NINE

Sunday, July 22nd, 1984
Belle Chasse, Louisiana

Arnie had driven about halfway to Belle Chasse when he turned to Rachel. "I guess he really has strong feelings for you."

"Travis said he was drunk."

"True, but he was trying to help."

"Have you ever made one of those late-night drunk calls to an ex-girlfriend?"

Arnie laughed. "I think just about every guy and a lot of ladies have too. Some people might say that this is how he really feels about you."

"Or it's just the rantings of a drunken liar."

"Okay, but why don't you give him a little credit for getting us this information?"

"How should we play this, Arnie?" Rachel changed the conversation to another topic.

"Let's find the marina. We'll check around and see if we can find a boat named Jessica."

THE SAINT-MICHEL DE BELLE CHASSE MARINA was closed when they arrived. Arnie shone his flashlight around, illuminating about two dozen yachts, sailboats, and cruisers. The boats were docked along wooden piers. Using the flashlight, they went up and down the docks until they found a cruiser named Jessica. "No lights, I bet he's not here."

"We came all this way, we should at least make sure it's his boat," whispered Rachel. "Should we take a look down below?"

Arnie sniffed the air. "I smell a cigar." He took a deep breath and began to step over the bow of the Jessica, but stopped short when he saw the red end of a cigar nearby. He shone his flashlight at the cigar, revealing a man sitting in a chair on the boat deck watching them.

"I wouldn't move too quick, mister. I have a gun pointed at your balls."

"Okay, don't shoot me, at least not in my privates. Is this your boat?"

The embers of the cigar grew bright, then the man said, "I'll ask the questions. What are you doing here, and who's that with you?"

"My name's Arnie Sims, and this is Rachel Henderson. We work for a private detective agency. The case we're working on involves a boat called the Jill. This might not be the same boat, but we came down to check it out."

The man stood up, and from the light of Arnie's flashlight, they could see that he was a portly man wearing a French beret. "The name's Simon Villemarette. This boat is called the Jessica now. Name kind of sucks the big one, if you ask me. I wanted to call it the Naughty Yachty, but I got outbid. Is your case about the Mardi Gras Killer, who died a couple of years back?"

Arnie shared a look with Rachel. "Yeah, why are you on this boat if you don't own it?"

"I swapped with the owner for a couple of weeks. You see, I own this castle east of New Orleans."

CHAPTER EIGHTY

Sunday, July 22nd, 1984
Irish Bayou, Louisiana

Something's changed. He just snapped and called me an ungrateful bitch. He's turned onto a dirt road. I can't see any lights now. The road's bumpy, and he's having trouble steering. "Where are we going, Charles?"

"To visit my Aunt Edna and maybe some old friends of mine. Don't worry; you'll all get along just fine."

"I'm sorry for calling you a bad name."

"A little late for that."

"It's never too late Charles. We can be together. We can still run away to Cuba."

Charles was momentarily distracted, having to concentrate on keeping the vehicle on the path.

Sitting up quickly, Star looped her arms around Bouvier's neck and pulled back with all the force she had, bracing her knee against the back of his seat. She had timed it right and caught him by surprise. She started madly wrenching his head from side to side as he struggled to control the vehicle while driving. The vehicle careened off a tree and then Star pushed him forward with all her strength and his head collided with the steering wheel. The vehicle sped up and veered to the right, coming to a stop after a few moments, tilted on an angle.

The headlights went out, plunging everything into near blackness. There was no sound coming from the front. Star guessed Charles Bouvier was out for the count. *I have to get the fuck out. He could wake up any minute.* Panic fueled her as she tried the doors, only to find that they were wedged closed. She tried to roll the window down. It took precious minutes before she figured out how to do it with her hands tied.

She eventually got the window lowered and started hoisting herself out face-first. At any minute she expected an angry Bouvier to wake up and grab her from behind. As she dangled out the window, she saw something moving in the darkness below. She suddenly realized that the vehicle had veered into the swamp and was partially submerged in the water. The idea of sliding into the bayou terrified her, almost as much as being caught by Charles Bouvier. Taking a deep breath, Star let herself slide down into the blackness.

Ben turned the truck onto the rutted road leading into the Bayou.

"Why here, Ben?" asked Gabriel.

"Just a hunch. It's out of the way. He grew up on the bayou. It means something to him."

Gabriel nodded. He looked over his shoulder at Rutledge, who was sitting in the back seat, double-checking his ammunition. He remembered what Suzanne Collings had said about him during their interview and spoke up. "If he's here it would be great to take him alive. There's a lot of families looking for closure."

"Job One is making sure Star is okay," replied Rutledge. "If Bouvier gets in the way, I won't hesitate to take him out."

Gabriel turned his attention back to Ben. "This is a pretty big area. If he took Star here, where are we going to look?

"I'm going to head towards where he dumped the Jeep. If we don't find anything, then we'll go over to where he dumped his Aunt Edna."

It was slow going, with nothing but the headlights to guide them along the narrow trail. As they neared the big tree signaling the end of the line, Ben suddenly reached over and grabbed Gabriel's shoulder. "Hey, look at that!" He pointed to where a truck lay half-submerged in the swamp. "That wasn't here the last time."

They all got out of Ben's truck and carefully approached what appeared to be a Chevrolet Suburban tilted at a forty-five-degree angle. Ben shone his flashlight into the vehicle. "Nothing." He tried to open the back door, but it was stuck.

Gabriel waded into the swamp on the other side of the truck, where he could see a window was down. He hoped the alligators were tucked in for the night as he moved in the brackish water. Gabriel shone Ben's flashlight into the backseat and spotted something lying on the seat. He hoisted himself partially in through the window, trying to grab the object. "There's something on the seat. It's a star necklace. She was here!"

"They couldn't have gone far. We only have one flashlight, so we'll need to stick together." Ben ordered.

"Watch where you walk," reminded Rutledge.

After twenty minutes, they had still found no trace of Star or Charles Bouvier.

CHAPTER EIGHTY-ONE

Sunday, July 22nd, 1983
The Irish Bayou, Louisiana

Star landed face-first in waist-high, oily water. Pushing herself off the mucky bottom, she righted herself. Her pressing thought as she stood up was to get as far away as possible from the Suburban. In the darkness, she thought she saw a log in the water moving towards her. *Logs don't swim.*

She tried to scramble quickly to the shore, but her feet were stuck in the thick mud. A hissing noise made her look back over her shoulder. The log was now only a few feet away. *A gator*! Its long scaly snout was opening. She tried desperately to pull her feet from the muck. She could smell the creature almost on her. She screamed and was startled by a gunshot from behind her. The next thing she felt was someone grabbing her t-shirt and pulling her backwards out of the swamp.

"Your hunch was pretty good Ben, what now?" Rutledge asked as the three men made it back to the truck.

Ben shook his head, so Gabriel spoke. "I think Star did something to cause the truck to go into the swamp. Maybe she was able to knock Bouvier out. I think she crawled out of that window and left the necklace to tell us she was alive."

"And where's Bouvier?" wondered Rutledge.

"She might be on the run from him," replied Gabriel.

"I'll drive us out of this place," Ben said. "You guys use my flashlight to keep an eye out for her."

They got back to the highway without having seen Star along the way. "I hate to say it, but they could both have become alligator food," said Rutledge.

Ben ignored the comment. "Star's on foot so she couldn't have gone far. I say we go right, and if we don't see her after a mile, then we'll double back and go left."

"Okay, sounds like a plan," Rutledge agreed.

"What are those lights over there?" Gabriel pointed ahead at a couple of lights flickering about thirty feet off the ground.

"That's the Irish Bayou castle," answered Rutledge.

"Do you think he could have taken her there?" asked Ben.

Charles pulled Star out of the swamp. He threw her to the ground, looking quickly behind him to make sure the alligator wasn't following them on land. "Now, listen. I don't want to hurt you. But I've learned my lesson. If you scream or try to run away, I'll put a bullet in your head." To punctuate his threat, he cocked the Colt and pointed it between her eyes. "Get up, we need to leave."

THE ACCESS to the castle was a gravel driveway about 90 yards up the highway. They decided to park along the road and travel on foot. Ben grabbed a coil of rope from the back of the truck, along with his flashlight, and led the way.

While they were walking, Gabriel whispered to Rutledge, "What's a castle doing in the middle of a bayou?"

"A developer built it last year as an attraction for the World's Fair. No one lives in it, and so far, it's been a bit of a bust. You can't really see it very well in the dark, but it has the ramparts and the watchtower. The owner was a bit of a nut for authenticity. It has all kinds of medieval trappings inside."

"Do we just go knock on the door?"

Rutledge shrugged. "They might not even be there."

Ben turned around and told them to be quiet.

When they got to within ten feet of the castle, Ben turned on his flashlight and illuminated the structure. "Smaller once you see it up close. Those walls have to be thirty feet high." The castle bordered a large body of water and looked deserted, other than two lights - one from a window about ten feet over the door, and another higher up in the watchtower.

Ben checked the front door and found it locked. To the right of the door was a barred window. He looked in, but the room was completely dark. "I'm going to circle around the castle and see if there might be another window or door; you two try to think of another way to get in."

Ben returned and shook his head when he discovered Gabriel and Rutledge arguing.

"They may not have come this way," Rutledge was saying.

"They could be walking along the highway towards Slidell. Maybe one, or both of them are hurt."

"If that's the case, there's no reason not to knock," replied Gabriel. "It looks from that light that someone's home."

"That's kind of announcing ourselves. Hello Mr. Mass Murderer, can you come out and play?" countered Rutledge.

Ben gestured to the next closest window, which was at least twenty feet off the ground. "I've got some rope. Anyone fancy themselves, Errol Flynn? With my bum shoulder, I doubt I could lift myself that far."

Gabriel looked doubtfully at Rutledge, who had to tip the scales at over 300 pounds. Looking up at the window, he noticed that the bars only went half way up. "If we could hook a rope up there, I can try to climb up to that window."

"Once you hoist yourself up to the bars, you might be able to reach through and see if the window's locked." Ben made a loop in the rope, and while Rutledge held the flashlight, he flung the rope at the bars covering the window. It took a few tries, but eventually he was successful.

Gabriel spat in his hands and grabbed the rope. He used his legs to crab walk up the castle walls. It took him the better part of five minutes, but he was finally able to grasp the bars. He hoisted himself up so that he could look in the window. An imitation torch illuminated an empty bedroom containing a four-poster bed and a wooden armoire. There was a boar's head above the head of the bed. He reached through the bars and tried the window. When it opened, he flashed a thumbs-up sign to Ben and Rutledge. Thanks to his small stature, he was able to climb over the bars and through the window. A couple of moments later, he reappeared at the window and pantomimed that he was hearing noises coming from the watchtower.

Ben made the down sign to Gabriel and pointed at the

door. Minutes later, Gabriel opened it and greeted them, carrying a shield and a long sword. The doorway opened into a small foyer with a high ceiling. A wooden staircase stood off to the right, leading to the second floor and another, narrower staircase that led to yet another floor, presumably to the watchtower. They looked around the room. It was decorated with medieval shields and weapons along with a suit of armor.

CHAPTER EIGHTY-TWO

Sunday, July 22nd, 1984
Irish Bayou, Louisiana

Charles gazed down at Jessica. Her arms and legs were shackled to a metal bed. He looked around the round room. *A castle for his beautiful princess.*

On the walk from the bayou, she'd tried her best to distract him.

"Where are we going? I think I twisted my knee in the accident." She turned around to face him. Blood was running down the side of his face from a gash on his forehead.

"Just keep walking."

"If you let me go, I promise not to say anything. You can get away, sail to Cuba with all your money."

"You don't get it, Jessica. Life is not worth living without you. Now that we're together, I'd rather we die in each other's arms than spend another minute apart." Charles nudged her forward with the gun.

Jessica had turned and resumed walking. After another

five minutes, Charles' flashlight illuminated a big structure. "What the hell is that?"

"Your castle, my dear, where we will consummate our vows."

When they got to the front door, Charles handed the keys to her and gestured for her to unlock it. They entered, and he flicked a switch. The foyer was immediately lit by electric torches on the walls. He pointed to the stairs and nudged her again with the gun to start climbing.

Once she reached the landing, he pointed to another set of stairs. "Your home awaits, my queen." The stairs opened up to a round room which had an iron bed equipped with metal shackles on each post. "Lie down." He shackled her legs first before untying her hands and stretching her arms out so that she was spread-eagled. "Do you know the struggles I have gone through to find and rescue you?"

"Untie me, my prince, and we can be together. *You'll eventually make a mistake, and then I'm going to kill you.*

Charles laughed. "I'm going to go downstairs and secure the door and windows. I wouldn't want anything to interfere with our lovemaking."

Jessica struggled in vain against the shackles after he left. *I have to be strong. As difficult as this is, I have to play along until there's an opening. No one is coming to rescue me. Arnie and Rachel must be out searching, but Travis said they found the boat. They're probably on their way there now. If I'm going to survive, I have to outsmart him.*

A few minutes later, Bouvier reappeared with a smile on his face. "We're all alone, my sweet." He sat down on the bed and ran his hand up her leg. "Don't worry; your lovely hair will grow back. In the meantime, maybe I can get you a wig." He leaned over her and tried to kiss her. Star struggled, trying to avoid his lips, but he clamped his hand on her head and forced his mouth on hers. She tugged against the shackles and realized that resistance was futile. She opened her mouth and kissed him. The move emboldened him, his hands traveling her body. Star moaned and used her tongue to tease him. He straddled her, continuing the kiss, moving his tongue with hers. She was teasing him, drawing him deeper.

A wave of revulsion came over Star, and she fought hard against nausea before suddenly clamping down hard on his tongue. He tried to pull away, but she bit down harder. She could feel him try to scream as he attempted to pull away. He used his fists on her. Bouvier continued to flail his arms until Star finally let go. Blood was dripping down his face. She smiled as she spit out a chunk of his tongue.

As Charles staggered around the room, holding his hands to his mouth and howling in pain, Jessica thought she heard a noise downstairs. The noise became the sounds of footsteps and a door opening. Charles heard the sounds as well. He picked his gun up from the table where he'd left it and went to investigate. The next sounds she heard were gunshots.

CHAPTER EIGHTY-THREE

Sunday, July 22nd, 1984
Irish Bayou, Louisiana

While Gabriel and Ben were listening for sounds coming from above, Rutledge was looking at a suit or armor. There were two quick gunshots; the first hit Gabriel's shield before ricocheting. Gabriel turned quickly to warn Rutledge. As he did, he saw Rutledge's head explode in front of him.

"Get cover," Ben yelled, shocking Gabriel into action. Gabriel bent down and grabbed Rutledge's arm, attempting to drag the big man under the staircase. "Leave him, he's gone," yelled Ben, grabbing Gabriel and pulling him under the stairs. Ben pointed upwards to where he thought the shots had come from.

They were at a stalemate. Ben figured that the killer was directly over them. It was hard for either the killer or them to move without exposing themselves. Ben looked at Rutledge's body; the bullet had blown half of his head away. *Rutledge risked his life for me. I talked him into retirement, and then to work at the Agency.* Seeing Rutledge lying lifeless was like a cruel hand squeezing his heart. *All Rutledge ever wanted to do was help people.*

Ben's thoughts were interrupted by Gabriel calling out, "Hey Bouvier, let's talk."

"What duh yuh want?" Bouvier had a speech impediment and was hard to understand.

"I know you love Jessica; let her go; you don't want her to get hurt."

"No."

"The local cops are on the way. Let's start by throwing your gun down. You've already killed a man. I promise not to shoot you."

"I've killed plenty. You're up next. Show yourself, and you'll die quickly." They heard spitting followed by a groan.

"Hey, shithead," yelled Ben. "There are families out there who need closure about the missing girls. Before we kill you, will you at least tell us what happened to them?"

There was a long moment of silence punctuated by the sound of someone spitting. "They're dead, all dead."

"Did you kill Heidi Gesche?" asked Gabriel.

There was a pause punctuated by another spit. "Who the fuck is that? Enough talk, I hab to take care of Jessica."

Gabriel guessed that Star was in the watchtower, a bullet away from death. One of the last things Rutledge had said was that saving Star was job one.

Gabriel still had the shield in his hand. He moved closer to the bottom of the staircase, pointed to the shield and gestured for Ben to use his gun. When Ben nodded, Gabriel came out from under the stairs, trying to make himself smaller and holding the shield up for cover. A gunshot pinged off the shield. A second bullet whizzed by Gabriel's ear. Then Ben was out from under the stairs returning fire. They heard a groan and the sound of something falling to the floor above them

A moment later, Gabriel peeked from behind the shield and saw a figure stagger towards the small staircase leading to the watchtower. Gabriel dropped his shield and emptied his revolver.

Ben and Gabriel raced up the wooden steps where they found Charles lying facedown on the wooden floor. Blood was pooling into a dark red lake around him.

"Fucker killed Bass," said Ben, nudging the body with his foot to make sure he was gone.

"Wait a minute. Bass?"

"Bassington Rutledge the III. He hated it. Threatened to kill anyone in the precinct that called him that."

Gabriel nodded. "Did you hear Bouvier say he killed all those girls?"

Ben nodded. "Yeah, that's what I heard. At least the families can now get some closure. He also said he didn't know Heidi Gesche. That's some hope for Mrs. Gesche."

"If he was telling the truth."

They were interrupted by screaming coming from the watchtower. "Hey! What the hell's going on down there? Jesus, are you going to come up here and get these chains off me?"

They ran up the narrow stairs and found Star shackled to the bed, her mouth covered in blood.

"He's dead," said Gabriel.

"Are you sure, this time?" A piece of what looked like a bloodied tongue lay on the bed beside her.

"We put a dozen bullets into him," said Ben, finding the keys on the bureau and unlocking her shackles.

Once loose, she started to cry and held her arms out for a group hug. "I can't believe this fucking nightmare is over."

EPILOGUE

Although Rutledge had no real family to mourn his passing, he'd spent over forty years combined, between the Biloxi and the New Orleans police forces. His funeral drew police from counties all over Louisiana and Mississippi. The priest who delivered the eulogy spoke about the honor of public service and the humanity of dedicating one's life to others. Ben was one of those chosen to speak, and he talked about Rutledge's courage and how in the years they were partners he'd always known that his partner had his back. He only wished that he could have had Rutledge's back.

After the funeral, Gabriel and Jacqueline stopped in Slidell to visit with Esther Gesche and told her that the killer had denied knowing Heidi. Once again, Gabriel thanked her for saving his life and promised that he would find out what happened to her.

One of the ceremonies Gabriel didn't attend was for Lana Gadzinga. The Sons of Silence were there in force. The local news covered the procession of Harleys, flying the gang's colors down Beach Boulevard to the cemetery. Based on the conversation at the trailer, Ben concluded that Frank Reznikov had hired Petr to drug Gabriel and add him to the list of witnesses who couldn't testify. Petr was brought in for questioning, but he denied any knowledge of Reznikov or involvement in Gabriel's abduction. He also claimed to have never heard of Keith Jager. In a surprise move, the Harrison County Sheriff declined to pursue any charges against Petr for drug dealing, or for helping to defraud Edna LeGrand.

The judge overseeing the trials of both Reznikov and former Mayor Baxter granted a continuation to D.A. Laura Ryan, due to the suspicious deaths of two of the State's witnesses. He also denied them bail once again, ensuring that the two defendants would spend Christmas behind bars.

There was a great deal of press shoving microphones in his face, but Gabriel declined to talk about what had happened at the castle. Suzanne Collings even visited, asking for an exclusive in return for a ton of free publicity, and hinting at other perks. He knew that one day the story would all come out.

The families of the missing girls, emboldened by Gabriel's testimony, sued for the proceeds of the Bouvier estate, including the remaining funds that were on deposit at the Bank of Louisiana. A search was made of the trailer and the boat, but no other money was found. Attorney Rod Smith, who was attending the proceedings, reported that they stood a very good chance of winning.

Rachel made up with Don "What's His Name," who claimed no memory of his late-night call to Travis. He told Rachel that he had decided to pull his name from consideration for the Senior Investigator position. Rachel figured that the woman who had been in the running had received the promotion over him.

Simon Villemarette eventually took ownership of the Jessica, renamed it the Naughty Yachty, and parked it at his castle. Months later he expressed disappointment at the public's lack of interest and put both the boat and the castle up for sale.

Jessica tried to reconcile with her parents, but when her father continued to sermonize about her loose hippy-like morals, she escaped and visited Sheri-Lyn in Hattiesburg. Saddened at seeing her friend a mere shadow of her former self, she donned the monk's tunic and moved back to the camp.

The bodies of Captain Rosman, Nelson Gallant, and Freda Furlong were never found, despite a continued police effort to search the Irish Bayou. Travis Franklin decided to finish his history assignment and put off thoughts of running for President. He told Gabriel that he would be on call in case another case needed to be solved.

The wedding at St. David's took place in the fall of 1984. Chevon looked beautiful in her gown. Ben wore a lime green tuxedo with a powder blue shirt. Chevon's mother was so moved by the ceremony she gave Ben a hug. Jacqueline, Gabriel, and Ben were the only white faces in the church. They were shocked to see pictures and statues of Jesus as a black man. Later over a dinner of Chinese food, they all agreed that their surprise was a reflection of how they'd been raised and that the color of a person's skin was insignificant.

The real development happened with the business. Both Jacqueline and Chevon issued their husbands an ultimatum. They'd had enough. They no longer wanted to stay up worrying about whether their husbands were safe. If the men didn't give up the Agency, they threatened to join Star at the camp. Eventually they relented after hearing that Rachel was willing to take over the business, on the condition that Gabriel and Ben stay on as consultants. When Arnie heard the news, he asked if he could take over for Rutledge in the New Orleans office. Apparently, he was motivated to get away from a female stalker named Bernice.

– THE END –

IRISH BAYOU CASTLE

ABOUT THE AUTHOR

Joe lives in Hamilton, Ontario, with his wonderful wife Anita and two of his three kids. (The ones that haven't flown the coop). He also lives with his three dachshunds. Initially attracted to owning the breed so that he could make wiener jokes in bed, he has come to love them and respect their many talents. Here he is with Pumba who is asking him to edit out all of the wiener jokes. After retiring from a long career in banking, Joe decided to take up writing. His short stories have appeared in numerous publications. This is his sixth novel. He can be found at www.joehamilton.ca

www.ingramcontent.com/pod-product-compliance
Lightning Source LLC
Chambersburg PA
CBHW060929030726
47503CB00003B/529
9780993999956